LEAD

LEAD
PARA-MILITARY RECRUITER™ BOOK 04

RENÉE JAGGÉR
MICHAEL ANDERLE

DISRUPTIVE IMAGINATION®

This book is a work of fiction. All of the characters, organizations, and events portrayed in this novel are either products of the author's imagination or are used fictitiously. Sometimes both.

Copyright © 2023 by LMBPN Publishing
Cover by Mihaela Voicu http://www.mihaelavoicu.com/
Cover copyright © LMBPN Publishing
A Michael Anderle Production

LMBPN Publishing supports the right to free expression and the value of copyright. The purpose of copyright is to encourage writers and artists to produce the creative works that enrich our culture.

The distribution of this book without permission is a theft of the author's intellectual property. If you would like permission to use material from the book (other than for review purposes), please contact support@lmbpn.com. Thank you for your support of the author's rights.

LMBPN Publishing
PMB 196, 2540 South Maryland Pkwy
Las Vegas, NV 89109

Version 1.01, March 2025
ebook ISBN: 979-8-88878-124-1
Print ISBN: 979-8-88878-125-8

THE LEAD TEAM

Thanks to the JIT Readers

Christopher Gilliard
Dorothy Lloyd
Zacc Pelter
Dave Hicks
Wendy L Bonell
Diane L. Smith
Rachel Beckford
Peter Manis
Paul Westman
John Ashmore
Jackey Hankard-Brodie
Jan Hunnicutt

Editor
The SkyFyre Editing Team

CHAPTER ONE

Julie Meadows jogged across the entrance hall of the Para-Military Agency's headquarters. She was chasing her partner and still clutching her cupful of chocolate mousse. It *had* been doctor's orders to have a rich dessert, so she wasn't going to give it up, even if their boss was demanding an urgent briefing.

"Taylor, wait up!" she yelled.

"Come on!" Taylor Woodskin barely glanced over his shoulder to make sure she was still following. His dark hair bounced around his slender pointed ears.

Drama queen, Julie grumbled inwardly.

The Panama hat on her head tightened briefly around the crown, and Hat's faintly British voice filled her mind. *Kaplan must be in a mood for Taylor to be this rushed.*

When is Kaplan not *in a mood?* Julie asked.

Good point, Hat conceded.

Instead of jumping into the elevator at the end of the entrance hall as Julie expected, Taylor dashed down a hallway to the right that Julie hadn't seen before.

"Where are we going, Taylor?" Julie yelled after him.

Taylor didn't look back, just kept jogging. Julie sighed,

pausing at the corner of the hallway for a spoonful of mousse before sprinting after him again. "I'm beginning to feel like Alice in Wonderland chasing the White Rabbit!" she shouted.

Taylor stopped. "In here," he gasped, then pushed open a door and led her into an unfamiliar room.

Julie had expected to be taken to Captain Kaplan's office, which was where their briefings-slash-chewing-out sessions were generally held. Instead, she stepped into a sleek conference room.

It had no windows, but the long LED strips on the ceiling provided plenty of light. There was a massive screen at one end of the room, and a table ran down its length, flanked by leather chairs. Most of the chairs were occupied by individuals in green uniforms. Julie spotted a gaggle of fae, two or three dwarves, a few elves, and a gigantic, furious man sitting at the head of the table.

It looked as though the entire recruitment department was here. Captain Jack Kaplan could transform into a tiger at will, and it was obvious from the way his amber eyes glowed when they spotted Julie and Taylor sneaking into the room.

"Now that the rest of our department has seen fit to join us, we can begin the briefing," Kaplan rumbled. His voice echoed around the large room without effort.

Julie winced as she and Taylor slunk into chairs at the far end of the table. "I see why you were in such a hurry," she whispered to him.

Taylor grimaced. "We're in trouble."

"Well, it *has* been slow around here," Julie pointed out.

They got a battery of glares from the other recruiters. Julie kept her eyes trained on Kaplan. Two bright pink spots had appeared on the weretiger's chiseled cheeks, and he rifled angrily through the pile of paperwork on the table in front of him.

"As you all know, recent events have led to instability in Avalon," he snapped. "I don't need to explain what they are."

He doesn't? Julie hissed inwardly.

Hat hesitated. *There's been...unrest.*

Unrest? Julie raised her eyebrows.

Taylor nudged her in the ribs with an elbow. "I'll explain later."

"The Eternity Throne is going to need the support of the Para-Military Agency in the coming months, and perhaps years, more than ever." Kaplan grabbed a pen and squeezed it in a giant fist, then tapped the end on the table. "Recruitment efforts *need* to step up. We have to boost our numbers if we're going to maintain peace, stability, order, and freedom for paranormals in every dimension."

The recruiters were silent. Julie didn't see anyone nod. A few exchanged glances, while others looked like they'd tasted something bitter. Remembering how she'd been drafted into the PMA and threatened, albeit emptily, with death if she didn't produce a recruit in the first week, Julie couldn't blame them.

"Recruitment quotas will be established—and *adhered to*—for everyone in this department." Kaplan's eyes swept across his staff. He jumped to his feet, shoving his chair back, and leaned on the table with both hands. "Expect an email with your quotas shortly," he growled. "This department needs to up its game, or there will be consequences. Not just for you, but for the Eternity Throne and for all paranormals."

His eyes narrowed. "Dismissed."

The recruiters got to their feet, and a chorus of grumbling filled the room as they shuffled toward the hall. Julie had just risen when Kaplan snapped, "Meadows! Woodskin!"

"Great," Taylor muttered beside her. "Just great."

Julie felt a twinge of anxiety in the pit of her stomach. She'd been watching the clock lately to hurry home to her ailing landlady Lillie, and Kaplan wasn't happy about it. Together with Taylor, she plodded to the head of the table as the door swung shut behind the last of the other recruiters.

"Sir." Julie nodded at him.

"Meadows." Kaplan paced in front of the large screen, his teeth grinding audibly. He spun and faced her. "How is Lillie?"

Julie blinked. She hadn't known that Kaplan knew her landlady's name. "Uh, she's doing better, sir. Thanks for asking."

"Good." Kaplan waved a giant hand. "Now. You two are my best recruiters by a long shot. The last few weeks have been quiet, though. You haven't brought me anything since the six Weres from Montana."

"Not true, sir." Julie put her hands on her hips. "I recruited Malcolm Nox at his handfasting little more than a week ago."

Kaplan sighed. "Fine. Nothing since Nox, then, and his usefulness is debatable." He snorted.

Funny how Kaplan calls his godson by his last name, Julie observed internally.

Hat snickered in her mind.

"My point is, I know I can count on you two to deliver," Kaplan continued, jabbing a massive finger at them. "So do it. We need more people, and we needed them *yesterday*."

"What's going on, sir?" Julie asked.

Kaplan blinked. "Don't you read the news?"

Taylor stepped forward. "Not the *Avalon Chronicle*, sir."

Kaplan huffed. "You saw what the Sylthana Elves were like at Qbiit's trial, Meadows. They've been causing even more unrest than usual lately."

"Why the Sylthana Elves, sir? What do they have against the Eternity Throne?" Julie asked.

Kaplan glared at her. "You can't be serious."

"I'm totally serious." Julie held his gaze. "*Sir*."

Kaplan sighed and redirected his glare to Taylor. "Did she get the full history of the Eternity Throne, or did you half-ass her training?"

Taylor froze.

Kaplan waved a hand. "I don't have time for this. Get your

asses to the training orb. This time, make sure she learns *everything*, Woodskin."

Julie hadn't been back to the training room since her first day on the job a couple of months ago. It was as white and featureless as ever, except for the small pedestal in the middle, topped by the blue sphere that glowed softly. It was covered in the handprints of every paranormal species.

Hat squirmed on Julie's head as the door opened. *Ugh. This place makes me uncomfortable. I could just have explained everything to you.*

Unhappy in the presence of a stronger magic than yours? Julie teased.

Hat snorted. *As if!*

She slipped him off and handed him to Taylor. "So, same as before? I just put my hands on the orb?"

The elf nodded. "Yeah. This time, it might take longer than ten minutes, though." He turned gray, as he did when he was embarrassed. "I...uh, Kaplan's not wrong. I did half-ass your training. I thought you'd be mind-wiped and sent on your merry way by the end of the week." He rubbed the back of his neck.

"That was then." Julie winked. "Before you had your own bank account and drove yourself to work."

"Don't even remind me." Taylor let out a strained chuckle. "I'll just be in the next room, monitoring the orb."

"What do you mean, 'monitoring the orb?'" Julie raised an eyebrow.

He shuffled his feet. "There's a control room next door. I tell the orb what to tell you. I kind of didn't the last time you were here."

"That was a long time ago, Taylor. Quit feeling bad about it." Julie walked up to the orb. She hesitated for a moment, remembering how trippy this had been the last time, then took a deep breath and placed both hands in the human-hand-shaped indentations on its surface.

In the split second before the orb began to work, Julie thought, *Human hands. Are they even human?*

Then she was standing in a long, low hall, its walls wattle-and-daub. The dingy interior was lit by a series of torches set in wooden brackets in the walls. She looked at a wooden throne at the end of the hall. A tall figure strode up to it, wearing a fur-lined cloak that flared around him as he moved. She leaned closer, trying to see his face, and stumbled forward a few steps. Surprised, Julie looked down. She was in the hall, though she could swear her feet had made no sound on the mud floor.

As she stepped forward, Julie glanced at the other people in the room. A crowd had gathered, wearing furs and cloaks. None of them looked like they'd been dyed. There was an official-looking warlock wearing a gold medallion around his neck and a rumpled, pointy wizard's hat. Beside him, a page—a tiny elf with pointy ears poking out of his mop of silver hair—held a nest of leaves and feathers in both hands. It was empty except for a heavy circular impression.

The cloaked figure continued toward the throne. Julie stepped in front of the page and waved a hand in front of his face. He didn't react. This was a scene from the orb, long ago in history.

Julie turned back to the throne as the cloaked figure reached it. He spun, and his cloak flowed around his limbs. He was wearing a tall, spiky crown that glittered as though it were carved from a single diamond. Sapphires and emeralds, rubies and onyxes glowed in the edge of it, and a giant purple amethyst was set in the middle of the highest spike at the front.

The Eternity Crown! Julie gasped. She gasped again when she looked into the eyes of the Eternity King. She'd expect a Lunar Fae with a commanding presence and sharp eyes like the judge who had presided over Qbiit's trial last week. This guy had pointed ears, silver hair that reached his hips, and flashing blue eyes. He was a Sylthana Elf.

Taylor's voice echoed into the throne room. "Hello? Is this thing working?"

Julie looked up as if she expected to see speakers in the thatched ceiling. "Uh, hi?"

"Okay. Great." Taylor cleared his throat. "So, this is one of the first Sylthana Elf kings. They took the throne after the first Lunar Fae dynasty collapsed when a usurper killed the last Lunar Fae king. The other six royal families—Copper dwarves, Aether and Sylthana Elves, Lords of the Deep, Orcs of Ruin Guard, and Nox vampires—fought to drive the usurper underground."

"Cool." Julie stepped forward. "Where are we? Scandinavia?"

"Middle Europe. The Sylthana Elves are an ancient family, but this was their first Eternity King. He was instrumental in unifying the royal families to drive out the usurper."

Julie couldn't help smiling as Taylor's voice boomed around the scene like an old-fashioned narrator's. "The Sylthana Elves are still one of the most numerous races, right? How come they lost power?"

"We'll need to skip forward a few centuries for that." Taylor quit speaking and everything spun around her, making her stumble back even though the floor under her feet felt solid.

When the world lurched to an uncomfortable halt, Julie's stomach felt like it was going to launch out through her mouth. She swallowed against it and found herself staring at the towering form of a dragon. It shimmered silver and light glowed from between its scales, which clanked like metal as it lowered its giant head toward where Julie stood. Her heart flipped in her chest, and despite the wisps of smoke that curled from the dragon's nostrils, she couldn't resist raising a hand toward its muzzle. It could have swallowed her car without a second thought.

The dragon stepped forward, snaking its head past her, and Julie turned to see a line of young people. They were in a moonlit forest glade, and apart from the queue, a small crowd had amassed near the back. Most were Sylthana Elves, though Julie spotted a stout form that must have been dwarven and a swarthy-skinned elf who looked a lot like Taylor.

The dragon looked past the people queued in front of it. It huffed out a smoke ring that drifted over their heads and settled over a cloaked figure in the crowd. The figure raised its head, the cloak fell back, and Julie gasped. It was a fae girl.

When the moonlight touched her skin, it seemed to soak into it, lending her an inner radiance. Her bright eyes widened, sparkling as they met the gaze of the dragon.

"Esmerelda," Taylor's voice announced. "Our current queen. She is the first Lunar Fae to rule after the collapse. She was a commoner then, as all Lunar Fae were. Their species became pariahs after their civil war almost tore the paranormal world apart. When she was chosen to take part, no one expected her to pass the test, much less to become the Eternity Queen."

"Whoa," Julie muttered as the girl stepped forward to join the line of young people, visibly trembling. The other royals shuffled away from her as though they were desperate to get away from her.

She only had eyes for the dragon.

"This was the start of Queen Esmerelda's rule, three hundred fifty years ago in Earth time. She changed the paranormal world in many ways. Good ways," Taylor went on.

"Queen Esmerelda, who's dying," Julie murmured, remembering what Hat had told them after Qbiit's trial.

"Exactly. With no heirs in sight between abdications, mysterious disappearances, and natural causes." Taylor cleared his throat. "Wait, I'm getting ahead of myself. Once Queen Esmerelda took the Eternity Throne, conditions improved for commoners across the paranormal world. There was a real decline in elitism, and she brought about the end of segregation."

Julie tried to imagine segregation of the species in the paranormal world and shivered.

"Not everyone was happy about it, though. The Sylthana Elves suddenly found themselves far less popular. Many embraced the changes and still held important positions in the government, but not all," Taylor went on.

The forest glade scene spun out of focus, and when Julie's vision cleared, she was standing in a plaza. She was surrounded by vibrant market stalls—wooden tables with brightly colorful canopies. Paranormals in ruffled dresses, stockings, and polished leather shoes with big brass buckles sold cheese, produce, and live chickens.

When Julie wandered across the plaza, she spotted an auction ring in the middle, where an elderly pegasus with a droopy bottom lip was being auctioned to a knot of farmers gathered around. There were plenty of straw hats around, and sandstone buildings with elegant gabled roofs surrounded the plaza.

The place was familiar. When Julie looked up, she spotted it: the spires of the Eternity Palace glimmering on the distant hilltop. "Is this Avalon Village?"

"That's right," Taylor boomed. "In the late eighteenth century, Earth time."

"Whoa," Julie murmured.

A cloaked figure hurried past her, almost bumping into her. She turned to watch it go. It was tall, and she glimpsed a strand of silver hair drifting out of the cloak. She followed it through the crowd. The figure reached a large sandstone building studded with gargoyles where several other tall, cloaked individuals were waiting. Each was wearing a steel medallion, and when one of them turned, Julie spotted the insignia on it: a smile-shaped sliver. A slender crescent moon, she realized.

The new moon.

The cloaked figures looked at their leader. When he turned, Julie glimpsed his face. It was a Sylthana Elf, and his face was set in grim lines. He held up his hand and spat an unfamiliar word, and blue fire flared in his palm.

"No!" Julie yelled.

The Sylthana Elf spun and extended his hand to the building. Fire leaped from his palm to lick the roof. As screams echoed across the plaza, the other elves scattered. Blue flames appeared everywhere, devouring the stalls and snatching at clothing. Rearing in panic, the old pegasus ripped away from his handler and burst through the crowd, knocking a family of dwarves to the ground.

Julie threw up her hands and staggered out of the way as the pegasus galloped past. When she looked up again, the plaza was on fire, the flames roaring and crackling all around her. Through the smoke, a flag snapped in the breeze, and its pole rammed into the blazing rubble of a stall. It was all black except for that one scrap of crescent moon.

"The Dark Moon League," Taylor murmured. "They were an extremist Sylthana Elf group that opposed Lunar Fae rule. Esmerelda's forces largely crushed them about a hundred years into her reign, and they faded into history."

Julie didn't want to look at the burning plaza anymore. She turned away, swallowing. "I've got a feeling there's an 'until' coming."

"I'm afraid so." Taylor sighed. "Discontented Sylthana Elf supremacists have always been around. There have always been mutters of bringing back the Dark Moon League—the League, for short—and assholes posting shit about how they should come back on the paranormal dark web, that sort of thing. It was all just bullshit, though. Well, until recently."

Julie flinched. "Let me guess. That bunch of Sylthana Elves in the gallery at Qbiit's trial. The ones who made a scene about the judge being a Lunar Fae."

"They're part of it," Taylor told her. "They'd never gone so far as to call themselves the Dark Moon League until then."

The burning plaza wobbled in front of Julie's eyes, and she clenched her teeth and rode out the disorientation as the scene melted and was replaced by a familiar one—the front of the courthouse in Avalon. A lectern had been set up on the steps, and a bunch of reporters crowded around it as a handsome male Sylthana Elf strode up to the microphone. He wore his long silver hair in a single neat braid down his back and a suit so black it seemed to suck the sunlight into it.

"Was he at the trial?" Julie asked, watching among the crowd.

"No. This is Prince Lotan, the Sylthana Elf heir. He wasn't there, but he sure had plenty to say about it," Taylor grumbled.

Lotan was making a speech about how Judge Penelope, the Lunar Fae who had presided over Qbiit's trial, had botched the whole thing. In his eyes, anyway.

"I speak for all Sylthana Elves when I say the trial was conducted in a manner that appears incompetent at best and, frankly, biased at worst." Lotan's sky-blue eyes swept the crowd, and Julie shuddered as they passed through her, though she wasn't really there. "I speak, too, for the entire paranormal world when I say that we all had hoped to see real justice served. The tragic story of Qbiit was not fully told."

"Tragic!" Julie snorted, her hands clenching into fists. "Qbiit mind-controlled hundreds of yetis, killed at least six people, and injured many more!"

"It is a symptom of the collapsing system that Qbiit was unable to testify at his own trial. How can we know that the geas placed upon him was not put there by Eternity Throne agents seeking to cover their own involvement in this?" Lotan shouted to a crowd that was yelling and cheering.

"The Para-Military Agency admits that it was *their* technology that enabled the mind control of the unfortunate yetis. If the Eternity Throne cannot control its military, does it deserve to continue as it has done?"

The crowd roared, "No!." Julie clenched her fists.

"It is time for the weak to leave this throne!" Lotan continued, throwing a fist in the air. "It is time for the strong to return to power for the safety and peace of us all!"

More yells from the crowd. Julie groaned. "What an ass. Typical politician."

"Lotan's not the worst." Taylor's tone was grim. "Look at this."

The world spun again, and when it stopped, Julie was standing in front of a building that burned with blue fire. Her heart stuttered. The roof blazed and the blue fire consumed sheet metal effortlessly. She could barely see the insignia over the doors: the sign of the Para-Military Agency.

A firetruck roared up the street, siren yowling as it skidded to a halt in front of the building. The doors banged open and a troop of paranormals jumped out, wearing dragon-scale armor. A hatch on the top of the truck opened and a female siren, still yowling, rose from the hatch, dripping wet, and extended her hands toward the building. Water arced through the hatch beside her and sprayed on the flames.

"Is this... When was this?" Julie gasped.

"Saturday night," Taylor murmured. "No one was killed, but the PMA branch in Avalon South burned to the ground."

"Who did it?" Julie demanded, her gut clenched.

Taylor sighed. "Turn to your right."

Julie did. Snapping against the stars was that black flag.

When Julie stepped out of the training room, she realized that her hands were sweaty and shaking. Taylor was in the hallway. His eyebrows rose when he spotted her. "You okay, Julie?"

"The Dark Moon League is back." Julie gritted her teeth.

Taylor nodded. "It looks that way. That's why Kaplan's so determined to get more recruits."

"Well, then we'll get him those recruits." Julie thought about the panicked screams in the burning plaza. "We need high-level ones, too. Werefoxes aren't going to cut it."

They headed toward the elevator as Taylor checked his watch. "There's not much we can do today. We've got a bunch of paperwork to finish, and it's already four o'clock. Best we get to work tomorrow morning first thing."

He held Hat out to Julie, and she slipped him onto her head, feeling better because of his presence.

"You with us on this, Hat?" she asked.

"Oh, yes," Hat growled. "I've seen the League in action, and I'm not keen on their return."

"Let's meet first thing tomorrow morning, then." Julie followed Taylor into the elevator. "How about breakfast at that diner on Staten Island you like?"

Taylor grinned. "Sounds like a plan to me."

It sounded like breakfast, and it would not be close to enough to stop the Dark Moon League.

It's a start, though, Hat soothed her.

Julie folded her arms. A start would have to be good enough for now.

CHAPTER TWO

Julie leaned back in the driver's seat of the 1971 Mustang Mach 1 and stomped on the gas. The car responded with her usual throaty roar and surged away from the now-green light, tires squealing as they took the last corner and accelerated up the narrow Bay Ridge street Julie called home.

Easy. Easy! Hat yelped, skidding across the dashboard.

Sorry. Julie scooped him up and popped him onto her head. *This day has sucked. Genevieve was just cheering me up.* She patted the steering wheel fondly as they rumbled down her home street.

Hat snorted. *Okay, fine, but can she cheer you up a little more slowly and without crashing?*

Julie leaned forward and stared through the window as they approached the cozy house halfway down the street. There was a large white van parked in front with its back doors open, and a guy in a uniform and a ball cap wrestled a cardboard box out of the van and staggered to the garage with it.

"Oh, no, no, no, no, no," Julie moaned. "Tell me that's not a U-Haul."

Hat snickered.

Julie turned Genevieve into the garage with a last roar of the engine, only to find that there was almost no room to park. Nearly every inch of available surface was covered in boxes, blocking the wooden steps that led up to Julie's apartment. The back door of the main house stood open.

As Julie stepped out of Genevieve, Ball Cap Guy set down the last box and slapped his hands clean. He gave Julie a quick look, then scampered to the U-Haul and drove away with alacrity.

"Mom?" Julie yelled, scrambling through the boxes to the back door. "Lillie?"

"Oh, hello, Julie." A tall man appeared at the back door and smiled at her. He was wearing square glasses.

Julie's heart thudded. *"Ernesto?* What are you doing here?"

Her stepfather sighed. "Whatever your mother tells me to do, honestly. Good seeing you, kid."

He stepped past her, picked up a box, and headed back through the door. Julie considered banging her head on the doorframe a few times. Instead, she followed him into the living room, where her little old landlady was sitting on the sofa, watching the proceedings with interest. She held her small, scruffy dog in her arms.

"Lillie, what's going on?" Julie groaned.

Lillie Griswall grinned. "You remember how you told me some time ago that your mom can be 'a bit much?'"

Julie grimaced. "Yeah?"

"I think we're experiencing a bit of her muchness." Lillie laughed merrily.

Julie moaned. She hurried after Ernesto and into the spare room, and her head sank even further. Two boxes, already emptied, were stacked neatly in the corner. The rest of the room was crammed with her mother's things: her vomitous pink-and-green bedspread, her disproportionately huge vanity, her three gazillion books on natural living and holistic remedies, her ugly jade vase that Julie hadn't even been allowed to look at when she was a kid, let alone touch.

"Right there, Ernesto. Thanks, honey."

Rosa stood in the middle of the room, rising from the chaos like a genie of terror. She reached into an open box to pull out a huge framed photograph from Julie's middle school graduation. Horror of horrors.

"Oh, hey, Julia!" she trilled. "Look what I brought!"

"Mom, what are you *doing*?" Julie protested.

"Well, honey, since Lillie's being sweet enough to let me stay in her spare room, and there's all this empty space, I thought I'd have a few of my creature comforts brought over." Rosa beamed.

Ernesto appeared with another box. He set it on top of the first one and wandered off again.

"A *few*?" Julie gaped at her mother. "How long are you planning on staying?"

"As long as Lillie needs me to!" Rosa turned the picture around and gazed at it. "Aw, look how cute you were with your chubby little cheeks, honey."

Hat gave an unhelpful snicker. *So cute.*

Shut up! Julie hissed inwardly. She helplessly looked at the chaos. "Are you sure you need *all* of this stuff?"

"Well, baby, since I'm going to be staying here a while, I may as well do it in comfort, right?" Rosa smiled smugly. "Oh, and I needed my stocks of aloe vera juice. My customers rely on me, you know! I got three months' worth, just in case."

"Three *months*?" Julie gasped.

Rosa's face fell. "Oh, honey! I-I thought it was helpful for me to be here."

Julie took a deep breath. "It's really helpful, Mom. I didn't mean it like that." She felt a pang of guilt and reached over to touch Rosa's arm. "Thanks for being here."

Her smile returned. "Where else would I be except supporting my baby?" Rosa crowed, throwing an arm around Julie's neck and suffocating her with a hug.

Julie peeled herself away and went back into the living room, almost crashing into Ernesto as he carried another box. He was beaming like a cat that had just gotten the cream of a house to himself for a while. Her landlady was still watching from the sofa. Julie flopped down beside her. "Lillie, are you sure all this is okay with you?"

Lillie patted her knee. "Okay? My dear, I've been dreaming of having this many people in this house since my children moved out, and that was a long time ago."

Julie smiled at the light in Lillie's eyes. It seemed as though she'd shaken off the worst of the illness that had landed her in the hospital for a week, even though she'd only been home for a couple of days. "As long as you're happy."

"I'm perfectly happy, dear. Just getting a little tired, holding Pookie like this." Lillie held up the dog. "Would you mind taking her?"

Julie pulled out Genevieve's keys and spun them around her finger. "I have a better idea."

Lillie's eyes brightened.

Lillie threw a wrinkled hand out of the window as Genevieve sped down the interstate. "Woohooooooooo!" the old lady whooped, her creaky old voice surprisingly strong.

Julie laughed, not that it was audible with *Thunderstruck* playing at full volume on the radio—Lillie's choice. The I-495 was wide open in front of them. There was almost no traffic at half past six, and Genevieve surged down the fast lane, the needle of her speedometer moving between sixty and eighty.

On the backseat, Pookie, wearing her collar and harness, was fast asleep. Julie guessed that, given the dog's advanced age, this wasn't her first road trip in Genevieve.

The song came to an end, and Julie turned down the volume.

Lillie leaned back in the passenger seat, grinning, and soft laughter burst from her. "It's so good to be free again."

Julie kept her eyes on the road. "Hey, I'm really sorry it took so long for me to take you out for a road trip like I said I would. I promise that I'll take you on a real road trip soon, not just a mini one."

"Don't apologize, dear." Lillie patted Julie's arm. "I haven't been outside the city in years. Short Beach is a treat for me."

"As soon as I have an open weekend and your strength is back, I'll take you farther." Julie grinned. "Maybe out to the Finger Lakes, like you told me you used to do with the kids."

Lillie smiled. "Ever been there?"

"Nope."

"Then it's high time you went. There's a few excellent spots for skinny dipping." Lillie leered.

"Lillie!" Julie gasped.

Lillie cackled. "Come on, girl. You can't tell me this is the best pace you can get out of Gennie." She gestured at the speedometer. "Put that pedal to the metal!"

"I'm doing seventy!" Julie protested.

Lillie scoffed. "Where's your inner hellion? Don't worry, I'll explain to the cops." She paused. "Although I doubt flashing 'em is gonna work as well as it used to, except to scare 'em off."

Julie couldn't help laughing. "Inner hellion." That sounded like something it would be cool to get in touch with. She pressed Genevieve's accelerator to the floor and the Mustang surged forward, the gauge whipping up to eighty, ninety, then a hundred. The faster she drove, the more Lillie laughed.

Julie hadn't known it was possible to drive from Bay Ridge to Short Beach, Smithtown, in sixty-three minutes, but they did.

She was breathless as Genevieve purred into the parking spot beside a charming seafood restaurant overlooking the bay.

"*That's* how you drive a Mustang." Lillie beamed as she released her seatbelt.

Julie glanced at the backseat. Pookie was still soundly asleep. She was relieved that she'd decided to leave Hat safe in her apartment. He wouldn't have enjoyed the speed she'd achieved at one point on the interstate.

"I hope you're hungry." Julie stepped out of the car. "The Google reviews said that this place had amazing clam chowder."

"You know I love a bit of chowder." Lillie opened the door and got out. As she rose, she let out a gasp and clutched at Genevieve's roof.

Julie's stomach flipped. She rushed to Lillie's side and grabbed the old lady's arm. "Lillie? Are you okay?"

Lillie impatiently waved her away. "Don't fuss, dear. I'm fine." However, her cheeks were pale, and strands of her white hair blew around her face, mussed by the wind.

"Maybe we should go home," Julie hedged.

Lillie snorted. "Don't be silly. You promised me clam chowder." She winked.

Julie studied her, then forced her smile back. "Okay! Clam chowder it is." She offered Lillie an arm, hooking Pookie's lead over one finger. The little dog trotted alongside, and they slowly walked to the little restaurant.

They had almost reached the door when the faint buzz of wings caught Julie's attention. She glanced to her right and froze. A pixie strolled toward them, muttering in a language Julie couldn't understand. Her wings whirred frantically on her back as she walked. She was looking down at a smartphone, clutching it in both hands since it was almost the size of her torso. A gossamer dress woven of cobwebs blew gently around her slim figure in the sea breeze.

"Oh!" Lillie clutched her arm. "That child looks lost, don't you think?"

Julie glanced at Lillie, then at the pixie. Of course. Thanks to the Veil, Lillie couldn't see the pixie for what she was.

"We should help," Lillie murmured.

Julie cleared her throat. "Hi! Are you lost?"

The pixie looked up at her, waving the smartphone in both hands. "Stupid thing doesn't have any reception down here!" she snapped.

"Where are your parents, dear?" Lillie asked.

The pixie glanced from Lillie to Julie, then shrugged. "They're at Short Beach, ma'am. Please, can you give me directions to find them?"

"We should drive her to her parents, Julie." Lillie's grip tightened on Julie's arm.

"I'll be all right, ma'am." The pixie sighed. "I just need directions."

Julie gently disentangled her arm from Lillie's hand and crouched beside the pixie. "Can I see your phone?"

"Sure." The pixie handed it over and folded her arms, tapping one foot as she looked around impatiently.

Julie held up the phone and got a couple of bars. The route appeared on the screen, neatly marked in blue, and she crouched again to hand it back. "There! You had it on airplane mode," she fibbed for Lillie's benefit. "Now, are you going to call your parents?"

The pixie glanced at Lillie, then nodded. "Yes, ma'am. I sure am."

"Good. Will you be okay?" Julie asked.

"Yeah, I'll be fine." The pixie simpered at Lillie. "They're close by. They'll come and get me."

"Okay." Julie took Lillie's arm again. "Good luck."

She led Lillie toward the restaurant, but the old lady stopped and looked back as the pixie strode off. "She's so young," Lillie protested. "We should drive her."

"Her parents will be here soon," Julie consoled her. "I'm sure she'll be okay."

Lillie gave a last glance back, then shuffled onward. "I trust your judgment, dear."

Julie had had to make her peace with keeping the truth from Lillie for her own safety.

"Oh, hey!" the pixie shouted.

Julie looked back. The pixie had tucked her smartphone into a backpack that hooked over her wings. She'd spread them, and they sparkled in the evening light.

"Thanks," the pixie called.

Julie waved goodbye, and she and Lillie went into the restaurant.

It was dark by the time Genevieve purred into the garage. Lillie groaned, placing both hands on her stomach as Julie brought the car to a halt. "Ooh! Gently. This old lady is very full of that excellent clam chowder."

"It *was* good, right?" Julie laughed. "You didn't seem all that full when you urged me to do a hundred on the interstate again."

Lillie chuckled. "Speed's never bothered me."

Julie got Lillie and Pookie out of the car and into the living room. Rosa was in the kitchen, packing an obscene amount of aloe vera juice into the cabinets.

"We're home, Mom!" Julie called as she got Lillie settled on the couch.

Rosa popped her head into the living room. "Oh, hey, you two. Did you bring me some of that chowder you promised?"

"Of course." Julie held up the plastic bag.

Leaving Lillie contentedly watching *Judge Judy* on the couch, she brought the bag into the kitchen, stepped over boxes of aloe vera juice, and set it on the table. "Where's Ernesto?"

"He just left for home, sweet thing." Rosa opened the bag. "Ooh, this smells good. Thanks for getting Lillie out of the house. She needed it, and I unpacked in peace."

"It was fun." Julie hesitated. "I'm heading upstairs to bed, but thanks for doing this, Mom."

"Anytime, baby." Rosa pinched Julie's cheek. She stifled a groan and fled upstairs.

When she stepped into her cozy apartment, Julie let out a breath of relief. It wasn't a big space, just enough for her kitchenette, a single bed pushed into one corner, a bathroom, a comfy chair, and a copious number of bookshelves, but walking into it felt like wrapping herself in a cocoon.

"Home already, are you?" Hat snarked from his spot on the back of the comfy chair.

"Shut up, you." Julie poked his crown to annoy him. "I'm taking a shower."

"Go shower, smelly human," Hat retorted.

"Speak for yourself, stinky hat," Julie yelled over her shoulder.

She showered, leaving Hat to attempt to smell himself without being in possession of a nose. She pulled on silky PJs and her unicorn slippers, then stood in front of the window that overlooked the street. It only provided a view of some garbage cans, the neighbor outside working on his ever-broken old car, and some walls, but she could see a few city lights blinking in the darkness. Stretching luxuriously, Julie rolled onto the balls of her feet, arms extended over her head.

"You looked very worried about the political situation," Hat quipped.

Julie sank into her comfy chair, scooping her book into her lap. "It was pretty scary seeing everything in the orb this afternoon," she admitted. "But it's not bothering me for some reason."

Hat plopped onto her head, slithered down her shoulder, and landed on her knee. "I have my theories as to why."

Julie raised an eyebrow. "I'm sure you'll share them."

"It's because you have a plan in place to help." Hat wriggled, making himself comfortable. "You feel like you can do something about it."

Julie nodded slowly. "You know," she murmured, "it feels like I've found my niche. Like I belong." She rubbed his crown with her knuckles. "Thanks for being part of that."

"Don't get all sentimental," Hat grumbled, but he cuddled in her lap like a happy cat as she picked up her book and began to read.

CHAPTER THREE

Julie straightened Hat on her head with one hand as she scampered down the stairs with Genevieve's keys jingling in the other. She paused at the bottom of the steps to pop her head around the back door. Pookie wagged her tail from the sofa. Rosa's and Lillie's voices came from the kitchen.

"Mom! Lillie!" Julie yelled. "You two okay?"

Lillie appeared in the doorway, beaming. "We're fine, dear. I'm teaching your mother my scone recipe."

"It's very good!" Rosa shouted from the kitchen.

"Okay. I'm heading out for breakfast. See you tonight!" Julie called.

"Julia! Wait!" Rosa shrieked. "You forgot your morning juice!"

Julie pretended not to hear as she closed the back door and hustled over to Genevieve. Hat jumped from her head to the dash as she started the engine. "Ignoring your mother? Classy."

"You don't have a tongue." Julie backed Genevieve out of the garage. "You don't know what aloe vera juice tastes like."

Still, she felt guilty as she drove away and realized she wouldn't be heading to breakfast with Taylor right now or meeting with him about how they were going to change the world if it wasn't for her mom staying here to help with Lillie.

Julie still felt vaguely guilty about pretending not to hear her mother as she pulled into the parking lot at Jingles. After she got out of Genevieve, she shot her a quick text.

Have a nice day. Thanks for your help!

She added flower emojis since moms seemed to be addicted to those.

The bright fifties-style diner was crammed with breakfast eaters sitting in the booths by the large windows when Julie stepped inside, glancing at her reflection in the brightly polished red-and-white counter. Hat looked particularly fetching today as a purple beret with her white blouse and purple slacks.

Very cute, she told him.

Not too ugly yourself, he replied.

Taylor was sitting in the corner booth he liked, sipping a vanilla milkshake.

"What are you, ten?" Julie scooted into her spot opposite him.

Taylor rolled his eyes. "As if milkshakes for breakfast have an age limit on them. I ordered a bubblegum one for you."

"Seriously?" Julie frowned. "Hey, how did you know bubblegum was my favorite milkshake flavor?"

Taylor grinned. "Woman's intuition?"

Julie swatted him with a menu. "Get it together, Mr. Woodskin. We're supposed to be changing the world here."

"Okay, okay." Taylor chuckled and held up both hands.

A waiter came over, handed Julie her disgustingly blue milkshake, and took their orders for pancakes with extra maple syrup.

He wandered off, and Julie sucked at her straw, feeling vaguely weird.

"Right. Let's talk strategy." Taylor plucked out a notepad and slapped it on the table.

Julie raised an eyebrow. That was new, but she wasn't going to query her partner's sudden businesslike attitude. "I think we should go straight to a group that's been disaffected by the Sylthana Elves. You said the Lunar Fae improved life for a lot of the more 'common' species." She made air quotes. "How about we try some of those?"

Taylor sat back, studying her. "We're trying to avert an all-out war, remember? Not start it by taking sides."

Julie shrugged. "We already took sides. We work for the Eternity Throne."

"Yes, but at this point, the Sylthana Elves are not our enemies," Taylor shot back. "In fact, *I* think we should look at recruiting non-radical Sylthana Elves. A lot of them still support the throne, and they could be useful."

"'Could be useful?'" Julie raised an eyebrow. "We're going to need something a bit better than that, Taylor. Seriously, let's go to a community that we know is against the Sylthana Elves. We could recruit droves of them."

"Yes, and that could tip the political balance even more dangerously in the direction of conflict." Taylor folded his arms.

Julie snorted. "Kaplan would have warned us away from those groups if that was the case. Let's try the warlocks. They're super high-value, aren't they? Oh, and where are the Drow on this?"

"Warlocks? Drow?" Taylor shook his head. "It's not going to work, Julie. We should go for something realistic."

"I think we left 'realistic' behind when we recruited Ellie Feathertouch in a single week," Julie retorted.

Taylor frowned. "Can you trust my guidance on this? I've been in this world for longer than you."

Julie bridled. "Going to play that card, are you?" Her voice rose, and the words hovered on the tip of her tongue. *I'm more a part of this world than you know.* She'd managed to forget that Dr. Olena from the PMA medical unit had recently told her she might not be human.

Thinking back to the pixie who'd asked for help yesterday, she suddenly wondered why *she* had been asked for help. Why the pixie had kept glancing from her to Lillie, as though the pixie had somehow known.

Taylor ran a hand through his hair. "I didn't mean it like that."

Julie knew he hadn't, and she let the moment go. Dr. Olena had to be wrong. She *couldn't* be a paranormal.

Hello. Hello? Hat spoke in both their minds. *Forgetting something, are we? Such as a certain magical artifact that currently exists mostly to track down recruits, hmm?*

"Sorry," Taylor muttered. He lowered his arms. "I'm a bit edgy because of...well, all this."

"It's fine." Julie sat back. "Okay, what are your ideas?"

Get that pen ready, Taylor, Hat told him. *If you two don't want to take sides, let's choose more neutral paras. Shh! No protesting. Just hear me out. There are plenty of options.* He cleared his throat. *I hope you're writing, Taylor.*

"Uh-huh." Taylor clicked his pen.

Let's start with the griffins, Hat began.

Taylor jotted down the word. "Intimidating, but a strong sense of justice. It worked out with Cironius."

"No, it didn't," Julie muttered. "We recruited the Weres, not the centaur."

Taylor inclined his head.

Now, now, children, Hat snapped. *Next, let's look at the unicorns. Excellent creatures to have on your side in a fight and pure of heart.*

"Yes, but violent," Taylor pointed out, scribbling down the word. "Also some of the wildest creatures in the paranormal world."

Julie suppressed a pang of disappointment. She'd seen a

unicorn once in Avalon Village, but she wouldn't mind seeing one again.

Next, the elementals, Hat ordered. *Also the tree and water spirits. The Green Man. Banshees.*

"The Green Man?" Taylor wrote it down. "Seriously?"

Don't interrupt, Hat barked. *I'm throwing out ideas here. Also add the Djinn, the sprites, and the brownies.*

Taylor stopped writing as the waiter returned with their breakfast. Taking a bite of her pancakes, Julie looked at the list. "Okay, how about the unicorns? What were you saying about them?"

Taylor shook his head. "They're very reclusive and loners too. Finding one would be nearly impossible, let alone getting to talk to it. Even then, they're more likely to kill us than join us."

"Yeah, I'd rather focus on recruiting groups *en masse* if we can." Julie leaned forward, reading. "Elementals sound cool, but my training is telling me they're difficult to find and communicate with." Julie grunted. "Pity. Considering the Sylthana Elves' penchant for fire, we could use a water elemental."

Taylor crossed out unicorns and elementals. "Naiads might not be elementals, but they're also water spirits, and they often live in the same woods as dryads. And the Green Man." He glanced at Hat. "Crazy as that is. He's not interested in mortal minutiae."

"Worth a try," Julie decided.

Taylor circled the last three names. "The Djinn?"

"Scared of being put into lamps?" Julie quipped.

Not far off the truth, Hat told her. *They're wary of capture and slavery, understandably. Also tend to be powerful and dangerous to approach.*

Taylor crossed them off.

"How about sprites?" Julie asked.

"Yeah, they're tricksters. More trouble than they're worth."

Taylor crossed them out. "Brownies are easy and useful for logistics if they can be found."

"I think the griffins, dryads, and naiads are our best bet." Julie propped her chin on one hand.

"Or we could try for something more traditional," Taylor growled. "Whatever happened to recruiting elves, fae, Weres, orcs, and dwarves? They're easier to find."

Julie shook her head. "We'd be better off leaving the easy signings to the rest of the department."

Yes, you heard Kaplan. Hat preened. *We're the best he's got.*

Taylor opened his mouth to protest, then shut it, shaking his head as he shoved another forkful of pancakes into his mouth.

"Hey, what about dragons? I'm sure one of those would be great to have on our side in a fight." Julie couldn't stop thinking about that shimmering silver dragon.

Taylor burst out laughing and almost choked on his pancakes. Hat sniggered. Julie glared at them while Taylor spluttered and slapped his chest.

"A Lord of the Deep deigning to get involved in the OPMA?" Taylor shook his head. "No way." He held out a hand. "I don't mean to disrespect you or anything."

Julie's cheeks reddened, but she waved a hand. "Whatever. Let's just finish our breakfast. Where do we find griffins and the tree and water spirits?"

"All in Avalon, outside the village," Taylor told her.

"Well, then we'd better submit some paperwork for a trip to Avalon." Julie stabbed her pancake with a fork.

They ate the rest of their breakfast in silence.

Julie prayed that the pearl-wearing elf in the admin department would be in a better mood than usual. She was not.

Her back and hips ached when she and Taylor finally stumbled out of the department, having collected, filled in, and returned their paperwork for a work trip. This simple task had taken four hours.

"Kill me now," Julie moaned as they shuffled into the elevator.

Taylor hit the button for the ground floor. "I swear that elf wants me dead. She wants to kill me stone-dead with boredom."

"Or backache." Julie rubbed her lower back. "Seriously, we have lobster at least once a week in the cafeteria. Couldn't the PMA spring for comfortable chairs in the admin department?"

"Or a little magic to expedite things?" Taylor flicked a finger, and a pen flew out of Julie's blouse pocket and into his hand.

Julie took it back. "As simple as that. Or just let us fill in the forms online and email them! Is this the twenty-first century?"

Her stomach growled as they headed for the cafeteria, but they'd barely reached the doors when Julie's phone buzzed. Her heart jumped. *Lillie*. When she pulled it out, it was Kaplan.

"Hold up." She touched Taylor's arm to stop him as she opened the text.

MEADOWS, MY OFFICE. NOW.

BRING WOODSKIN.

KAPLAN.

"Does he know you don't have to sign texts?" Julie mumbled. "And what's with the caps?"

"I'm guessing we're going to have to wait for lunch." Taylor sighed.

They headed back to the elevator, which took them up to the third floor. After striding into a large, communal office, they headed for the door at the back of the room.

They passed through it into a roomy office with high windows. An equestrian portrait of a burly figure on a rearing horse occupied the back wall. Kaplan sat behind his desk, glaring at his computer screen, almost as annoyed as the battle-ready Kaplan in the portrait.

He looked up as Taylor closed the door. "Ah, if it isn't my two favorite red flags." He gestured at the armchairs by his desk. "Sit."

Julie's gut clenched. *I should have expected a Kaplan confrontation.* She sighed inwardly as she sank into one of the chairs. *I'll bet he's going to say the same thing Taylor did—that we should focus on the "traditional" groups.*

Hat sighed. *The Eternity Throne has stood for diversity since the rise of the Lunar Fae. I was hoping to further that agenda.*

Yeah, me too, Julie grumbled.

Kaplan folded his giant arms. "I've just received travel paperwork to Avalon for the two of you. Want to tell me what shenanigans you two have planned?"

"We're hoping to recruit groups of paras instead of one at a time, sir." Julie tipped up her face to meet his eyes. "We're thinking of targeting the griffins, the dryads, and the water spirits. Even talk to the Green Man."

Kaplan raised a huge, hairy eyebrow. "The Green Man? Which one?"

"What do you…" Julie stopped.

Taylor interjected, "Sir, there's a far greater concentration of paras in Avalon. It makes sense to focus our recruiting efforts there, especially since Avalon Village was directly affected by the League's actions. It might have inspired people to make a change. Or join the PMA."

Julie shot him a grateful look. That had been her idea.

Kaplan waved a massive hand. "Fine. Sounds good. You have the green light."

They were silent. Julie's "Yes, but" sat on her tongue, unused. She swallowed it. Taylor gave her a wide-eyed look.

"Don't look so startled," Kaplan grumbled, then turned back to his computer.

Julie cleared her throat. "When we were summoned to the office, we both thought—"

"I know what you thought." Kaplan curled his lips in a smile, revealing rows of very white, very sharp teeth. "I take pride in intimidating my recruiters."

Julie couldn't tell if he was joking.

"I just want to know what you're doing so I can preemptively cover your asses for when you invariably land neck-deep in shit." Kaplan waved them off. "Now, go out there and get me some recruits. Dismissed!"

Julie didn't need to be told twice. She fled toward the elevator, and Taylor was close behind her. Both were silent until the doors slid closed. The elevator jolted, heading for the ground floor.

"Is it just me, or was that super weird?" Julie asked.

Taylor burst out laughing. "That was *very* weird!"

"He didn't yell at us or try to stop us, and he even sort of gave us a compliment?" Julie threw up her hands, laughing. "Who is he, and what did he do with Captain Jack Kaplan?"

Taylor shrugged. "I don't get it either. Maybe you and Hat were right. This *is* a good idea." He lowered his head, sheepish. "Hey, I'm sorry about what I said. I didn't mean it that way."

"Forget about it." Julie waved a hand. "But I'm going to need lunch before I get seriously hangry."

"Same," Taylor agreed. "I hope it's—"

The elevator jolted to a stop and the doors swung open, allowing a gust of breathtakingly cold air and a swirl of snowflakes inside. Julie stumbled back, gasping with shock. She grabbed Hat to keep him from blowing off her head. Taylor reached behind his ear and held out a hand.

In front of them, snow and ice stretched in every direction. The sky was gray, and a howling wind swept a mountainside. Everything was white and gray, even the figures of the two orc guards standing just beyond the doors. They glanced at Julie and Taylor with little surprise.

It wasn't the first time Julie had seen Switzerland through the elevator doors, but it was always a shock.

"Shit!" Taylor grumbled, jabbing buttons. "This stupid confluence of magical dimensions can be so annoying."

"Wait!" Julie grabbed the doors to stop them. "Someone's coming."

Taylor reached behind his ear again and pulled out something the size of a toothpick. He clenched his fist, and with a hum, it transformed into a six-foot-tall magical staff.

"You're still carrying that?" Julie hissed.

Taylor shrugged. "It's handy."

Julie was beginning to wish she'd brought her gun. The two orc guards had drawn their weapons. Instead, she clenched her hands into fists and held them up by her jaw as the figure strode out of the swirling snow toward them. It was huge, hairy, burly...

"A yeti?" Julie lowered her fists.

"That's Randkluft." Taylor turned the staff back into its toothpick size again and tucked it behind his ear.

The yeti that stepped out of the snow was seven feet tall. Dense dark fur covered his entire body, except for two white tufts that rose on either side of his head. His dark eyes swept them as he approached. Julie realized that this was her first time seeing Randkluft, or any yeti, in his natural environment. Here, he didn't lumber. His giant feet crossed the snowdrifts with a loping liquid grace. His thick coat rippled in the wind, snowflakes starring the black fur.

When he got to them, Randkluft reached into a leather satchel by his side. He pulled out a white envelope and thrust it into Julie's hands.

"Uh, hi," Julie squeaked.

Randkluft just looked at her for a few moments. The depth of his gaze made it impossible to look away. Julie's fingers closed on the envelope, and Randkluft's lips twitched around his tusks, curving upward in a smile. Then he loped away and disappeared into the snow.

"What's that?" Taylor yelled over the howling wind.

Julie hit the button to close the doors. They slid shut, sealing the recruiters in sudden warmth, even though snowflakes still swirled around them. She held up the envelope. "I'm not sure." It was blank.

"I can read it," Hat told them. "Even if it's in yeti."

"Let's get back to our office before we go to lunch. We can stash it there and ask Kaplan about it if we need to." Taylor hit the button for the third floor.

Julie gently opened the envelope as the elevator began to move. She pulled out a piece of plain cream-colored parchment with smooth letters written on it in charcoal. They were unreadable but flowed attractively.

"To the one who fears not the sound of the thunder," Hat read. *"The Queen of the Wind and Sky calls you from the other lands to stand before her and speak of what has been done and what will be done. You shall journey to the Palace of the Ice Heart after three moons have risen and three suns have set."*

"So, a summons from the yeti queen?" Julie guessed.

"For Friday," Taylor added.

Julie winced when she remembered seeing a stalactite crash down on a cavern filled with yetis. She didn't know if any of them had been killed. It hadn't been her intention.

"Don't make that face." Taylor patted her shoulder. "You're the one who freed them, remember?"

Julie swallowed. "Yeah, but I also hurt a lot of them."

"She probably wants you to tell her what happened from your perspective." Hat briefly tightened on her head. "Yeti culture is based on storytelling, remember?"

"Yeah, and you'll have to tell it as long-windedly as you can." Taylor spread his arms. "You, the one who fears not the sound of thunder, were traveling with your companions, the one who loves his Audi RS in carbon-black and the one who snickers in a most annoying fashion when things go wrong."

"Hey!" Hat protested.

Julie grinned. "Maybe they want to tell *us* the story. It'll take a day or two."

"Or they want to have you both for dinner. Then I won't have to put up with you anymore," Hat grumbled.

"Nonsense. We both know yetis eat nuts and things." Julie snorted.

"Better hope you're not staying for dinner then, considering you don't like nuts," Taylor pointed out.

Julie threw up her hands. "My mom made me *live* on nuts for, like, two weeks, okay? She had this whole detox thing going on. It's not my fault."

Taylor was laughing as the elevator doors opened—on their floor, this time—and they headed for their office on the right side of the large room. Julie just had time to glimpse the cozy space with its ugly mermaid painting before Taylor's desk chair spun and a vampire tumbled out of it.

"Malcolm!" Taylor gasped. "Were you playing Minesweeper on my computer?"

"No! Yes. Okay, a little." Malcolm Nox's translucent cheeks colored faintly.

Julie grinned. It was good to see the young vampire looking so put-together, with his suit pressed and his hair neatly styled in a way that almost hid his faux hawk, which was still growing out. "Missing your old life, huh?"

"Oh, *no*." Malcolm laughed. "Being a vampire prince who does nothing but play online games all day was overrated." His eyes met Julie's. They had deep-crimson irises. "Working for Uncle Jack is pretty cool."

"So cool that you feel the need to hide in my office, playing offline games all day?" Taylor raised an eyebrow.

"I wasn't *hiding*." Malcolm drew himself up to his full height, tipping up his chin in a way that reminded Julie that he was the heir to one of the most powerful thrones in the paranormal world. "Sire asked me to talk to you, actually."

"Oh?" Taylor blanched.

Julie grinned. "How *is* your dad?"

"He's fine. Pretty pleased with me being here at the PMA, in fact." Malcolm grinned. "He wanted me to ask you and Taylor to come to dinner tonight."

"Tonight? What time?" Julie checked her watch. "It's already past three."

"At six, or earlier if you can make it. After work was what he said." Malcolm waved a hand.

"I don't know—" Julie began, but Hat's crown tightened around her head, stopping her. *Tell him yes,* he murmured.

Why? Julie demanded.

Just trust me on this, Hat insisted.

Julie said nothing, and Taylor took her silence for assent. "Thanks, Malcolm. We'll be there."

"Great." Malcolm's phone played Taylor Swift's *Love Story*, and he plucked it out of his pocket. "Oops, it's Cassidy. See you."

He scampered off, answering the phone in a high-pitched voice.

Julie plucked Hat off her head and glared at him. "Uh, dude, I have to get home to my sickly landlady and my crazy mother."

"I don't think you understand." Hat paused. "Dinner with Julius Nox is like breakfast with anyone else. It must be urgent if he wants you there."

"Us?" Taylor frowned. "We're nobody."

"Hey, speak for yourself," Julie shot back.

"You saved his son from certain death at Qbiit's hands," Hat pointed out. "He trusts you. This might be important."

Julie sighed. "Fine. I'll call my mom. Hopefully, she'll be okay with Lillie for tonight, but if it sounds like they need help, I'll have to cancel."

"Cancel?" Taylor squawked. "On Julius Nox?"

Ignoring him, Julie flopped into her chair and pulled out her phone. Lillie didn't answer. Her heart clenched in her chest as she dialed her mother's number. It seemed to take an eternity before Rosa's voice screeched in her ear.

"*Juliaaaaaaa!*"

Julie leaned back in her chair, pinching the bridge of her nose. "Mom. Are you guys okay?"

"We're *fine*, sweetheart! When are you coming home?" Rosa cooed.

There was music in the background. Was that *Under Pressure*?

"What are you guys listening to?" Julie blurted.

Rosa giggled. "Just taking a little trip down memory lane."

Someone laughed in the background. Lillie. Julie couldn't help smiling, wondering when the old lady had last had this much company.

"Okay. Hey, Mom, I'm sorry, but I, uh, have to work late tonight. Something came up." Julie clenched her fist, fingernails digging into her palm. She couldn't tell her mother that the vampire king had invited her to dinner. "I'll see you guys late if you think you two will be okay. Otherwise, I'll come right home."

"Honey, don't you worry about *us*. We're having a whale of a time. Lillie's fine, and she's taking her medicine and drinking some of that ginger tea. It's making a big difference." Rosa sighed. "I just worry about you working so hard. Is that company paying you overtime?"

Julie thought about the hitherto-unthinkable amount of money in her bank account after her recruitment bonuses for the past few weeks. "Yeah, don't worry. They're treating me well. We just had a deadline pushed up."

"Okay, honey. Make sure you eat something! You really should have taken some of those cinnamon pills." Rosa sighed.

"I'll be okay. Don't worry. Taylor and I will get something for dinner." Julie threw the name out like a bone and instantly regretted it.

Her mother pounced. "Ooh! Well, in that case, take your time, Julia. He's quite the catch."

"Mom." Julie allowed her head to thunk on her desk. "I gotta go."

"Okay, baby. Take care of yourself," Rosa ordered.

"I will. And don't tire Lillie out, okay?" Julie added.

There was mad cackling from the other end of the line, and Julie shook her head, ending the call.

"Everything okay?" Taylor asked.

"Yeah, everything's fine." Julie stretched. "Let's do some research for the trip, at least. We can head out early tomorrow morning."

At five o'clock, Julie shut off her computer. She typed the Nox mansion's address in her phone's navigation app and winced at the blood-red line running through Staten Island's suburbs.

"Wow, the traffic sucks," she groaned. "We'll get there in half an hour even if we leave right now."

"Uh, we can't." Taylor cleared his throat, looking up from his screen. "I need to change first."

"Change?" Julie laughed. "Into what? You got evening wear stashed in your locker or something?"

Taylor's cheeks turned gray. Julie laughed harder. "Oh, my goodness. You *do* have evening wear stashed in your locker!"

"Who doesn't?" Taylor spluttered. He got up and strode over to their lockers on the other side of the office.

Julie gaped as he swung the door open and pulled out an elegant suit in forest green with tails and a bowtie. She snorted, tried to cover her laughter, and failed.

"What's so funny?" Taylor demanded.

Julie leaned back in her chair. "What's that for? Unexpected date nights?"

Taylor scoffed. "I *am* a prince of the Aether Elves, I'll have you know. Sometimes I have important stuff to show up for."

"Uh-huh." Julie chuckled. "Like, you've been to so many important things since I got to know you."

"Okay, fine." Taylor drew himself up to his full height. "I *did* have quite a few date nights since you asked. Also, I don't know anyone who doesn't have evening wear at work."

"You don't really know anyone," Julie pointed out.

Hat snickered.

"I get your point." Taylor hung the suit over the back of his chair and opened the locker again, rooting around for a shirt. "I mean, it's not like you're going to dinner at the Nox mansion dressed like *that*."

Julie glanced down at her neat slacks and blouse. "What's wrong with how I'm dressed?" she demanded.

Taylor laughed. "You slay me, Julie."

She folded her arms and stood up. "Seriously, what's wrong with this?"

Taylor glanced at her, his eyes widening. "Uh…"

"Just because *you* have fancy clothes stashed away in your locker doesn't mean every person in the world is fully prepared for a five-course meal in royal company, you know," Julie snapped. She smoothed her slacks. "And for your information, yes, I *am* going to dinner dressed like this."

Ouch, Hat commented.

Taylor ran a hand through his hair. "I didn't mean it like that, Julie."

"Whatever." Julie got up. "I'll meet you there."

She snatched Genevieve's keys, hooked her backpack over her shoulder, and strode away.

CHAPTER FOUR

Julie gave Genevieve an extra tap on the gas pedal as she turned into the courtyard of the Nox mansion. White roses bloomed around the courtyard, filling the air with their thick, sweet fragrance as she stepped out of the car.

Looks like I'm the first one here, she told Hat, glancing around the empty space.

Well, you wouldn't be here on your own if you weren't so annoyed with Taylor, Hat told her.

Julie snorted. *I'm not annoyed.*

Uh-huh. Sure you're not, Hat muttered.

Sarcasm? Really? Is that what we're doing now? Julie shot back, closing the door.

"Good evening, Miss Meadows."

Julie almost jumped out of her skin. When she whipped around, the Noxes' butler stood six inches away, wearing white gloves, a suit, and a top hat with a thin veil hanging over his face. Gerald Perkins' lips twitched in the closest thing to a smile she'd ever seen from him.

"Oh, hey, Gerald. Still sneaking up on people, are we?"

"I *am* a vampire butler, miss." Gerald sniffed. "Your keys, if you please."

"My keys?" Julie slowly held them out.

"Yes, miss. I will park your car and return it when you leave." Gerald held out a hand.

Julie dropped the keys into his palm. *Let's not tell Lillie I let a vampire drive her car*, she mumbled inwardly.

My non-existent lips are sealed, Hat assured her.

Gerald paused, turning to her. "Miss Meadows?"

"Yes?" Julie met his eyes.

His lips did twitch this time. "It's good to see you."

He slipped behind Genevieve's wheel, revved the engine expertly, and drove off with only a slight squeal of the tires. Julie walked toward the mansion, shaking her head and smiling.

She went through the rose garden and up to the front door, which was lit by little glass orbs containing perfect tiny gold flames that burned in mid-air. She followed the sound of soft music down the hall and onto the back porch, a wide space floored with polished redwood and surrounded by lilies that filled the air with their heady scent. More of the fiery glass orbs hung in mid-air over the table, stirring gently in the cool summer breeze.

Julie hesitated when she saw the table, trying not to let her mouth hang open. The centerpiece was living jasmine that grew across the pure white tablecloth, but this jasmine bloomed in shades of purple and blue. She guessed Julius had done some supernaturally creative crossbreeding in his hothouse again. The table was laid with more cutlery per plate than Julie had ever seen, and glowing letters that hovered in mid-air over each plate spelled out the names of the guests.

Taylor's hesitation about her choice of clothes didn't seem weird anymore.

You're fine, Hat whispered to her. *Don't worry.*

I thought it was just dinner, Julie whimpered inwardly.

Footsteps sounded in the hallway behind her. She looked up to see Taylor, immaculate in the forest green suit, and felt a pang of relief. "Hey," she hissed. "This is, uh, pretty nice."

"I'm looking forward to the food." Taylor smiled. Julie half-expected him to rub her nose in the fact that she was hopelessly underdressed, but instead, he offered her his arm. "Shall we?"

"Okay." Julie threaded her arm through his.

As they stepped out onto the porch, Julius Nox looked up. He was about to take his place at the head of the table. The porch was shaded by the surrounding plants, and the vampire king wore a simple cream-colored suit that made his skin look even paler. His jet-black ponytail hung neatly down his back. "Good evening, Miss Meadows, Prince Taylor." He nodded at them. "I'm glad you could come."

Julie smiled. "Thank you, Sire."

Taylor was ogling the names hovering above the plates, and she heard him gasp.

"Please, take your seats. The other guests have just arrived." Julius strode smoothly past them.

Taylor led Julie to two seats near the far end of the table. "Have you *seen* who's invited?" he hissed, gripping her arm tightly.

"I thought it was just us," Julie admitted. "Until I saw the table. Why? Who is it?"

"Important people," Taylor muttered.

He pulled out her chair for her. Julie gave him a faint glare, dropped into it, and scooted it into place herself. The last guy who'd pulled out her chair had decided to split the check at the last minute, leaving the then-unemployed Julie without the cash for a ride home. Taylor took the hint and sank into his chair beside hers.

"Important people like who?" Julie asked.

Taylor's eyes flicked up. Following his gaze, Julie watched as Malcolm and his wife Cassidy emerged from the house. Cassidy was wearing a tight red dress that hugged her curves in all the right places, and she knew it. Her hips swayed as she strutted over the hardwood in bright red heels. She shot Julie a grin as they moved toward the head of the table, and Julie waved.

"That's just Malcolm and Cassidy," Julie whispered to Taylor. "I mean, I know they're heirs to the Nox throne and all, but..."

Taylor nodded at the door. "Cassidy's parents. Adelaide and Terence Consta. Heads of the second most powerful vampire family in the world."

Julie could see where Cassidy had gotten her psycho-bitch side from. Adelaide Consta wore a tight black dress covered with sequins and gazed down her long nose at the table with the corners of her mouth turned down. She simpered at Julius, but when her eyes met Julie's, they narrowed. Beside her, a balding vampire seemed washed out by comparison.

"She looks like Kim Kardashian," Julie whispered to Taylor.

Taylor raised an eyebrow. "She's richer than any human billionaire."

"See?" Julie shrugged. "Kim Kardashian."

Taylor snorted. More guests arrived. It was a distinguished bunch: a handsome pair of Copper Dwarves and two well-dressed orcs. Kaplan followed them, wearing his dress uniform. Julie didn't think she'd ever seen him wear anything other than some form of PMA uniform.

"Amazing that he can do a full split in that," she whispered to Taylor, who snorted into his lemonade.

The lemonade had arrived a few minutes earlier, borne by silent, elegant waiters. It had a strange, tropical flavor Julie didn't recognize.

"Oh, no!" Taylor moaned, ducking his head.

"What?" Julie looked up.

Taylor grimaced. "My family's here."

A crew of Aether Elves strode onto the porch. She recognized Shae, Taylor's asshole brother, and Ilsa, his cool oldest sister. There were a few other sibling-age elves and—

"My parents," Taylor whimpered, burying his nose in his lemonade like that might save him from being seen.

Georgina and Benedict Woodskin, Julie's orb training told her. *The reigning king and queen of the Aether Elves.*

Reigning buttheads to their youngest son, Julie muttered inwardly.

Hat snickered. *Well put, but maybe keep that to yourself.*

Georgina was so thin that she looked as though she might blow away. In contrast, Benedict was a solid brick of an elf. The impression was heightened by his military hairstyle, cut perfectly flat on the top. He spotted Taylor and shot him a death glare that tempted Julie to blow him a raspberry. Instead, she death-glared back until Benedict broke his gaze and moved toward his seat near the head of the table.

Everyone sat, and the waiters arrived with the hors d'oeuvres, yogurt pannacotta drizzled with honey. Julius took the first bite. The rest of the guests followed suit, and Julie took a cautious nibble. "This is good," she whispered to Taylor. "Breakfast-y, though."

"This is breakfast when you're a vampire, remember?" Taylor smiled. "An early one, too."

"A sumptuous five-course breakfast for dinner? Sign me up." Julie grinned.

Julius cleared his throat, and silence instantly fell around the table. Even Benedict and Georgina Woodskin looked at him with wide eyes.

"Now that everyone and their heirs are here, let us begin." Julius inclined his head graciously.

Why am I here? Julie mused.

You did *save his son's life*, Hat reminded her.

Julius' eyes swept the table. "Those assembled here are the

individuals I trust most in any dimension." His voice boomed around the porch. "Trouble brews in Avalon, friends, and it is guaranteed to spill into the rest of the world. We are going to have to work together when it comes to preserving peace, not only within the paranormal world but in the world as a whole."

Julie's stomach clenched. She hadn't considered the possibility that the unrest in Avalon could affect this world. *Her* world. Mom's and Lillie's world.

"I shall not call this a council of war, for I hope that if we work together, it will not come to that. Consider this a council for the prevention of war." A smile flickered over the vampire's face.

There was a faint tap from Julie's right. She glanced over to see that the orc seated beside her was looking intently at her phone. She was tall and slim, with a swirl of tattoos over the dark gray skin of her cheeks. Small tusks barely peeked out from her bottom lip, which was bright purple with lipstick. Her phone had a pink cover and a silly pom-pom charm hanging from it on a thin chain. The orc's fingers flew over the screen.

Julius paused, his eyes narrowing.

"Kellian." The orc in the sparkling silver Armani suit sitting beside her put a hand on her shoulder. "Please. Put your phone away." His accent was British, and his enunciation was perfect.

Kellian sighed loudly and lowered her phone to her lap. She all but rolled her eyes. Julie quickly looked away, feeling embarrassed for the male orc. *Mazi Hagyar, orc councilor to the Eternity Throne*, Hat whispered in her mind. *He's part of the Ruin Guard family, the most powerful royal family of orcs. That's his daughter Kellian.*

Kellian looks like she'd rather be anywhere than here, Julie observed.

She's only forty-five. A teenager in orc years, Hat explained.

Julie peered surreptitiously at Kellian's phone. She was busy selecting one of what seemed to be an endless scroll of selfies to post on Instagram.

Amazing what you can do with filters these days, Julie quipped.

Hat snickered.

Julius' rising voice dragged Julie's attention back to him. "One of the most important measures we can take is to ensure that there is a strong, trustworthy candidate for the throne. One who will promote peace and diversity instead of the elitism and division the Sylthana Elves are so bent on causing."

Julius' eyes shot to Taylor's oldest sister. "Ilsanthia Woodskin is slated to be one of the first to take the test that will determine her worthiness to ascend to the Eternity Throne after Queen Esmerelda passes on."

Ilsanthia—Ilsa, as Taylor had introduced her to Julie at the Nox handfasting a couple of weeks ago—raised her chin. She was almost a copy of Taylor, with the same crinkles at the corners of her eyes and the same dark hair, which she even wore in a bob not very different from Taylor's side part. But where Taylor's eyes were a limpid chocolate-brown, Ilsa's held a note of steel.

"It is to be hoped that the queen's passing will not come for some time." It was Mazi Hagyar who spoke, the orc councilor. He flashed Ilsa a smile.

Julius nodded. "It is, Mazi, but preparations have to be made. There are...concerns for Ilsanthia's safety."

Taylor inhaled sharply, and Julie glanced at him. His face was ashen.

Georgina sat back in her chair. "Julius, I hardly think the fact that your son was kidnapped is cause to be worried." She tittered. "The troll was after vampire blood, and he's safely dead."

"We are as yet uncertain that Qbiit was working alone." Julius shot her a look. "What's more, with the Dark Moon League active once more, all royals might be under threat. We know from history that the League will stop at nothing in their bid to seize power." Darkness flashed across his face.

Julie glanced at Taylor, whose eyes were still fixed on Ilsa. The elf princess' chin was raised, and her eyes glinted.

"The Aether councilor has voiced concerns to me, too," Shae interjected. The arrogant elf sat next to Ilsa, his face a collection of hard lines. "There have been...concerns of late that not every Aether Elf royal has been conducting themselves with regard to their safety."

Taylor's hand curled into a fist around his fork. Julie gave him a sympathetic pat on the knee.

Julius met Shae's eyes. "I had hoped your uncle would be here, Prince Shae, instead of sending his aide."

"I am a prince of the Aether Elves," Shae retorted.

Benedict shot him a look that silenced him.

Julius gazed at him for a few more seconds, then turned to Georgina. "Your daughter needs training for the test, as well."

"Ilsanthia has been training for this moment all her life." Georgina smiled. "It has been the sole goal of her existence."

"Sounds grim," Julie whispered.

Taylor sighed. "More than you know."

"No one questions that. We only desire her training to continue as it has been so eminently done during her entire lifetime." Mazi Hagyar inclined his head.

Benedict's eyes flashed. "Rest assured that this will be accomplished."

"We are all hoping Ilsanthia's test will be successful." The speaker was one of the Copper Dwarves—a female, her fox-red hair streaked with lines of gray that made it shimmer more brightly under the gold flames. A thin beard, neatly braided and studded with gemstones, protruded from the point of her chin. She had a wide, smiling Emma Watson kind of mouth and matching blue eyes that glittered with intelligence. "An Aether Elf upon the throne will bring neutrality and peace with it."

Sylvie Mackintosh, Hat murmured. *A dwarf of the Copper Clan and councilor to the Eternal Throne.*

"The Copper Dwarves do not lack a strong candidate for the Eternal Throne." Mazi's smile lit up his bright eyes.

Beside Sylvie, a young male dwarf, his beard and mustache an elaborate mass of braids and metal beads, let out a belly laugh. "Diplomatic of you, Mazi, but you know that most of us want the succession to be quick more than anything else."

Sylvie shot him a glance, but the young dwarf ignored her. "We're all desperate for peace and tolerance for all species. We're not picky about who gets to wear the shiny crown."

Julie couldn't help grinning at him. Taylor leaned closer. "That's Yondal Mackintosh. Mack to his friends. Sylvie's son. He's cool to hang out with at long, boring councils."

"The young fool isn't wrong," Kaplan rumbled. "The queen too prioritizes a quick and peaceful succession above all else."

Georgina's eyes flashed to Julie's for some reason, then returned to Kaplan. "Perhaps she should have kept her heirs in line, then."

"How can you presume to know what the queen wants, weretiger?" Adelaide Consta snapped.

"She even *sounds* like Kim Kardashian," Julie hissed. Taylor gave her a swift nudge in the shins to shut her up.

Kaplan held Adelaide's gaze with the confidence of a man who could transform into a five-hundred-pound Bengal tiger at a moment's notice. "Because I'm not here as the captain of the Para-Military Agency, Mrs. Consta. I'm here as the direct representative of the queen."

A murmur of shock ran around the table. Julius spoke over it. "What Jack says is true. In my house, we will accept his word."

Silence fell again. Even Mazi, Sylvie, and Shae, the queen's councilors or their aides, looked shocked.

"Why would the queen send Kaplan as her representative instead of one of the councilors?" Julie whispered.

Taylor shrugged.

The waiters reappeared, spirited away the plates, and brought smoked salmon omelets. Almost no one else had touched their hors d'oeuvres. Julie tucked into her omelet with glee. It was really good, and she wouldn't let it go to waste.

"Let us return to the matter at hand," Julius snapped. "Which is ensuring Ilsanthia's safety and the continuation of her training."

There was more tapping next to Julie. Kellian seemed to have picked the selfie she wanted and was composing the perfect caption for it. Mazi ignored her.

"Ilsanthia will continue her training in the safety of the Aether Compound." Benedict sat back, nodding as if this were decided.

"I disagree." Julius' voice was calm.

Sylvie spread her hands. "So do I, frankly. The compound might be secure, but it's the first place enemies would look if they sought to harm her. She should be moved in secret to an undisclosed location. Allow enemies to believe she's still at the compound and tighten security there so any attackers are apprehended."

Georgina bridled. "Are you suggesting we cannot care for our heir, dwarf?"

"I think Ms. Mackintosh is saying deception could be our friend when it comes to keeping your daughter safe, Queen Georgina." Mazi's voice fell over the tense situation as smoothly as cool water. "We all have the common goal of helping Ilsanthia achieve success in the test. To that end, it is reasonable to do whatever is necessary to ensure her safety."

"We *are* doing all that is necessary," Benedict snapped.

Julie glanced at Ilsa, who was sitting still, not saying a word. She watched the proceedings—the discussion about what would happen to her next—more calmly than most people would watch a football match.

"Come on, Dad." One of Taylor's brothers spoke. He was a plain-looking elf, his skin tanned darker than Taylor's and his voice very soft. "There are more secure places than the compound. We all know it."

Benedict silenced him with a glance. Julie noticed that the two other siblings, a sister and a brother, hadn't spoken. The brother gazed into the middle distance as if wishing he could be somewhere else while the sister kept glaring at Ilsa.

"She should go somewhere safe. Maybe even the Eternal Palace," Mack interjected. "What's safer than that?"

"In a war? Anywhere," Adelaide barked.

"Ruin Guard is one of the safest places in the world." Mazi's voice was still quiet.

"Ruin Guard? *Are you trying to hoard every good candidate, orc?*" Georgina shouted.

"The solution is simple." Kaplan's voice cut through the fighting, holding the edge of a snarl. "Ilsanthia should be brought to the PMA Headquarters."

There was silence. Georgina opened her mouth, then shut it.

"It makes sense," Mazi murmured. "The PMA is more politically neutral ground than any of our strongholds. Its security is undoubtable."

"'Undoubtable?'" Adelaide snorted. "I seem to recall six paras dying not long ago in a yeti incursion."

"An incursion that was quelled." Kaplan growled the last word. "The building is safe now, and security will be heightened around Ilsanthia. What's more, her training can continue unhampered there."

Benedict ran a hand over the back of his neck. "Kaplan, events at the PMA of late do not inspire confidence."

Mack chuckled. "Should we dissect every security breach the Aether Compound has ever had?" He ignored the glare Georgina gave him.

Sylvie spoke up. "The Dark Moon League has only been active in Avalon recently, not on this side of the Veil. That makes a New York City-based agency more secure than anywhere in Avalon."

"I see the point," Adelaide murmured.

Julius held up a hand, silencing all of them immediately. "Debate could continue forever. We need to take action *now*. I suggest we put this to a vote." He cleared his throat. "As is customary, the senior members of the family will vote. All in favor of keeping Ilsanthia at the Aether Compound?"

Georgina and Benedict's hands shot up.

"All in favor of having Ilsanthia moved to the PMA to be kept safe and to continue her training?" Julius raised his hand.

Sylvie, Mazi, Adelaide and her silent husband Terence, and Kaplan followed suit.

"It is settled, then." Julius nodded. "Ilsanthia will move to the PMA tomorrow."

Again, Julie glanced at Ilsa. The elf princess nodded and turned her attention back to her omelet. Her parents shot glares around the table, but they didn't speak again.

Julie slammed her spoon down. To her satisfaction, almost everyone at the table jumped. Kaplan didn't flinch, and Julius just looked up, a smile tugging at his lips.

"Really? Just like that?" Julie snapped.

Julius raised an elegant eyebrow. "Would you have us debate the matter further, Miss Meadows?"

Surprisingly, Georgina and Benedict were silent.

"No. I'd have you consider a factor that you've all pretended doesn't exist." Julie pointed. "Ilsanthia's needs and desires! Doesn't she get to have a say in her own life?" She turned to the elf princess. "What do *you* want to do, Ilsa?"

Ilsanthia studied her. The corners of her mouth were turned down, but her voice didn't tremble. "My duty to my people. It's what I was born for."

The words seemed stiff to Julie. She opened her mouth again, and Hat tightened on her head. *You've said your piece*, he murmured. *Saying more might make things difficult for Ilsanthia.*

Julie closed her mouth and looked away, painfully aware of the many pairs of eyeballs trained on her.

Conversation dwindled as the main course plates were cleared and dessert—for breakfast!—was brought in. Julie didn't think she'd ever had a better meal. It was fruit sorbet, the flavors so fresh and cool on Julie's tongue that they made her gasp and distracted her from the chatter that ran back and forth across the table.

Taylor was very quiet and only picked at his sorbet. Julie lowered her spoon. "Hey, I'd be mad, too."

"Mad?" Taylor looked up. "Why?"

"You know. Because of how they're pushing Ilsa around it." Julie couldn't resist taking another bite.

Taylor set down his spoon with a sigh. "Oh, it's not that. I just didn't know she was a target. It makes sense, I guess. But I *like* Ilsa."

Julie raised an eyebrow. "You say that like it's not true of your other siblings."

Taylor shrugged. "I mean, you know how it is."

"Not really. I was an only child," Julie reminded him. *Or was I? Do I have paranormal brothers and sisters running around?* She shoved the thought away. She wasn't a paranormal. She couldn't be.

"I'd die for them, but I'm not their biggest fan." Taylor glanced at the rest of his family, who were eating in silence. "Shae's an ass. Second-to-eldest is Amaryl." He nodded at his other sister, the one with moody eyes. "She's got a complex about being second in line."

"I noticed the way she was looking at Ilsa," Julie remarked.

Taylor pointed his spoon at the brother who'd spoken earlier. "That's Ieuan. He's never around, always hiking or fishing or something. It's his escape. Then there's Rohan." He flicked the spoon toward the last brother. "He's just quiet."

Julie nodded. She didn't think Rohan had said a single word since he'd arrived. "Wait. Rohan, like in *Lord of the Rings*?"

"It's an ancient Aether name." Taylor sniffed.

Julie held up a hand. "Sorry to offend your heritage," she joked, but Taylor didn't laugh.

"It's not right." Julie shifted gears, sending Genevieve purring over the Verrazzano-Narrows Bridge toward home. "She shouldn't be treated that way."

Hat sat on the dashboard. He shuffled around to face Julie and let out a laugh. "'Treated that way'? You do know that Ilsanthia has had the best of everything for her entire life as befits an heir to one of the most powerful thrones in the world, don't you?"

Julie waved a hand. "There's more to life than *stuff*."

"It's more than stuff, Julie. It's education, society, and parental attention. Ilsa has had everything, emotionally, from her parents that Taylor never did." Hat's brim curved down.

Julie shook her head. "I don't agree. Taylor says he had it better since he was farther from the throne, and he was right. Just look at what happened tonight. Ilsa's whole future, the place she lives, what she's supposed to do every day, and her safety? A bunch of random people just decided it for her. She wasn't allowed to say a word. She wasn't even a pawn in their game, just a tool."

Hat's brim curled up in a shrug. "That's how it's always been for royalty, both in the human world and ours."

When she reached the end of the bridge, Julie turned left, then cruised to a halt at a red light. She gripped the steering wheel tightly. "That doesn't mean that it's okay. In fact, I think it's high time I started trying to help Ilsa the way I helped Taylor be more independent."

"Taylor was one thing," Hat pointed out. "Sixth in line, so it was easier for him. Encouraging Ilsa to be independent is a dangerous game, Julie. It's best not to cause trouble with powerful royalty. Trust me on this one."

Julie shook her head. "I don't care. Ilsa has a right to live her life, even if she's beholden to the Throne."

Hat sighed. "I want to argue, but I know that voice. I'm not going to stop you, am I?"

Julie grinned as the light turned green. "Nothing is." She stomped on the gas, and Genevieve bellowed homeward.

CHAPTER FIVE

Julie fumbled with the thin strap on the carry-on bag as she tucked it over her shoulder, cursing the lapse of judgment that had made her pick a bright purple bag instead of the one with the comfier strap.

It was a treat to yourself, Hat pointed out. He was a cute little straw boater today, which went well with her bell-bottom jeans and plain white T-shirt. *It didn't have to be practical.*

I did tell myself I'd enjoy this on my next work trip. Julie finally sorted out the strap and began to cross the porch.

"You forgot your juice, Julia!" Rosa hurried down the hall, carrying three bottles of the stuff.

Julie plastered her best smile into place. "I'm sorry, Mom. I can't take it. I'm just taking a small bag on the plane. Just uniform and toiletries." She was taking a portal, not a plane, but her mother didn't know that. "I'll just have to drink some extra when I get back."

Rosa lowered the bottles, the corners of her mouth drooping.

"I did pack the cinnamon pills, though," Julie added.

Liar, Hat snorted.

I did! She doesn't need to know I'm not going to take them. Julie kept her smile in place.

Rosa sighed. "Okay, baby. Just take care of yourself." She wrapped Julie in a hug.

Julie returned it. "Thanks, Mom. And really, thanks for staying with Lillie. I appreciate it so much."

"Of course, honey. You're making a great career for yourself." Her mother kissed her cheek.

An engine hummed, and a shimmering silver BMW M8 Competition Convertible sped down the street, coming to a sharp halt at the front gate without so much as a squeak of tires.

"Oh, *my*." Rosa pressed a hand to her heart. "How many cars does this young man have?"

"I'm just going to say bye to Lillie." Julie lowered her bag.

"No need, dear." Lillie doddered through the doorway, her eyes eagerly scanning the street. "I'm not going to miss the opportunity to admire this view!" She cackled at the look on Julie's face.

Taylor had stepped out of the driver's seat. He was wearing a pair of nice black chinos and a pale blue button-up shirt, the sleeves rolled up past his brawny forearms, and there was a collective sigh from Rosa and Lillie.

"Gross," Julie moaned. "Bye, you two disgusting old ladies."

"Bye, honey. Travel safe." Rosa waved.

"Have *fun*!" Lillie leered.

Julie stifled a groan and bumped down the porch steps. Taylor met her at the bottom, smiling faintly as he reached for her bag. "May I—uh." He stopped.

Smart boy, remembering how much she'd disliked him pushing in her chair. "I'm okay. Thanks." She flashed him a quick smile. "Let's go."

"Hello, Taylor," Rosa called in a singsong voice.

Taylor looked up. Rosa gave him a little wave and a Cheshire Cat grin.

"Hello, Rosa." Taylor cleared his throat. "And hello, Ms. Griswall."

"Nice ride you've got there, boy." Lillie grinned at the BMW. "She's got a twin-turbo V8 under the hood, doesn't she?"

"Uh-huh." Taylor grinned. "Six hundred seventeen horses."

"Ooh!" Lillie whooped. "I'd cause some trouble in that baby if I was thirty years younger. Or forty years younger."

Taylor gave a little bow. "I hope you're feeling much better."

"All the better for seeing you, dear." Lillie's eyes traveled up and down the length of Taylor's body.

"Okay, *bye*, you two." Julie shook her head. "Come on, Taylor."

He waved goodbye to the incorrigible older women in Julie's life and opened the back door for her to stow her bag. As soon as they were both seated and the doors safely closed, Julie groaned, slamming the back of her head against her seat. "Dude, I'm sorry. Mom was ogling."

"Your *mom*?" Taylor laughed, putting the M8 into gear. "Lillie was doing her fair share, too."

"Oh, she's more attracted to your car, don't worry. Mom's the one who was really checking you out." Julie giggled.

He flashed her a smile as the M8 purred down the street. After executing a smooth U-turn, he revved the engine a few times for Lillie's benefit as they passed her house again. The old lady gave a fist-pump as they drove past.

"It's good to see her like this again," Taylor observed.

"Yeah." Julie remembered the week Lillie had been in the hospital and shuddered. "Hey, thanks for all the help when she was sick."

"Anytime." Taylor grinned, then hesitated. "Listen, about last night. I hope you don't think I'm mad at you since I didn't support you when you spoke up about Ilsa making her own choices."

Julie folded her arms. "I did sort of wonder why you didn't have my back."

Taylor shrugged. "It's just that there's no point in trying to change my parents. Not when it comes to Ilsa. She's supposed to secure the future of our whole family. Our whole species."

"I'm really sorry for putting you in an awkward situation with them." Julie hesitated. "But I still believe you two *both* deserve to make your own choices."

Taylor glanced at her as he turned onto the freeway. "I don't disagree. I just don't see a way to make that happen for my sister." He grinned. "But I'm ready for a couple of days' break from my parents. Do you want to see what this baby can do?"

Julie sniffed, raising her nose. "She's nothing like my Genevieve."

Taylor laughed and put his foot down, and the M8's six hundred seventeen horses all reared and plunged at once, speeding toward Central Park and the portal to Avalon Village.

Something had changed in the air of the village.

Julie felt it the moment the disorienting, spinning sensation of the 110th Street Bridge's magic portal through the Veil had faded. The sight of the plaza made her stomach tighten, remembering that two-thousand-year-old raid that had left the place burning.

The plaza was now lined with brick-and-mortar shops adorned with colorful signs, neon lights, and snappy slogans. It was also cobbled in many different colors, some of which shone like gemstones, and bright flags snapped in front of every building.

Julie glanced at the flags, expecting to see the thinnest of crescent moons. It wasn't there, but Julie still felt a chill down her spine.

"It's so quiet here today," she commented as she and Taylor

crossed the plaza. "Last time I was here, this place was bustling with paras."

"I know." Taylor nodded at a cafe on the corner. "I've never seen that place so empty."

The last time Julie was here, a gaggle of pixies had been sitting at one of the tiny tables on little pedestals around the cafe. Now, it was empty except for a wrinkled old orc reading a newspaper.

RETURN OF THE DARK MOON? its headline demanded.

A cool wind blew across the plaza, shoving a handful of leaves over the cobbles. Julie spotted a young woman heading their way, pushing a long pram that contained four toddlers. One of them kept transforming into a wolf cub and back, seemingly at random. The werewolf's eyes widened at the sight of Julie, and she ducked into the first shop she reached.

"Why was she scared of *me*?" Julie hissed.

Taylor sighed. "Qbiit's trial was televised, remember? Everyone knows we work for the PMA, which stands against the Sylthana Elves. Most ordinary people here don't want anything to do with a brewing war."

Julie shook her head. "It's sad to see the village like this."

"I agree." Hat sighed. "I haven't seen it this quiet in centuries."

"Way to flex on your age, Hat," Julie quipped. "You said we were going to the PMA office, right? Didn't it burn down?"

"The Avalon South branch did. The North branch is bigger, and it's fine. We need to get some transport from the motor pool." Taylor nodded at the far end of the plaza. "It's a few minutes' walk down Sixth Street."

"Are we going past Iris' boutique?" Julie sighed at the memory of the gorgeous blue ball gown Taylor's best friend had sold her.

Taylor ran a hand through his hair. "We are. I thought I might stop by and say hello if you don't mind."

"I don't mind." Julie grinned. "I'd love to see Iris. We wanted to connect the last time I saw her, but we never got around to it."

Taylor raised an eyebrow. "Probably a good thing. You two together would just be dangerous."

"Dangerously *awesome*," Julie shot back. Taylor could only shake his head and laugh.

Don't stare, don't stare, don't stare. Julie repeated the words like a mantra, but as usual, she couldn't stop staring once she'd walked into Iris Fashions. Between the roomy, airy feel of the place, the incredible eucalyptus smell that floated through the air, and the tinkling music that seemed to come from everywhere at once, Iris Fashions was breathtaking even before Julie laid eyes on the mannequins. She couldn't stop gaping at a gown that sparkled golden, scattering light from its skirt even though it was hanging on a mannequin by the window.

Iris Wingfinger was behind the counter, scribbling on a huge sketch pad. She looked up as they came in, and her wide grin leaped easily to her face. "Tay! Julie! How amazing to see you!" she trilled. She jumped up and hurried over to them.

Julie easily accepted Iris' fragrant hug. "It's nice to see you, too."

Iris squeezed Taylor in a bear hug, too. "What's the occasion?" she asked, taking her friend's hand and twirling him like a girl. "Another handfasting?"

"We're not here to shop today, Iris." Taylor had turned his most embarrassed shade of pale gray. "I just wanted to check on how you were doing. The village seems so quiet."

"Business has been slow." Iris sighed and leaned on her counter. "Saturday's debacle scared people off, you know. But it was the weirdest thing." She frowned. "The night before last, Monday night, the palace guards were all over the village."

"Wait, palace guards?" Taylor raised his eyebrows. "From the Eternal Palace?"

"That's right."

Julie frowned. "What were they doing?"

"Arresting paras. A bunch of them." Iris shrugged. "No one I knew, but it seemed strange."

"Arresting people?" Julie demanded. "Do they have jurisdiction to do that?"

Iris shrugged and held up her hands. Taylor shook his head. "I don't know. It doesn't seem right."

"No one seems to know why the paras were arrested, either. And they weren't all Sylthana Elves. We all thought maybe the guards were looking for the League, but surely the PMA would do that?" Iris sighed. "It's a scary time, Tay. I'm not gonna lie."

Taylor's mouth drooped. "I'm sorry, Iris. If you ever need somewhere to go..."

"I don't. I'm not leaving my boutique." Iris' grin bounced back. "Sure you don't need anything?"

"I'm sure. We're on a work trip," Taylor explained.

"Yeah, we've got to go." Julie gave Iris a hug. "Stay safe, okay?"

"You too!" Iris waved as they left the shop, and Julie couldn't help looking back as the elf bent happily over her sketchbook again.

She fell into step beside Taylor, and they headed down Sixth Street. "What do you think all those arrests were about?"

"I have no idea, but Iris is right. Things do seem fishy." Taylor paused. "Hey, Hat, do you think you'd be able to work something out?"

"I could ask Malcolm. He'll have access to bags of information, being Kaplan's assistant." Hat hummed busily for a few moments. "It's going to take a little while to get the info, but I've sent the request."

"Spotty connection across dimensions?" Julie guessed.

Hat chuckled. "More like Malcolm Nox isn't used to being an office grunt yet."

They all laughed.

"Why *would* the guards be making arrests instead of the PMA?" Julie frowned. "Could someone in the Eternal Palace have a hidden agenda?"

"It doesn't make sense." Taylor bit his lip. "The PMA answers to the Eternity Queen. If she wanted people to be arrested, she'd ask the PMA."

"Unless she wasn't having them arrested for legal reasons," Julie suggested.

Taylor glanced at her. "Queen Esmerelda? It doesn't sound like her."

"Maybe one of the councilors is involved." Julie thought hard. "Mazi and your uncle and Sylvie are councilors, right? So there has to be a Sylthana Elf and a vampire councilor, too. And a dragon. Any of them could be responsible."

"Not Uncle Arion." Taylor laughed. "He wouldn't hurt a fly."

"She might have something to hide for a non-sinister reason," Hat pointed out. "Maybe she's trying not to cause a panic."

Julie scoffed. "Having a bunch of guards arrest paras for no reason isn't the best way to go about avoiding a panic."

Taylor stopped, giving a little flourish with one arm. "The Avalon North offices of the Official Para-Military Agency," he announced.

Julie looked up. There was a castle in front of her—a real one, with gray stone walls and battlements and a drawbridge over a moat of perfectly clear water. Their feet rang hollowly on the wood as they crossed it. Julie leaned over to peer at the moat. An octopus the size of a school bus looked back, its tentacles waving gently in the water.

Julie gasped. "Is that a kraken?"

Taylor followed her gaze. "A juvenile one, yes."

"*Juvenile?*" Julie jogged after him and glanced at the portcullis over their heads. Its sharp iron spikes made it look like it was still painfully functional.

They crossed the courtyard beyond and headed through a

pair of heavy oak doors into the main hallway of the keep, which had rushes strewn over the floor and tapestries on the walls and boring wooden reception desks. Taylor avoided those and led Julie down a spiral staircase, and *not* into a creepy, cobwebby dungeon. Instead, there was an ordinary door with a glass window and the words REQUISITIONS DEPARTMENT on a sign beneath the window.

Taylor pushed it open, and they stepped into a small room staffed by a droopy old orc sitting at a desk that looked too big for him. He looked up at them with yellowed eyes, his lips barely twitching.

Julie recovered enough to pull their paperwork out of her backpack. Taylor handed it to the orc, who gazed at the papers for what seemed to be a very long time.

"ID," the orc growled.

They flashed their IDs, and the orc pushed a set of keys across the table toward them. "In the motor pool." He jerked a thumb at the door behind him and turned his eyes back to his computer.

Julie followed Taylor through the door. This time, they emerged into a huge space carved into the bedrock on which the castle rested. Streaks of some glowing green ore shone in the walls and the rough-hewn floor, which was neatly painted with white lines that demarcated parking spots on the left of the cavern. Julie spotted several carriages, a shining black steam train, and a massive red-and-gold sleigh.

On the right, the cavern was divided up into large stalls. A series of heads looked over the stall doors at them; a few were equine, but in the nearest one was a lion chewing contentedly on a femur the size of Julie's entire body. It had a goat head sticking out of its back. The goat head nibbled at the straw.

Something soft nuzzled Julie's cheek. She jumped, then laughed. "Aw, hi, Sleipnir." Julie petted the head of an eight-legged horse. "I wondered where you'd been. I don't have sugar for you today."

"He normally bites." Taylor backed away from him.

"Sleipy? He's a sweetie." Julie kissed the silky muzzle. "I'll bring you sugar when we get back, big boy."

Taylor checked his keyring. "Spot D35. Let's see what we've got."

Julie experienced a beat of wild excitement as they walked toward a silver DMC DeLorean, but that turned out to be in Bay D34. Right next to it was—

"A minivan?" Julie's hands fell to her sides. "You've got to be shitting me. We could be riding Sleipner or a chimera or going in one of those spooky carriages, but we're driving a *minivan*? I should have brought Genevieve."

"All transport runs on magic here. There wouldn't be any gas for her," Taylor pointed out, but his shoulders slumped as he unlocked the white minivan and opened the driver's door. He straightened abruptly. "Whoa! Julie, get in here. You're going to want to see this!"

Julie slid the side door open and gasped. The inside had the dimensions of an RV. Everything was in soothing tones of brown and cream, with a series of lights set into the roof and sides that filled the space with warm light. Near the front, where Julie stood, leather seating was grouped around a polished wooden coffee table. The back was occupied by two bunks separated by a curtain. Between was a fully functional kitchenette hardly smaller than the one Julie had in her apartment, complete with a tiny stove, multiple cabinet doors, and a little table with a bench on either side.

"There's a whole bathroom back here." Taylor appeared through a door at the back of the bus. "It's epic."

"I take it back." Julie laughed. "The minivan's fine." She stepped farther in and opened one of the cabinets. It turned out to be a refrigerator that held milk and various fruits and a packet of bacon and a bottle of champagne. "Dude, this is a *fridge*!"

Taylor chuckled. "Ever been on a tour bus before?"

Julie closed the fridge and went over to one of the bunks, flopping down on it. "Whoa. This mattress is nicer than the one I have at home." She bounced. "And yeah, I've been on a tour bus, but it had holey seats and smelled like old cheese."

"A *luxury* tour bus, I mean." Taylor grinned.

Julie got up and headed to the front, where she tested one of the leather chairs. "This is amazing. I've never been on anything like this."

Taylor shook his head. "Ah, poor little Brooklyn human. I went on school field trips in ones like these."

"Poor little rich boy," Julie shot back, sticking out her tongue.

He laughed and spun the keys around one finger. "Just for that, I'm driving for the first hour."

"Done." Julie stretched out on the leather seat. "I'll just stay here and read."

"Nuh-uh. It doesn't work that way." Taylor gave her a swift poke in the ribs that made her jump up, squealing. "You're shotgun. You've got to navigate and DJ. Don't you know *anything* about road trips?"

"Not road trips in one of these," Julie pointed out. She pulled Hat off her head and made him comfy on one of the leather seats. His brim went floppy like he was melting into it.

"A road trip is a road trip is a road trip." Taylor clambered into the driver's seat. "Bring snacks."

"Snacks? From where?" Julie opened a kitchen cabinet. "Oh, man, there are, like, five different potato chip flavors in here."

Taylor laughed. "Bring them all!"

Julie chose the sour cream and chives flavor to start, and they crunched on chips as Taylor steered their magnificent vehicle—which handled like a minivan despite its interior—up a ramp, out from under the castle, and into the streets of Avalon Village.

It wasn't long before the village dwindled into the distance behind them and the minivan was swallowed by the countryside. They followed a winding road paved with a material that looked like stone but was as smooth as asphalt, and farms stretched to the horizon on either side of the road. Julie couldn't stop staring at the fields. In one of them, huge blue oxen contentedly grazed together. Another contained a flock of sheep with shimmering golden fleeces.

They passed a farm covered in what appeared to be ferns, except that each had a single massive bud rising from the middle on a long green stem.

"What are those?" Julie asked, pointing.

Taylor glanced over his sunglasses. "Plants? I don't know anything about agriculture."

Hat had made himself comfortable on the dashboard as a festive pink straw beach hat with a pink leopard-print band. "*Chervona ruta*, or fern flowers. They're a major source of luck."

"Luck?" Julie raised her eyebrows. "Like, good fortune?"

"Oh, yes. They bloom on the summer solstice, and the farmers harvest them that night. They press them whole for their luck and sell it bottled." Hat's brim curled in a shrug. "I'm told it's a good industry if you can get them all harvested in one night, and if you spray them with the right products to keep the evil spirits off."

"I didn't know that was a fern flower. A friend of mine drank a bottle of their luck once. It allowed him to talk to animals," Taylor commented.

Julie gasped. "I *need* some!"

"Oh, no. I hear it's got awful side effects. My friend could understand animals, but he could only insult them back." Taylor shook his head. "Things were never the same between him and his dog after that."

"That's awful." Julie connected her phone to the minivan's

sound system via Bluetooth and sat back in her seat as instrumental pop covers from the Piano Guys flooded the bus.

Taylor raised an eyebrow. "Really? This is your road trip music?"

Julie folded her arms. "You got something against piano music?"

"It's just not road trip vibes." Taylor changed gears as the minivan rumbled up a hill. "Come on. Give us something upbeat!"

"Fine, fine." Julie laughed. "Is this better?"

She hit play on her phone, and the thumping beat of George Ezra's *Shotgun* pounded through the van. Taylor laughed and stomped on the accelerator. "That's more like it!"

Hat stretched out. "Two hours to go. Wake me when we get there."

Julie relaxed in her seat. Avalon extended around her, and the minivan carried her deeper into a new world with every mile.

"Wake up! There he is!"

Something prodded Julie's shoulder. She sat up with an unladylike snort. "Huh? What?"

"Sorry to wake you." Taylor laughed. "Look, a griffin!"

Rubbing the sleep from her eyes, Julie leaned forward and peered through the windshield. The landscape had changed since she'd fallen asleep half an hour ago. Then, they'd been traveling through hill country covered in farmland. Now, the minivan was surrounded by a dense tangle of forest. Julie could smell the sea.

"Where?" Julie couldn't see him.

"He's circling. You'll spot him in a...*there*!" Taylor pointed.

Julie gasped. Apart from the dragon, she'd never seen anything so huge and alive airborne before. A massive feline shape soared through the air above the minivan, with giant feathered wings extended on either side that flashed gold in the sunlight. Then there was a piercing eagle's shriek, and the griffin banked to the left and vanished over the treetops.

Griffins: a proud and fierce race that lives in coastal forests, Julie's orb training told her. *Known as guardians and protectors. Often employed as bodyguards for dignitaries. Capable of sensing lies, they place a high value on the truth. Keen sense of justice, high intelligence, and a stern culture give griffins little patience for those who act with nefarious intentions.*

"They sound scary," Julie admitted.

Taylor nodded. "Two griffins guard the Aether Compound. I wouldn't mess with them." He grinned. "They have a weakness for laser pointers, though."

"I'm guessing you found this out in calm conversation with one?" Julie raised an eyebrow.

Taylor turned a faint gray. "Hey, even princes get up to shenanigans sometimes."

Julie spluttered with laughter.

A sudden gust of wind made the minivan buck on the road. Taylor gasped and slowed down as he gripped the wheel. Hat slid off the dash and into Julie's lap with a thump, then wings obscured Julie's view of the sky. As Taylor skidded to a stop, a thundering rustle of feathers filled the air. Two griffins landed on the road in front of them with feline grace.

Julie's heart jumped into her mouth. The griffins had the bodies of lions if lions were the size of horses. Both were almost as tall as the minivan at the shoulders. Their wings would span Julie's apartment. Gold feathers shimmered as they turned to face the minivan. One had a windblown black-and-golden mane that blended into the coppery feathers covering his neck and head. The other was a little smaller and lacked a mane, but they both had the palest amber eyes Julie had ever seen and massive leonine heads. The male panted as they paced toward the minivan on giant soundless paws. His open jaw revealed fangs that rivaled Kaplan's in his tiger form.

"Okay, I'm scared," Julie squeaked.

"You'll be fine," Hat told her as he turned into a serious black fedora. Julie squashed him onto her head.

The griffins flanked the minivan. Swallowing audibly, Taylor rolled down his window. Julie hastily did the same. The female griffin gazed at her with those sharp eyes for a few long seconds before speaking.

"Are you for or against the Eternity Throne?" Her voice rumbled.

"*For!*" Julie and Taylor shouted in unison.

Julie's hands shook a little as she pulled her ID from her pocket. "We're on Para-Military Agency business. We, uh, we'd like to speak to your leaders."

The griffin's eyes bored into hers for a few seconds longer before a smile touched her lips, which looked strange in her feathered face. "Very well. I will escort you to the eyrie."

The male griffin shook his mane and loped down the road a few strides, then threw open his wings. His powerful hindquarters bunched as he launched into the air, and his wings thundered down, paws treading air. In seconds, he was over the trees and gone.

Julie started as Taylor started the minivan again. The female griffin ran down the road, her tail rippling behind her, the feathers down her sides mingling with the black fur at its tip and fanning out as her tail swayed from side to side. They drove after her, and Julie glanced at Taylor. "Did you also just shit yourself a little bit?"

"A little." Taylor chuckled. "And I'm used to them."

"We'd better recruit some. They'd make great agents and soldiers." Julie grinned.

The griffin led them through the woods and out onto a road that wound along the edges of towering clifftops over the sea.

The wind had picked up, and the sea was gray and whipped into a fury, pounding against the cliffs.

"There's the eyrie. Straight ahead," Hat announced.

Julie dragged her eyes away from the sea to the fortress that rose ahead of them, a menacing tower of stone. It engulfed a cliff that stood in the ocean, separated from its fellows by a narrow channel. There was only one door on the ground floor of the fortress that Julie could see, a huge drawbridge that faced the mainland, but it was hundreds of feet up the cliff—too high for anyone to reach unless they had wings.

There were griffins everywhere: swooping in vast circles around the fortress, landing on the platforms by the high doors, and taking off and swan-diving toward the sea.

"It's been a while since the last time I was here," Hat murmured.

As they approached the drawbridge, the griffin leading them raised her head and let out a long cry that resounded like a bald eagle's. The drawbridge began to descend slowly, and by the time the minivan reached a cliff edge, it had been lowered to the ground on huge iron chains.

The griffin strode onto the drawbridge. Taylor gulped and put the minivan in first gear.

"No rails, huh?" Julie muttered.

"Oh, a couple of griffins could catch us if we fell," Hat breezed.

There was a slight bump as the minivan mounted the drawbridge. Julie stared out the window and down an unfathomable drop to the leaping ocean at the bottom and felt sick. Taylor let out a long breath through his teeth when they reached the other side and drove into a courtyard where, amazingly, several other cars were parked alongside a chariot drawn by two goats and a pegasus who dozed as he stood tied to a ring in the wall.

Griffin guards watched them in silence, not from the ground but from pedestals set into the fortress. They lay on their bellies, huge paws draped over the edges of their pedestals, eagle eyes unflinching.

Taylor parked the van next to the goat chariot. Julie screwed Hat onto her head tighter as she stepped out, stretching her stiff legs. The air was filled with the fresh tang of the ocean and the not-so-fresh smell of goat.

Their guide waited for them by a huge arch. "This way," she purred.

They followed her down a long, dark hall that was tall and wide enough to admit griffins in flight. When she reached a guard at the end of the hall, the griffin spoke to him in a series of purrs and chirps. He slipped away and returned a few moments later to glance at Julie and Taylor with a nod.

"The Matriarch and Patriarch will see you now," the female griffin told them.

The guard pawed at the double doors, and they swung open. Julie and Taylor walked into a massive hall, which had columns marching down its length and hundreds of huge niches in the walls. It was seating for griffins, and many were occupied. In the shadows, Julie could make out the griffins' forms and their shining eyes.

Benches lined both sides of the hall as well. Sunlight poured into the huge room. When Julie looked up, she saw a massive iron grille standing open in the ceiling. A griffin was flying out of it.

In the center of the pool of sunlight sat the Matriarch and Patriarch of the griffins. The Patriarch's mane was longer and more luxurious than those of the male griffins Julie had seen so far, and his gold feathers were edged in a black that shimmered beetle-green where the sunlight caught it.

He sat very erect. His chest was as broad as Genevieve, his enormous paws were motionless against the stone, and his tail curled around them like a cat's. The Matriarch was a little smaller, but her eyes looked through Julie's soul.

Go down on one knee when you reach them, Hat ordered. *These are serious people.*

Julie didn't need him to tell her that. When they reached the edge of the sunlight, she sank awkwardly to one knee. Taylor did the same with fluid grace, bowing his head.

"Julie Meadows and Prince Taylor Woodskin of the Aether Elves," their griffin escort announced. "Recruiters from the Para-Military Agency, Your Majesties." She bowed her head and left the room on silent paws.

The Patriarch inclined a head the size of an anvil. "Rise," he rumbled.

Julie did so slowly. The Matriarch was still studying her in silence.

"What is the meaning of this visit?" the Patriarch asked. His voice made the floor tremble.

Julie cleared her throat, scraping together the memory of the pitch they'd rehearsed yesterday at the PMA. "Your Majesties, our agency seeks to keep peace throughout the paranormal world. To do that, we need agents and soldiers who are both intelligent and physically powerful. More than that, we need paranormals with a keen sense of justice."

Taylor stepped forward. "Griffins are ideal candidates to join our agency. We would like to present that opportunity to any who would be interested, with your permission, Your Majesties."

The Patriarch looked around the hall, feathers stirring in his mane. The Matriarch did not remove her gaze from Julie.

Hat stirred on Julie's head.

"We thank you for your presence, young elf," the Patriarch growled. "Yet we must decline. We can feel the nearness of war, and our first and greatest duty is the protection of the throne."

Julie bowed. "A great priority, Your Majesty. However, please consider that the PMA exists to protect the throne, too."

Smooth, Hat chuckled.

Julie forced down a smile. *Thanks.*

"I do not deny your point, young one, yet for generations, we griffins have worked directly with the queen to guard her life and the lives of her councilors. Our role is defined." The Patriarch stood. "One of the guards will show you to refreshments and a place to rest after your journey."

Hat hummed on Julie's head, but she didn't hear him speak into her mind. The Matriarch sat up taller, eyes widening, and for the first time, she spoke. "Wait," she purred. "This...changes things."

"What does, Your Majesty?" Taylor asked.

The Matriarch didn't answer. She looked at the Patriarch and murmured something to him in the chirping griffin language. He blinked and glanced at Julie, then nodded.

"Very well. You may present your case to my children. However, I cannot order them to fight for a cause they have no duty to protect." The Matriarch's voice was soft, yet it echoed through the entire hall.

There was a *thwump* of wings. Julie looked up as a griffin leaped from one of the niches, swooped over her head, and landed neatly on the ground a few yards from her. It was a younger male, his mane still pale and thready. He bowed low, his tail arching over his back. "Your Majesty, by your leave, I wish to join the PMA and become a soldier. I am too young to guard the queen, so let me make myself useful in other ways and gain good experience in the meantime."

The Matriarch nodded. "You have my permission and my blessing. Go well, young one."

More wings fluttered, and five other griffins landed beside the first. "We're all friends, Your Majesty," a young female told the Matriarch. "We would like to go with him."

The Matriarch repeated the same blessing to the other young griffins, and the first young male turned to Julie. He grinned, his amber eyes sparkling. "Where do I sign up?"

Julie plopped onto one of the bunks in the minivan/tour bus, toweling her hair briskly. "Not gonna lie. It was nice of the griffins to invite us to stay, but their fortress is spooky."

"I know!" Taylor was fishing around in the fridge. "I can't believe we signed *six* griffins." He glanced at the stack of recruitment forms on the little table, each signed with an enormous paw print. "Kaplan's going to have a field day."

"I'd like to see those Sylthana Elves trying to light a PMA building on fire when it's guarded by griffins." Julie grinned.

Taylor chuckled. "We did a good thing today."

"We did, but I'm not sure how we did it." Julie directed a stare at Hat, who sat at the end of her bed.

"What? What are you looking at me like that for?" Hat spluttered.

"You said something to the Matriarch back there." Julie ran her fingers through her damp hair. "Something that changed her mind. What was it?"

"Oh, that." Hat's brim curled in a shrug. "I just reminded them of what you said, that anyone who joins the OPMA is serving the Eternity Throne."

Julie narrowed her eyes, but Taylor slammed the microwave door before she could say anything and switched it on. "Okay, we leave first thing in the morning for Fernwood Deep."

"Why tomorrow? It's not sunset yet. We could probably make it before it's too late," Julie pointed out. "Also, maybe it would be better to park in the woods than on a random stretch of road halfway between the eyrie and Fernwood Deep."

"Oh, no." Taylor chuckled. "This is much safer. The trees get annoyed if you disturb their beauty sleep."

CHAPTER SIX

They had breakfast the next day at a little roadside stall run by a friendly centaur and her husband. Julie was pleasantly stuffed when she got into the minivan and clipped on her seat belt, glancing at the gauges in front of the minivan's steering wheel. "Dude, where's the fuel gauge? We drove for hours yesterday, and I didn't see any gas stations."

Taylor reclined the passenger seat and stretched out, patting his full stomach. "It runs on magic, remember? You only need a magimechanic to charm the engine every ten thousand miles or so, and you're good to go."

Julie raised an eyebrow. "Remind me why I live in Brooklyn and pay four dollars a gallon when I could be here?"

Taylor chuckled. "Because it costs about the same per mile to get the charm done, but it's better for the air." He waved a hand. "Sentient trees get really annoyed about chemical garbage in the air."

Julie shook her head and put the minivan into gear. It felt like driving a cruise ship after her agile, zippy Genevieve. "Pity our trees can't talk in the human world. They'd probably do a lot of cursing."

"Extra snarky today, are we?" Hat quipped from his spot on the dashboard.

Julie grinned. "That's what happens when I have to bite my tongue like I did at the eyrie."

"Oh, great. Snark buildup." Taylor snorted.

"It's not because you're nervous about meeting the dryads?" Hat asked.

Julie raised an eyebrow. "Why would I be nervous about meeting thousands of pounds of wood that walks around on its own?"

Taylor folded his arms, closing his eyes as he leaned back in his seat. "Clearly, the orb didn't tell you about the Dryad Wars."

"What were they about? Deforestation?" Julie quipped, but there was an unpleasant flutter in the pit of her stomach.

Hat chuckled. "He's teasing you. There were no Dryad Wars."

Julie gave Taylor a soft punch in the arm.

The morning wore away, the minivan chewing up the miles at a steady pace. The hill country gave way to moorlands grazed by herds of silver-white ponies that shimmered in and out of visibility.

"Backahasten," Hat explained. "River horses. Apex predators. Don't follow them on dark nights."

As they passed, one of the ponies raised its head and yawned, revealing long white fangs.

"Look. Fernwood Deep." Hat's words dragged Julie's attention back to the road. It ran very straight toward a dark line on the horizon. As they got closer to the forest, Julie saw that it was very different from the griffins' woods. These trees didn't look like anything she'd ever seen before.

She slowed the minivan and brought it to a halt at the edge of the forest and gazed at the towering trees. They looked like ferns the size of redwoods, their stems as sturdy as trunks. The tips of the leaves stirred faintly, ripples of movement rushing through the forest although there was no wind.

Goosebumps rose on Julie's arms. She rolled her window down and took a deep breath. The air smelled of damp dirt and dead leaves.

Taylor sat up with a snort. "Oh. We're here." He glanced at Julie. "We can just head into the woods. We'll find what we're looking for. He'll find us, rather."

Taylor's words did little for her rising nerves. She laughed to cover them. "Cryptic much?"

"Seriously, that's how it works." Taylor gestured. "Onward, noble steed."

Julie scoffed and drove slowly into the shadows of the trees. The road began to wind, bending its way among the trunks.

"I've never seen anything like these trees," she whispered.

"Why are we whispering?" Taylor asked.

"I'm not whispering." Julie sat up straighter. "Are you going to tell me about these trees or what?"

"They're not trees, technically. They're dryads." Taylor leaned forward, hands on the dash, peering up at them. "Incredible beings. It's said that the older ones hold all the wisdom of the world, but they can't share it with us. Time moves differently for them. Years pass like seconds. They can't really interact with those on a mortal timeline."

Nearer the ground, Julie noticed a handful of bright green saplings. They were also fern-shaped and taller than the minivan, but they were walking among the trunks of the giant dryads with slow, flowing movements, branches rustling. One of them turned to the minivan, and among the tangle of leaves and buds near the top, Julie thought she saw a face. It raised a branch like an arm and waved its leaves. Julie waved back, gaping.

Taylor grasped the steering wheel with one hand and gently straightened the van. "Try not to run us off the road, okay?"

"Sorry." Julie blushed. "What were those? Also dryads? Why were they moving faster?"

"They're filled with growth energy when they're younger. They experience time more like we do," Taylor told her.

Julie glanced at them in her rearview mirror. They disappeared after she negotiated another bend in the road. "That was cool, but I thought we were here to find the Green Man. We getting a two-fer?"

"A three-fer, actually." Taylor grinned. "There's a brownie village a few miles into the forest. Also, it's *a* Green Man, not *the* Green Man. There's more than one."

Green Men, Julie's orb training piped up. *Caretakers of magical forests. As old as the land, and often bound to their homes. In possession of strange and secret magic that enables their forests to flourish.*

"So, we're looking for Tom Bombadil?" Julie grinned. "That's epic. He *so* should have been in the movies."

"Don't let Mazi or Kellian hear you talk about *Lord of the Rings*," Taylor warned.

"Hey, I'm just saying, Tom Bombadil deserved the screen time. He was one of Tolkien's best characters," Julie retorted.

A voice came from ahead of them and rustled like the wind. "Where do you think Tolkien got the inspiration?"

Julie stamped on the brakes as a figure emerged from the forest. About six feet tall, the Green Man moved with the same slow grace as the dryads, but his hands and neck and broad shoulders and the sturdy calves that ended in yellow boots were undeniably flesh. When he stepped into the sunlight in front of the minivan, though, his hair and beard were shaggy bursts of foliage. Leaves dripped from his beard as he smiled, revealing startlingly white teeth. Creepers hung over his forehead like bangs. Behind them, bright blue eyes sparkled.

Julie didn't move as the Green Man strode unhurriedly to the van and bowed his head, then scrutinized Julie with those bright eyes. His lips curled up in a smile under a grassy mustache. "Hmm. Interesting. What brings you to Fernwood Deep?"

Julie swallowed. "My name is Julie Meadows, and this is

Taylor Woodskin. We're from the Official Para-Military Agency, and we're here to recruit paranormals to the agency."

The Green Man nodded. "Ember Floraison. I hope you're not here to recruit *me*, Miss Meadows." He chuckled, a deep, cozy sound.

Julie's smile came easily. "You'd be very useful to us, Mr. Floraison, and there's an excellent salary and benefits package."

"Ember, please. And I'm sure there is," the Green Man boomed, "but I will not—cannot—leave my forest. I am bound to Fernwood Deep, body and soul." He gazed at the forest for a few moments, smiling as though he'd never seen it before. "I think I can help you, though."

"How?" Taylor asked.

"Well, this is my forest, and everyone here knows me. If you wish to recruit some of my residents to your cause, brownies or young dryads, perhaps, I can act as an intermediary."

Julie grinned. "That would be great. We'd really appreciate your help, Ember."

"Of course. Fernwood Deep welcomes visitors, and the Eternal Throne has been good to us for centuries. The PMA too, by proxy." Ember bowed.

Julie leaned out the window. "Where do we start? Taylor mentioned a brownie village not far from here."

"I have an even better idea." Ember laughed. "Everyone will be at the Beltane festival. The celebration of the Spring equinox."

"Spring?" Julie glanced at Taylor. "It's summer back home."

"Time moves differently in Avalon, remember?" Taylor grinned. "Are you suggesting we go, Ember?"

Ember's chuckle made his beard rustle. "Indeed I am, young elf. The celebration is tonight. I can take you there at once. The preparations are being made."

"We'll go. Thank you so much," Taylor gushed.

Ember inclined his head. "Follow me." He turned, but instead of striding off, he let out a soft whistle between his teeth. The wind roared through the trees and dryads, whipping their branches, and an enormous leaf the shape of a maple leaf but as big as the minivan swooped out of the trees on an eddy of wind. It hovered in front of Ember, who stepped onto it, and it swept him down the road at a steady pace.

Julie drove the minivan after him, shooting a glance at Taylor. "We'll go to Beltane, will we? We're supposed to be working, and I don't have another change of clothes. I thought we were going home this afternoon."

"You've clearly never been to a Beltane festival." Taylor was beaming. "I got to go once or twice as a kid, but I was never allowed to join in because of guards and protocol and stuff." He squealed softly, punching the air. "I can't believe we're going to Beltane!"

"Isn't it a Celtic festival?" Julie grumbled.

Taylor laughed. "Oh, you'll see. It's so much more than that. And don't worry—there's no greater gathering of paranormals in Fernwood Deep. There will be plenty of opportunities for recruiting."

Ember's leaf settled onto a stretch of grass in a wide clearing an hour's drive into Fernwood Deep. Julie parked the minivan beside it, gaping at a group of white deer that grazed contentedly at the edge of the clearing. They wore headstalls woven from blooming vines that linked them to a picket line between the trees. Gold saddles and bridles lay in a pile around the bottom of one of the trees.

Ember didn't give the deer a second glance as Julie grabbed Hat and hopped out of the van. "This way to Beltane," he boomed, throwing his arms wide and letting out an earth-shaking chuckle.

Taylor pushed past Julie and scrambled after Ember, skipping with excitement.

What's with him? Julie grumbled, following her guides up a footpath among trees that inclined steeply.

He's finally getting a chance to live his life. You can't blame him for being like a kid on Christmas Day. Hat chuckled.

They climbed steeply for a few minutes before the trees suddenly ended. Julie stepped out into the golden rays of the setting sun. They were standing on a high hilltop crowned with a stone circle akin to Stonehenge. A natural spring welled from the center of the circle, and the water ran in clear streams down the sides of the hill.

In a circle around the spring, large rough-hewn tables were set with wooden cups and plates. There were yellow flowers in bunches on the tables, blooming underfoot, and creeping and blossoming over the enormous stones that made up the circle. In front of each of the standing stones, an unlit bonfire was ready, the wood piled higher than Julie's head. A crowd of paranormals had gathered. Julie saw elves, pixies, dryad saplings, Woodland Fae, and others that she'd never seen before: satyrs and minotaurs, fauns and naiads, leprechauns, and goblins with long green fingers. They mingled around the tables, sipping cocktails served by elven waiters in yellow robes.

"Wow," Julie murmured.

"Make yourselves comfortable, friends." Ember inclined his head and stepped back. "I must attend to some of my other guests, but I will see you later. The feast begins at sunset."

He strode into the woods. Julie took a step closer to Taylor. "I've never seen so many different paras in one place," she hissed.

"Isn't it amazing?" Taylor bounded toward the stone circle. "Let's get cocktails!"

"We're on duty!" Julie complained, trailing after him.

He took a couple of piña coladas from the nearest tray and

handed her one. "C'mon, Julie. You're always telling me to live a little." He grinned.

Julie laughed. "Clearly, I'm making progress with you, Mr. Woodskin."

"Clearly you are, Miss Meadows." Taylor clinked his goblet against hers.

Julie sipped her cocktail as she scanned the crowd for likely recruits.

There. Nine o' clock, Hat hissed. *A bunch of aimless-looking young brownies.*

Julie looked. Three young brownies were sitting together, using a stump that couldn't have reached as high as Julie's knee as a table. Their cocktails were full-sized, Julie noticed, and the little folk had to hold their glasses with both hands. They were spindly creatures no taller than Julie's hip, and all had rosy cheeks and scruffy straw-colored hair.

"Taylor." Julie tugged at his arm. "Let's go talk to those brownies while they're relatively sober."

"Julie and Taylor! Is that you?" a familiar voice drawled with a thick Western accent.

Julie looked up. "Cironius!"

The centaur strode out of the crowd, grinning from ear to ear. His equine half was as black and glossy as ever, and his hooves thudded softly on the grass. As usual, he wore a khaki shirt and a black Stetson, his brown hair spilling over his shoulders from beneath it.

"I didn't think I'd be seein' you two here!" Cironius boomed. "What are y'all up to this time?"

"Recruiting, as always." Julie grinned as she gave Cironius a warm handshake. "And you?"

"Visitin' some family for Beltane, y'know." Cironius shifted his weight from hoof to hoof. "Ain't happy leavin' the horses, but I got a kid lookin' after 'em. Ambush had her foal, by the way.

Most beautiful little gray colt you ever did see." He beamed. "All happy and healthy, thanks to y'all."

"We should be the ones thanking *you* for letting us help you with your werewolf problem." Taylor laughed. "Those six Weres are shaping up to be good soldiers, and they had our backs in a fight with yetis a few weeks ago."

"I heard about that yeti business. A bad thing. Very bad." Cironius shook his mane, then raised his head and beamed. "Aha! The sun's gone down. First time at Beltane, Julie?"

"Yeah," Julie admitted.

Cironius clapped her on the shoulder with a force that almost knocked her over. "It's gonna put hair on your chest, kid." He laughed uproariously. "They're lightin' the fires!"

Julie looked up. She noted for the first time that they weren't alone on this hill. Seven hills sprouted from the forest near them, connected with pathways. Each was decorated exactly like this one. The sun had slipped down the horizon, and Ember now stood in the center of their stone circle, his arms spread wide.

"Friends!" he thundered. "Welcome to Beltane!"

CHAPTER SEVEN

A hush fell on the crowd. Ember reached into his pocket and drew out something small and bright that moved this way and that on his palm, quick as a lizard.

A salamander, Hat whispered.

It didn't look like any of the salamanders Julie had seen on National Geographic. This little creature was patterned in orange and red, and it let out a soft chirp as it scampered to the end of Ember's fingers. Then it leaped into the nearest wood heap.

As it jumped, flames burst out all over its body. When it landed in the stacked bonfire, the logs roared into flame. As if in response, flames burst out of all the bonfires stacked around the stone circle. The fires on the other hills ignited, and the dark forest was studded with flame.

Ember's face was ancient and wild as he turned to the spring, the leaping flames and stirring leaves etching shadows across his skin. His eyes glowed. "Naiads!" he thundered.

The spring bubbled. Water rose in pillars to human height, then shifted, changed, turned to flesh, and became two pale girls standing in the spring, their long blue dresses still splashing and babbling and almost transparent. Taylor's eyes widened. Julie had an absurd urge to cover them.

Ember chuckled and stepped forward, raising his arms. "May the streams run with wine and mead!" he boomed. "Beltane begins!"

One of the naiads grinned and bent to touch the surface of the water with her finger. The other followed suit. Where the first naiad touched the water, it turned crimson; the other naiad turned her half of the stream into something honey-gold.

A cheer roared from the crowd and the waiters reappeared, this time with gold goblets. Taylor grabbed two from the nearest tray and bent to fill them from the stream. "Wine or mead?" he asked, holding them out.

"I've never had mead." Julie took the goblet of honey-gold fluid and sipped cautiously. It was vaguely beery and unbelievably sweet.

Giggles erupted from the two naiads. They flung themselves into the stream and paddled up and down, shifting from flesh to water and back. The crowd filled their goblets from the stream, and the volume of the party rose.

Julie sipped more mead. "Are we going to talk to those brownies now?"

"Okay." Taylor nodded, wiping wine from his upper lip with the back of his hand.

They headed to the stump. The brownies had discarded their cocktails and were taking shots of wine and mead from acorn tops. The only brownie female in the group seemed to be the least inebriated, so Julie addressed her. "Good evening! We're from the Official Para-Military Agency, and we'd like to offer you a job."

The brownie huffed and crossed her skinny arms. "No, I'm not going to skim your milk, sweep your floors, or polish your shoes." She made a shooing motion with one hand. "I don't care how many bowls of milk you put on your hearth."

"How about working in the logistics division of the PMA and getting a decent salary with plenty of benefits?" Taylor asked, then stepped away to talk to a couple of dryads who had come up to him.

The brownie raised her eyebrows. "Wait. You're offering me a job? A real job? For money?"

"Of course," Julie told her. "And no pay cuts due to stature, either. All our paras are paid equally."

The brownie rubbed her chin. "Fine. I'm in. My two knucklehead brothers, too."

One of the brothers belched and fell off his chair.

"Maybe we'll sign the papers in the morning, though." The brownie sighed.

"Done." Julie grinned and handed her a business card.

Ember's deep, full voice rolled over the hilltop. "Let us feast!"

Taylor appeared beside Julie, followed the dryads, who held their wine and mead goblets in long, twiggy fingers. "C'mon, Julie!" He gestured with his goblet. "Let's eat!"

Julie followed him to one of the long tables. She wasn't sure she'd seen food being brought out, but the dishes were full, and the smells were enough to make her mouth water. Perching on a giant toadstool that was knee-high and surprisingly strong as well as very spongy to sit on, Julie took her place beside Taylor and stared at the food. Mounds of leafy greens drizzled with something that smelled exotic and tangy. Huge bowls of fruit salads, berries and peaches and edible flowers, with slices of emerald green and amethyst-purple fruit that Julie couldn't begin to recognize. When she bit into them, they burst in her mouth with floods of ripe flavor.

There was also a whole roast boar with an apple in its mouth, and when the waiters carved thin slices of the meat from it, it was softly pink and so tender that it fell apart on Julie's plate. She heaped her plate with it. There were interesting hints of mint and orange and rosemary woven in with a flavor that seemed more gamey and full than pork, and she groaned with pleasure at the first mouthful.

There was a dark chuckle across the table from her. "Enjoying him? He was a fighter. It took all four of us to bring him down, and he almost killed one of the deer."

Julie looked up. A painfully beautiful male faerie sat across the table from her. His skin was moon-silver, his dark hair was gelled into spikes, and his eyes were so dark that they were almost black. His pointed features were harmonious, and his ears were far longer and more pointed than Taylor's.

True faeries, her orb training whispered in her mind. *An older, wilder, and more savage people than the fae. Considered one of the most dangerous beings in the paranormal world.*

Julie raised an eyebrow, glancing at the bracelets of living vines on the faerie's wrists and the golden bands on his fingers. "Were those your deer in the parking lot?"

Taylor gaped. The faerie grinned, revealing a black mouth and teeth as pointed as a cat's. "Good guess. Except for mine—it was wounded in the fight with this boar. Tusk to the legs." He carved another slice of meat from the boar's shoulder. "I put my spear through his skull once we ran him tired."

Julie felt a faint shiver down her spine.

"Don't frighten the human." A female faerie spoke from beside him. "It's too early in the night for that." She laughed, an eerie cackle as wild as the night wind. Two faerie girls next to her joined in.

The male faerie held Julie's gaze. "I don't think she's so easily frightened."

She figured she *should* feel a little frightened. She was the only human here, and maybe the only human who had ever been to Beltane. *Or am I human?* Would a human feel like she belonged here? Like she'd been waiting her whole life to be here?

She shoved the thought down. "That spear of yours." She

nodded at the giant hole in the boar's skull. "Tell me, can you use it for more than hunting boar?"

The female faerie sat up straighter and met Julie's eyes. "Do you have bigger quarry for us?"

"I do." Julie grinned. "How about the enemies of the Eternal Throne?"

Taylor's jaw dropped. "Are you trying to recruit *faeries*?"

"I'm not trying to recruit them. I *am* recruiting them." Julie raised an eyebrow. "You'd be paid handsomely, and you'd be preserving peace in the paranormal world."

The male faerie scoffed. "Peace! We've had our fill of peace."

"We want battle!" One of the young faeries punched the air.

"You might see some if you join the PMA." Julie pulled out a business card. "There's good medical insurance, too, and a nice salary. I'm sure there are stalls for your deer, or pastures or something."

"Both," Taylor croaked, staring at the business card.

The female faerie grinned and took it. "We might accept your offer, human."

The arrival of a selection of pies brought an immediate end to the conversation. These were savory and buttery and stuffed with sumptuous venison or something green and leafy that looked like spinach but had a sweet, fresh pop on the tongue that took Julie by surprise.

By the time the dried fruits and nuts came, followed by wedges of something that might have been black forest cake but had a sharply spicy aftertaste and had definitely been soaked in rum, Julie was too stuffed to move. She sagged on her toadstool.

"Dude, I'm dying," she groaned to Taylor. "But I'm dying happy."

Taylor's nose was buried in his wine goblet. He looked at her over the brim. "I hope you saved some space. There will be more dessert after the dancing."

Julie gaped. *"Dancing?"*

A musical note rang across the seven hills. Julie whipped around as a bronze-skinned figure capered from the woods, his bare feet so light on the grass that the blades hardly bent where he trod. His head was a wild mass of brown curls. His body was a lithe, sinewy collection of muscles, naked but for some strategically placed leaves.

There was a long staff under his arm, intertwined with growing leaves and tiny living white flowers, and he held a flute to his lips. He blew another note, his wild dark eyes raking the tables, and the whole of Fernwood Deep stood to attention and listened.

"Is that *Bacchus?*" Julie hissed.

Ancient woodland spirit, her training supplied. *Ruler of the forest as the Green Man is its protector.*

"Bacchus!" cooed a duo of high-pitched voices. The naiads stumbled out of the stream, soaked to the skin and hiccupping as they leaned on one another, fawning over Bacchus.

He grinned at them and played another note, then another. Then he was off across the grass, his feet so quick that Julie could barely see them, playing fluidly. A cheer rose from the tables and the dryads followed him, then the faeries. The hill was encircled by a blur of dancing.

Julie realized her goblet was empty. She gripped it and got to her feet, waiting for the world to stop spinning before she stumbled to the stream for a refill. Taylor followed her, avoiding two of the dryads who followed Bacchus, their leaves rustling in time with his flute.

"Enjoying Beltane?" Taylor yelled over the music, steadying her with a hand on her arm when she bent to refill her goblet.

Julie raised her dripping goblet from the stream and took a long swig of mead, then held it up and grinned at him. "Beltaaaaaane!" she whooped.

Taylor chortled and raised an arm to clink his goblet against hers. "Beltaaaaane!" he echoed.

Julie turned to head back to her toadstool and almost slammed into a bare and exceptionally well-muscled chest. She stumbled back a step, tipping up her chin to look up at the faun standing in front of her. He wore nothing except the thick, white fur that covered him from the waist down. His legs ended in cloven goat hooves that had been painted gold.

"Forgive me, madame." The faun bowed low, then straightened to grin into her eyes. His curly white beard tumbled down to his chest but his face was smooth. His eyes were a breathtaking shade of pale gray.

"That's okay." Julie staggered up the bank of the stream.

The faun made no move to refill the empty goblet hanging from between his fingers. He smelled raw and animal and faintly goat-y, but not in a bad way. In a musky pheromone-laden way.

"What brings someone like you to Beltane in Fernwood Deep?" he asked.

Julie waved her goblet. "We're here to recruit people to the OPMA. Paras, I mean."

"Intriguing." The faun's eyes played over her face. "I doubt I've ever met anyone like you."

Julie snorted. "Met a lot of humans, have you?"

"No." The faun's grin returned, and he held out a hand. "I've never danced with one, either."

The faun's silvery eyes and the wild music drew Julie in, her heart thumping madly in her chest. Then she took another swig of mead. "You won't be dancing with one tonight, either."

The faun shrugged. "Very well." He winked at her. "You can always find me later." He refilled his goblet and sprang off, clicking his cloven hooves together before joining the mad circle of dancers.

Julie turned to Taylor and paused. His brows were drawn together, and the look on his face was... She'd never seen him look that way. It made her feel weird.

Julie could think of one way to fix that. She took a deep

breath, raised her goblet to her lips, and chugged it. When the last of the honeyed mead slid down her throat, the weirdness had melted, replaced by a warm, floaty feeling.

She grinned at Taylor. "I'm gonna dansh."

"What?" Taylor peered at her over the rim of his goblet.

"Dansh." Julie tried again. "*Dance.*"

He giggled. "I thought we were here for work." He waved his arms.

"I don't wave like that. My arms." Julie waved them.

"Yesh. You do," Taylor slurred. "You said we were here for work." He did the stupid waving thing again.

"You're annoying," Julie spluttered. She jabbed a finger at him. "An-noy-ing. And I'm gonna dance."

She stumbled toward the dancers; They were following Bacchus in a snaking line around the hill, and the last one in the line was a young dryad, her shoots the tenderest green. Her right arm was linked to the satyr's next to her, and Julie grabbed for her left arm as she came past, her fingers finding bark and twigs.

The dryad folded her arm around Julie's and they were away, whisking across the grass, jumping and spinning and skipping after Bacchus. Julie's limbs moved of their own accord in perfect time to his flute.

The dance grew faster. A hairy arm slipped through Julie's; she wasn't sure whose. A circle formed in the center of the stone circle, surrounding the bonfires. Smoke and sweat and the scent of trampled grass filled her nostrils as they danced faster still. The circle changed direction, broke apart, and reformed. Julie performed each step in the dance as though she'd practiced it.

Bacchus broke the circle and led them in a long line down a footpath that disappeared into the woods, his wild music echoing around the trees. Up the next hill, their dance joined with that of the next stone circle, then the next and the next until every paranormal at Beltane was dancing together.

The world spun, and the stars sparkled. Julie's head became a mad whirl of wildness.

Something damp brushed Julie's face.

She swiped at it. "Uh-uh."

The dampness went away. When it returned, it splashed on her cheek, over her forehead, and into her ear.

"Nooo," she groaned. The vibrations of her voice went through her head like someone was slamming it against concrete. She let out a soft moan instead, which merely made her eyeballs feel like they were about to pop out.

More...*licking*? Julie's heart palpitated. What had *happened* last night? Her eyes snapped wide, and she looked into a pair of big brown eyes as lips began to explore her nose.

She shrieked and sat bolt upright even though the movement sent a lance of agony through her head. The deer that had been licking her face sprang back, let out a bleat of terror, and bolted into the woods, the underside of its white tail held high.

"*Crap*," Julie moaned, covering her face with her hands. "Tell me that was just a deer. A standard-issue, ordinary old deer."

"Oh, yes," Taylor bellowed in her ear. "It was a non-magical deer."

Julie clapped her hands over her ears and curled up, pressing her forehead to her knees. "Quit *yelling*."

"I'm not yelling. Do you want some breakfast?" Taylor asked.

Julie's stomach lurched. She opened her eyes as slowly as possible since every beam of sunlight seemed intent on slicing through her eyeballs and into her brain like bits of glass. Something rustled on her shoulder as she moved, and she grabbed it before it could fall to the ground. A jacket that smelled like the earth after rain.

Taylor must have covered her with his jacket when she'd

fallen asleep. She peered around at the ring of toadstools surrounding her. Where had *they* come from?

"Where are we?" Julie croaked.

"In a clearing close to where we parked the minivan. Ember's making breakfast. You want mushrooms with your bacon?" Taylor sat on a stump a few yards away, wearing Hat, who was a cheerful straw boater today. Ember was cheerfully frying things in a cast-iron pan over a campfire.

"Why are you so peppy?" Julie groaned. "Why do you want food? Why are we awake?"

Taylor raised an eyebrow. "We need to get back to the PMA soon, remember? We have that audience with the yeti queen. There's no time for sleeping in."

Julie let out a sigh and tipped back her throbbing head, closing her eyes. Audience with a queen? All she wanted was to throw up, then sleep for a week.

"It's barely dawn," she growled.

"We'll be late if we don't get going." Taylor gripped Hat's brim and flicked him toward Julie like a frisbee. She yelped, barely catching him, and squashed him onto her head.

Don't squash me! Hat protested.

"Ow. Ow. Ow." Julie pressed her knuckles to her temples.

Taylor gave a painfully perky laugh. "Be glad you didn't go with that faun last night. You'd be feeling even worse now."

Julie frowned. "How much mead *did* I drink last night?"

"Definitely not enough before you recruited a family of scary-ass faeries." Taylor chuckled. "They came to the minivan this morning and signed their paperwork, by the way. So did the brownies. And the dryads. And the satyrs."

"Satyrs?" Julie frowned. She barely remembered a couple of satyrs staggering up to her, leaning on each other and singing *Glimmering Light* from *A Midsummer Night's Dream*. "Did you recruit those two idiots?"

"Hey, satyrs are very hardworking and intelligent." Taylor folded his arms. "When they're not wasted."

Julie tried to be happy about all the recruits and failed. She flopped onto her back on the dewy grass, trying to decide which direction to vomit in.

Ember abruptly straightened, smacking his hands clean. "I think you've had enough misery for now." He chuckled deeply and picked a palm-sized leaf from the nearest tree. Using the leaf, he scooped a thimbleful of dew from the tree, strode over to Julie, and offered it to her.

She took the leaf, and her hesitation vanished when she looked at that crystal-clear dew and felt thirst burning the back of her throat. Putting the tip of the leaf to her lips, Julie sipped. Instantly, the fogginess in her head and nausea disappeared.

"Whoa." Julie blinked. "What was *that*?"

"A magical hangover cure." Ember grinned. "It actually works."

Julie scrambled to her feet. The earth felt reassuringly solid beneath them, and she raked a damp hand through her hair. Suddenly, the food in that frying pan looked amazing. "Okay, that was *awesome*. And yes, I *would* like mushrooms with my bacon, please."

"We'll have to take it to go, though, or we'll be late." Taylor turned to Ember. "Mr. Floraison—"

"Ember." The Green Man beamed.

"Ember." Taylor smiled. "Thank you so much for inviting us to Beltane. I had the time of my life, and we recruited so many paras!"

"It was incredible." Julie nodded. "Thank you."

Ember bowed. "I am pleased to have served you." His grin returned, and he slipped back into informal mode. "Besides, many of those young paras needed something productive to do. They are trying to live as though every day is Beltane."

He scooped their breakfast into two big bowls woven of leaves, and they ate in the minivan, Taylor driving with his knees as they wound out of Fernwood Deep.

CHAPTER EIGHT

Julie studied her reflection in the mirror of the third-floor bathroom at PMA HQ. *How is it possible that I drank so much mead last night, and I don't even have red eyes?* She leaned closer to the mirror, prodding the smooth, tight skin above her cheekbones.

It's not called a magical hangover cure for nothing, Hat quipped.

Julie stepped back with a sigh and ran her hands over her rumpled clothes. They looked like she'd gotten ridiculously drunk and then spent all night dancing with a bunch of wild forest spirits in them, which she had. *I should have packed a change of clothing, even if the shower in the minivan helped.*

An amazing lack of foresight on your part, Hat commented.

Julie scoffed. *Gee, thanks. I hadn't noticed.* She pulled him off and put him down by the sink, then stepped into the nearest stall to change into her dress uniform. It was the only clothing she had had in her locker. She felt a twinge in the pit of her stomach at the thought of being the only idiot in the recruiting department wearing her dress uniform today.

When she stepped out of the bathroom, her dirty clothes stuffed into the backpack over her shoulder and Hat obligingly posing as a dress cap, Taylor was waiting for her outside the men's. His side-parted hair was still damp, and he was wearing his uniform for once—the green and silver of PMA recruitment.

"Well, look at you." Julie raised an eyebrow. "Looks like I'm not the only one who lacked foresight today, Hat."

Taylor held up both hands, laughing. Hat snorted. "I wouldn't be so sure about that. I know full well that you have a whole closet stashed in your locker. I was the one who helped you place the charm on it so that everything would fit."

Taylor's cheeks turned an embarrassed gray.

Julie chuckled. "I'm not judging. I want one!"

Leaving the bathrooms behind, they made for the elevator. Taylor's phone binged, and he pulled it out. "I'd almost forgotten that Ilsa's coming here later today."

"Your poor sister," Julie grumbled. "I mean, I love working here, but I'd hate to live here."

"Trust me. She'll be well taken care of." Taylor's smile was lopsided.

Julie snorted and pressed the button for Switzerland. "Yeah, because having all your freedom taken away and being forced to assume a role you never asked for is being well taken care of."

Taylor shrugged. "Ilsa could have abdicated, you know."

"And become a pariah for all eternity," Hat commented as the elevator surged upward.

Taylor's shoulders slumped. He looked down at his phone, drooping.

"I'm sorry." Julie bumped him lightly with her shoulder. "I know none of this is your fault, and I'm not helping. So, what does she say? Are we going to see her later today?"

"I'm going to ask Kaplan if we can help her get oriented when she gets here." Taylor typed on his phone. "I think she'd be glad to see a familiar face."

The elevator halted, and doors slid open. The guards turned around, and Julie laughed in recognition. "Isaiah! Chester! It's good to see you."

The two Weres, some of Julie and Taylor's earlier recruits, were both in wolf form. Isaiah was shaggy with golden fur, and Chester was enormously muscular and pale blond. They both grinned, pink tongues spilling over lupine fangs.

"Hey, Julie!" Chester wagged his tail. "We've got orders to escort you to the Ice Palace. How cool is that?"

"Aren't you guys still in training?" Julie shivered as she stepped onto the snow.

Isaiah nodded. "Technically, yes. Since we're military, our training is three months long, even though agents only get three weeks. But the OPMA is shorthanded, and now that there's peace with the yetis, they're using trainees for guard duty here."

"We're glad to see you." Chester transformed into his human form, which was equally muscular, and fished in a backpack. "You're the first things we've seen except for snow all day. I get why we have to guard the portal after the whole Qbiit drama, but it's dead boring." He pulled out a couple of fluffy fur coats and two pairs of snow goggles. "Put these on. It's a bit of a hike."

Julie slipped gratefully into the coat and pulled the goggles over her eyes. "Mush!"

Chester scoffed, then turned back into a wolf. "We're not sled dogs."

"Would be cool if you were," Julie retorted.

Isaiah chuckled. "Come on. It's not far to the portal."

"Portal?" Julie raised her eyebrows. "Don't the yetis live here?"

"Some do, but the Ice Palace is in the yeti lands in Avalon near where we had the fight with Qbiit," Isaiah explained over his shoulder as he paced across the snow. Taylor and Julie scrambled after him.

"There are two portals between the yetis' lands and Earth," Hat told her. "One in Switzerland and one in Tibet. That allows yetis to travel between Avalon and other communities here."

"I didn't know the yetis had that technology," Julie admitted.

Taylor smiled. "They don't. The Eternity Throne placed the

portals centuries ago to foster a connection between yeti communities in a time of famine."

Julie raised her eyebrows as they toiled uphill through the snow. "So the Eternity Throne *does* do more than just look pretty."

Taylor laughed. "Apparently."

The portal was tucked under a shelf of ice. At first glance, it just looked like a gap in the ice that led to more windblown, snowy landscape. When they drew closer, though, Julie saw that the scene through the portal was flat and still. They stepped through it, and when her dizziness cleared, she could see nothing but snow and ice in every direction. There was no wind here.

"The White Sea. A frozen lake at the edge of yeti territory," Hat told her. "The Ice Palace is dead ahead."

"I don't see anything." Julie squinted through her goggles and rubbed her stinging ears. It was even colder here.

Hat went *poof,* and fur extended over her ears. "Better?"

"Better." Julie smiled, smoothing him. He'd become a fur-lined deerstalker. "Thanks."

Isaiah raised his nose, sniffing. "Let's go."

The Weres trotted ahead, and Julie and Taylor plodded after them. The snow wasn't very deep. In places, Julie looked down into cool blue ice. Some of the ice stood up, cracked and jagged. In other spots, black rocks protruded through it.

"Wait a second." Julie peered at the ice under her feet. "Those caverns we were in..."

"Good eye." Hat extended a flap further over Julie's left ear. "They go under the White Sea, too."

"I thought there would be a village or something around here." Julie squinted around at the cold, empty landscape. "I mean, we haven't even seen a yeti."

Hat laughed. "You won't, either, not unless they want to be seen. They don't live in villages. They prefer their own company most of the time, except for storytelling gatherings on occasion."

"Except for the Ice Palace?" Julie asked.

Hat snickered. "Well, you'll see."

If the eyrie had been big, the Ice Palace was gargantuan.

They had been walking for half an hour when Taylor first spotted it. It took ten more minutes to be visible to Julie's human eyes. *If they are human eyes,* she added silently to herself. *No. Stop it!*

At first, it was only a vague blue shape jutting from the horizon. By the time they reached the walls of the palace, Julie was gaping open-mouthed. The Ice Palace sprawled over the banks of the White Sea, stretching in every direction as far as Julie could see. There were no battlements or arrow slits. It was a blank line of blue ice, impenetrable and immovable. There was a single door tall enough to accommodate yetis. Its ice grille stood open.

There was no sound, no movement, and no sign of yetis.

"Spooky," Julie whispered on a cloud of steam.

"It's like this place is abandoned." Taylor hugged himself as they approached the door.

Chester's nose twitched. "Oh, it's a long way from abandoned," he growled, blond hackles rising on his shoulders.

Isaiah shot him a cool look. "They're friends, Chester."

"I know." Chester's hackles smoothed. "Their smell just takes me back to the fight."

The Weres paced through the door in front of them into a giant courtyard with doorways and passages leading in every direction.

"Straight ahead," Hat told Julie, his voice echoing around the courtyard. "Into the main building."

There were so many turrets and towers and courtyards and doorways in every direction that Julie couldn't tell which was the main building, but she followed the Weres through a door that took them into a hall carved out of ice. Slits in the walls let in beams of sunlight that sparkled on the polished floor. Julie's feet skidded out from under her, and Taylor just managed to grab her arm to keep her upright.

"This floor is designed for padded furry feet." Isaiah chuckled, holding up one of his massive paws. "Step carefully."

"It still seems unoccupied." Julie half-expected cracks to spread in the walls at the sound of her voice. "Why is it so quiet? Does the queen live alone?"

"Oh, no. Her family lives here too, and there are plenty of craftsmen to maintain the ice," Hat explained as they walked slowly through the hall. "The palace has to be this size, so each yeti has enough personal space to be comfortable."

Julie shook her head. "They must have *hated* New York City."

Hat snorted. "Now you understand why I was so adamant that the yetis were acting out of character when the muggings began."

Julie nodded.

The door at the end of the hall was closed. Isaiah sniffed again. "This leads to the throne room. Chester and I will wait out here."

"Do we knock?" Julie asked.

"Oh, no. That would be rude!" Taylor gasped, wide-eyed.

"Sue me for not knowing." Julie held up both hands. "What are we supposed to do?"

Her raised voice echoed through the hall, and the doors, made of ice that looked like frosted glass, swung open. Finally, she saw yetis. A youngster stood on either side of the door, tusks just beginning to protrude from their bottom lips and their eyes milky blue as they watched Julie and Taylor step into the throne room.

They weren't the only ones. The room could have swallowed the entire third floor of HQ and left room for more. Blue columns of ice supported a vaulted ceiling that extended six or seven stories above Julie's head. At the far end, a single throne towered over everything, and a yeti with pure-black fur sat upon it.

Her massive feet, with toes the size of Julie's fist, were placed wide apart. Her hands rested on the wrought-ice armrests, and her brown eyes bored into Julie's even from this distance. The yeti queen wore no crown, but her tusks curved forward and up from her bottom jaw to the top of her head. They were covered in elaborate carvings. Three attendants stood on each side of the throne, with ten feet of space between each. They were motionless.

Randkluft appeared on Julie's left and gave her a grin. He called something in the gargling yeti language, which sounded like Wookie, and held up his hands. Julie expected a cheer, but the gathered yetis hummed together, a low sound like the wind over ice.

What are they saying? Julie hissed.

Randkluft announced you, Hat told her. *Well, both of you. The one who fears not the sound of thunder and the maker of the blue fire.*

Taylor grinned and touched the magical staff still tucked behind his ear.

Randkluft turned to Julie and gestured to the queen, warbling again. Hat translated as he spoke. "Honored guests who have come from the land of smoke and sound, you are presented to the Queen of the Wind and Sky, Empress of the Ice and Sea, Lady of the Snow and Storm. Queen Pereletok!"

More humming from the yetis. Pereletok rose to her feet and strode down from the throne with loping grace. She stopped at the base, folded her hands in front of her, and waited.

You can approach her now, Hat murmured. *But stay ten feet away.*

Six feet apart, huh? Julie quipped, swallowing hard as she and Taylor stepped forward.

Hat scoffed. *Six feet is considered to be an unforgivable invasion of privacy in yeti culture, reserved for the closest family. It'd be like grabbing the queen's ass.*

Julie looked at those tusks and remembered how effortlessly a young yeti had thrown her against the sewer wall in Brooklyn. *Noted.*

They stopped, though the space between them yawned. Pereletok studied them for a few more moments before raising both her shaggy arms, hands to the ceiling. A huge grin split her face, extending on either side of the tusks and showing her teeth. Her voice was high as she gargled a greeting.

"Welcome to the Land of the Wind and Sky!" she thundered, Hat translating. "You who stood by our people in a time of peril and pain! You who have shown courage and kindness! You who sought to succor and save!"

Relief washed over Julie. *Did she swallow a thesaurus?*

Seriously? Hat groaned. *You've just been welcomed with open arms by the queen of a species that rarely shows itself to strangers, and that is your reaction?*

Pereletok kept her arms high and her smile in place but spoke no further.

Taylor cleared his throat. He didn't bow, Julie noticed, but he replied very quietly, "We are honored by your presence, Queen of the Wind and Sky."

Hat must have translated telepathically since Pereletok's smile widened.

"How can we help?" Julie added.

Pereletok's eyes flashed to her, and she shook her head. "You misunderstand, fearless one. I had you brought to me from the land of smoke and sound and across the White Sea so that my people could express their abundant gratitude to you, and to you, Maker of the Blue Fire, for what you have done for us. You broke the circle and saved my people."

The yetis hummed. The sonorous sound echoed through the room as they nodded in appreciation. Randkluft just grinned.

"My people are people of the wind and snow, and we wish to repay you for how you saved us from the direst fate of all," Pereletok went on. "We have none of the machines you make to transform your world, and we have no magic beyond that which is in our hearts, but whatever we have, we offer to you in repayment for what you have done for our people."

More humming.

Julie glanced at Taylor, who took a step back.

It's a sign of respect in yeti culture, Hat hissed.

Julie echoed Taylor's movement as the Aether Elf spoke. "Queen of the Wind and Sky, we cannot accept repayment for doing our duty."

"Yeah," Julie added.

Taylor shot her a look.

"I mean, yes, Queen. We were only doing what was right." She cleared her throat. "We could never accept repayment for our deeds."

Good effort for someone untrained in yeti speech patterns, Hat snickered.

Julie's cheeks warmed. *Shut up!*

Pereletok's smile widened, and she nodded. "Your tale will be told to generation upon generation of my people. Every yeti who lives and will ever live will know how the one who fears not the sound of thunder and the one who makes the blue fire saved my people from insufferable bondage. You will be immortal, your spirits set free in the stories of our race, the wind that blows from one generation to the next long after our bones are frozen in the White Sea."

Julie's cheeks warmed even more. "Thank you. We're honored."

Hat buzzed on Julie's head the way he did when he was busy. He warbled in Yeti for a very long time. Pereletok and the others nodded, beaming.

What are you doing? Julie hissed.

Saving your ass, Hat returned. *Short responses are considered very rude.*

Conversations must take a long time here, Julie commented.

Hat snorted. *Since most yetis only see each other once or twice a year, that is no surprise.*

Hat finally fell silent, and Pereletok spread her arms. "Go in peace. May the aurora dance forever over your heads. May the ice be firm beneath your feet, and may the wind always be at your back."

Julie cleared her throat, almost stepping forward before she remembered herself. "Queen of the Wind and Sky, may I be so bold as to make one small request of you before we undertake the journey back?"

Eh, could be longer, Hat remarked.

Shhh! Julie held her breath.

Pereletok nodded at once. "Speak, fearless one, for we are all listening."

Julie took a deep breath. "You asked if we wanted a reward, and we don't. But if I may take this opportunity, I want to let you know that if any of your people want to join the OPMA, we will welcome them with open arms."

Taylor glared daggers at her. Julie ignored him.

Pereletok ran a hand over her chin, touching the bottoms of her tusks with her thumb and forefinger. "Mine are not people of war or magic or science or any of the things your agency is associated with. We are people of the snow and stories. What is more, we are not people of violence, and while many of us are angry and seek justice not only from the Green One but from the one he served, we seek peace and silence and solitude above all things."

Taylor kept his voice very soft. "Your nature is an admirable one, Queen of the Wind and Sky, yet if you tell this story to your people, please tell them there are roles to suit every type of paranormal. Perhaps even roles where solitude is a necessity." He paused. "The yetis have been touched by war before. The Eternity Throne will try to protect you, but it needs all the help it can get."

Julie glanced at him as he slipped back into everyday speech, but Pereletok didn't look offended. She nodded. "I will tell this story to my people. We part as friends. May your journey back to the land of smoke and sound be filled with laughter and peace, and may the cooling north wind attend your way."

"Ilsa's here." Taylor looked at his phone as the elevator juddered toward the third floor. "And Kaplan said it's okay if we help her get settled."

Julie grinned. "I wonder if Kaplan's heard how many recruits we got this week."

Taylor chuckled. "Well, we haven't been called to his office to be chewed out yet, so I'm guessing he has. Anyway, we have to meet Ilsa in his office. She's just been brought in via portal for safety."

"Okay." Julie reached up and ran her fingers around Hat's brim. "Thanks for all the translations back there, Hat. You were great."

"I'm always great," Hat rejoined.

"Aaaand, moment ruined." Julie sighed.

The elevator doors opened, and they headed across the floor to Kaplan's office. Malcolm's desk outside Kaplan's door was unoccupied. When they entered the office, Malcolm shuffled papers at Kaplan's desk while the weretiger chatted with Ilsa, who was sitting in one of the leather chairs that faced him.

"Hey, Ilsa." Taylor held out his arms.

"Nice to see you, Tay." Ilsa got up and glanced at Kaplan, who nodded, before giving Taylor a hug.

Wow. Does she have to ask permission for everything? Julie grumbled.

Hat sighed. *That wasn't permission. She was just making sure that Kaplan could tell this really is Taylor by smell.*

Julie swallowed. Maybe the threat to Ilsa's life was more imminent than she'd realized.

"Glad you finally made it, Woodskin," Kaplan barked. "What did the queen want?"

"To thank us for our heroics." Julie gave him a big smile.

Kaplan studied her. "Fine." He opened his desk drawer and pulled out an elevator pass, which he held out to Ilsa. "This is the only way to access your suite. My most trusted agents will serve as guards, but you won't see them much except when you leave your suite, which I suggest you only do when absolutely necessary."

"Yes, Captain." Ilsa nodded. "Thank you."

"You're in safe hands with these three." Kaplan waved them away. "I'll keep an eye on you until you get to the elevator. Now, I need to get on with my day."

"Does that mean I can go with them, Uncle Jack?" Malcolm asked, brightening.

Kaplan glared at him. "I said *three*, Malcolm. Can you count?" He turned to his computer. "Dismissed."

"Come on, Ilsa." Taylor put a hand on his sister's arm. "Let's get you settled."

He led the way out of the office. Malcolm was just about to close the door behind Julie when Kaplan's phone rang. He held it to his ear, and before the door closed, Julie heard him growl, "*What?* They recruited *how many?* My budget for this quarter is *screwed!*"

CHAPTER NINE

"What did you guys do?" Malcolm demanded as they walked across the office. "Am I going to have to manage Uncle Jack's mood when I get back? Because it's not easy, let me tell you."

"Just snark at him," Julie suggested.

Malcolm stared at her. "I don't have a death wish."

"He won't be mad," Taylor told him with a grin. "We brought in a bumper crop of recruits from those two days in Avalon."

"Bumper crop? They're not corn." Julie laughed. "Although honestly, I think we were almost drunk enough to recruit a field of corn at Beltane if there'd been one."

Ilsa grinned. "Wait, this sounds like a story I need to hear. You went to *Beltane?*"

"We went to the eyrie first." Julie shivered. "That was scary."

Taylor hit the up button on the elevator, and they waited. "It was, but we got six griffin recruits," he told Ilsa.

"Six!" Malcolm's eyes widened. "You don't recruit them one by one, do you?"

"Oh, no." Julie laughed. "Then we tried to recruit a Green Man—"

"Ember Floraison," Taylor added. "Of Fernwood Deep."

"Yeah, but he was bound to the forest, so we wanted to talk to some dryads and brownies instead," Julie went on. "He invited us to Beltane. He said we could talk to people there."

"Oh, so you went to Beltane on a work trip." Malcolm snorted. "Sure."

"In my defense, I didn't know there was going to be so much alcohol involved," Julie countered.

Hat snickered. "You're not even legal, Miss Meadows. What were you thinking?"

Julie's ears warmed. Taylor gave her a gentle shove on the shoulder. "Don't look so stressed, Julie. Avalon doesn't have an age limit for human drinking, so you're okay. No laws broken."

"What was Beltane like without any guards or protocol?" Ilsa's eyes were wistful.

The elevator arrived.

"It was amazing." Taylor grinned as they shuffled inside. "I drank a *lot* of wine. I recruited some satyrs while I was drunk. They even remembered and came over to sign their paperwork."

"We recruited some brownies and dryads too. And faeries," Julie added.

Ilsa stared at them. "Faeries?"

"Oh, yes. Creepy, but cool in their way." Julie peered at the buttons. "Oh, hey, here's a new button. I'm guessing it's yours." It had the Aether Elf coat of arms on it. She pressed it, and the elevator did nothing.

The pass in Ilsa's hand chimed. "Oh, right." Ilsa stepped forward and swiped the pass at the button. It gave a cheerful *bing*, and the elevator doors closed.

The Aether Elf princess turned to Julie, grinning. "You recruited *faeries*?"

"And flirted with a faun," Julie added.

Taylor turned pale gray. Ilsa grinned at him, but to Julie's intense relief, she didn't comment. "It sounds pretty cool."

"Wait, I lost count." Malcolm held up his fingers. "You recruited six griffins and…

"Three brownies. Four faeries. Two satyrs." Julie ticked them off on his fingers. "How many dryads?"

"I don't remember," Taylor confessed. "There was a lot of wine involved by that point."

Ilsa grinned, draped an arm around Taylor's shoulders, and drew him in for a hug. "I'm so proud of you, little bro. I always knew you had it in you to do good in this world. Maybe our parents will start taking you seriously when they see you've found your niche."

"I hope not." Taylor's eyes widened. "I'm just starting to get my life how I like it."

Julie tried to hide her smile at that remark.

The doors opened, and though Julie was half-expecting a prison cell, they paced into a roomy suite tastefully decorated in shades of lavender and smoky blue.

"This is pretty nice," Julie admitted grudgingly, following Ilsa into a spacious living room. Couches, poufs, and armchairs were arranged around a coffee table, and a cabinet in the corner held a large TV. There was an open doorway to their right, and French doors on their left led onto a balcony.

"It'll do." Taylor shrugged. "I know you're used to more space, Ilsa."

"Oh, this is fine. It's only for a little while." Ilsa smiled, eyes crinkling, but Taylor didn't return her smile.

Julie wondered what Ilsa stood to lose if she failed the test. She felt a sudden swoop in the pit of her stomach.

Ilsa turned away. "At least there's a balcony."

"Is it safe, though?" Julie asked, following Ilsa through the French doors.

The scene below her didn't make sense, given that they were in the PMA building. The balcony looked out onto blue skies and green fields, leading to distant, misty mountainsides. A river wound through it all.

"None of it is real." Ilsa touched the air just above the balcony rail, but it wasn't air. It rippled like water. "It's magic. To make it feel a bit less claustrophobic in here, I guess."

Julie reached out, and her fingers met something springy and soft. "Feels claustrophobic to me."

Their eyes met, but Ilsa's smile didn't touch hers this time. "It's okay."

"Not really." Julie sighed. "I'm sorry for my outburst at the dinner party, but I still don't think it's right for you to be treated this way."

Ilsa shrugged. "This is how it's always been. Come on. I want to check out my new bedroom, and I'd love the company if you have the time."

Julie laughed. "We're about to get into trouble for being *too* productive, so I definitely have time. How did your stuff get here, anyway?"

"Magic." Ilsa waved a dismissive hand.

Malcolm and Taylor occupied themselves examining a panel in the wall that allowed Ilsa to order her food and drinks. "Want some food?" Ilsa offered. "It's almost dinnertime for you, but I'm guessing you didn't have time to eat in the yeti lands."

"How does it get here?" Julie examined the options. It looked like a touch screen.

"Household elves." Ilsa grinned. "They do more than repair shoes in the night, you know."

They ordered sandwiches and left Taylor and Malcolm in the living room as they headed into Ilsa's bedroom. As tasteful as the rest of the suite, it featured a queen-sized bed with lavender drapes forming a canopy. There was a window in one wall, as fake as the balcony's view. The breeze that blew into the room and stirred the drapes smelled like the sea.

"Smells like the beach," Julie commented.

Ilsa shrugged. She was sitting on the edge of the bed and gazing out the window. More sky, more mountains. "I wouldn't know. I've never been."

"Never been to the beach?" Julie poked her head through the door at the end of the room. It led to a walk-in closet bigger than her apartment. Whatever magic had brought Ilsa's clothes here had also hung them all neatly. She hurriedly withdrew.

Ilsa smiled. "My parents have always been pretty protective since I'm the heir."

"Seems like being the heir sucks." Julie took a seat on an ottoman by the window. "I'm sorry."

Ilsa raised her chin. "Caring for my people is both my birthright and my honor. It's got its downsides, sure, but I know who I am and what I was born to do. That's a privilege in my eyes, no matter what disadvantages it comes with."

I know who I am and what I was born to do. Julie tried not to let the words echo around her mind too loudly. *I don't even know what species I am.*

At least you're a species that can walk out of the building and do what you want with your life at the end of this day, Hat pointed out.

Julie's phone binged. She pulled it out and grimaced. "Sorry, Ilsa. I'll have to take a rain check on those sandwiches. Kaplan wants to see us in his office."

Taylor barged into the bedroom and spotted Julie with her phone in her hand. "Looks like we're going to be in trouble after all."

Behind him, Malcolm groaned.

Kaplan looked at the report in his hands, then at Julie and Taylor, down at the report, and up at them. The silence hung so heavily in the office that Julie was finding it hard to breathe. She tried not to openly bite her lip as the weretiger fixed them with a glowing amber glare.

"You've done it." Kaplan slammed the report on the desk with unexpected speed, making Julie jump. "You've finally done it."

"Recruited more people in a week than the rest of your department in a year, sir?" Julie offered.

Kaplan shot her a look, and Taylor cringed. The weretiger's eyes narrowed. "No, Meadows, what you've *done* is to make me speechless. I am not often speechless, but I am now at a total loss for words."

He fell silent. Taylor's eyes were popping out of his head, and Julie was beginning to wish the armchair would swallow her whole. *If I die, tell Mom and Lillie I love them,* she hissed in her mind.

Hat sighed. *I will. Any last words?*

"Don't piss off Captain Kaplan?" Julie suggested.

Hat snickered. *More like a pro tip than last words, but okay.*

Kaplan finally leaned forward and opened his mouth. "I won't complain about all the new recruits, but really? *Beltane?* You two went to Beltane in Fernwood Deep on the PMA's dime?" His shaggy brows drew together.

"We got most of our recruits there, sir," Julie piped up.

Kaplan snorted. "I'm not surprised. You can talk a drunken dryad into almost anything."

"They were all sober when they signed." Julie held his gaze. "Sir."

Kaplan huffed. "What am I supposed to do with all these signing bonuses? I assume you will demand a full bonus for every para you signed, Meadows?"

"For Taylor, too." Julie crossed her arms. "Or, you know, we could just give the Fernwood its recruits back, sir."

Kaplan scoffed. "You don't need to be sassy with me, Meadows. You two are both going to get exactly what you deserve for your behavior this week." His eyes narrowed.

Taylor sucked in a breath, and Julie felt a sudden pang of fear. If she got fired, would that be the end of her contact with the paranormal world?

Kaplan opened his desk drawer, pulled out two golden epaulets, and slid them across the desk toward them. "Congratulations. You're now Recruitment Officers of the OPMA."

Taylor's mouth fell open. Julie stared down at the epaulets, uncomprehending. "Uh, what?"

"That's 'Uh, what, *sir*?' to you, Meadows," Kaplan snapped. "Take those. Oh yes, and consider this the green light for all those PR ideas you had—the recruitment videos and such. You now rank directly below your commanding officer. You have six months to train the rest of your department on your recruiting methods."

Julie opened her mouth. Julie shut her mouth. Nothing seemed ready to come out. It took a few seconds before she could blurt, "Yes, sir. Do we get a raise?"

Kaplan raised both eyebrows. "Do you *think* you get a raise?"

Julie raised hers right back at him. "I should think so, sir, given that we won't be getting signing bonuses while we're not in the field."

Taylor gaped at her, still open-mouthed.

Kaplan sat back in his seat, folding his enormous arms. "Fine. Yes. You can have a ten percent raise. Happy?"

"Fifteen seems fair." Julie spread her hands. "I mean, considering how much our bonuses will be this month, it's difficult to justify accepting a new position for a worse salary."

Kaplan let out a snort. "Fine. Fifteen percent. Now, get out of my office and report to your CO immediately." He waved a hand. "Dismissed."

Julie took the golden epaulet and calmly placed it on her uniform, removing the silver one. "Thank you, sir." She got to her feet and strutted out of the office.

Taylor scurried after her, and Malcolm closed the door.

"So, where do we find this commanding officer?" Julie asked, striding across the communal office. "I didn't know we *had* a department head."

Taylor was still wide-eyed. "Did we just get promoted?"

"I think so." Julie grinned. "Where do we find our CO?"

Taylor shook himself. "Uh, this way. Two doors down from Kaplan." He grimaced. "I have to warn you. She's…intense."

Hat snickered.

"Intense?" Julie set off for the door Taylor indicated. "Compared to Kaplan?"

"Oh, yeah." Taylor groaned.

Julie laughed. "I didn't think that that was possible. What's she called?"

"Officer Hartshorn. Bianca Hartshorn." Taylor sucked in a breath as Julie grabbed the door handle and pushed it open.

The office was similar to theirs, except for having a single desk set across the front right corner of the office. There was a portrait on the wall here too, but it was a faun that looked uncannily similar to the one who had flirted with Julie, looking over his shoulder in a moonlit clearing with a leer of unmistakable intentions on his face. Thanks to the position of the desk, Julie had to walk into the office and turn to see Bianca Hartshorn for the first time.

Well, shit, she thought in shock. *Taylor was right.*

Bianca sat with her feet up on the desk, clad in knee-length leather boots with stiletto heels and laces. She reclined in her chair, sucking on a bright red lollipop while she scrolled rapidly on her computer screen, three-inch blood-red nails tapping her mouse. Her blonde hair tumbled over her shoulders in luscious curls. Curling horns like a gazelle's protruded from the top of her head, and her eyes were the brightest blue. She wore full leather leggings and a leather jacket with a white blouse daringly unbuttoned.

Taylor swallowed audibly.

"Uh, hi?" Julie tried.

Bianca sat bolt upright. Bat-like wings unfolded from her back, covered in fine dark fur, and she flung them wide with a devastating shriek that rattled the faun painting on the wall. Julie grabbed Hat to keep him from being blown off her head.

"Oh, sorry." Bianca sat back in her chair and folded her wings again. "I didn't see you there."

Succubus, Julie's orb training supplied belatedly. *A race of all-female paranormals. Long maligned as being demons and seeking to seduce men and kill them. Succubi are not spirits and are historically known for being fiercely devoted lovers, their fearsome reputation originating from their ferocious protectiveness for the people they love. They also have plenty of confidence and a killer dress sense.*

Bianca's glittering eyes locked on Julie. "You're Meadows, right? The number one person in my department I've been trying to avoid?"

"That's me." Julie put her hands on her hips, feeling scruffy despite her neat dress uniform. "Why are you avoiding me?"

"I do my best to avoid trouble." Bianca pointed her lollipop at the tottering stacks of files on her desk. "Does it look like I have time for trouble? Besides, Kaplan wanted to keep a personal eye on his human recruiter. So, what can I do for you?"

Taylor swallowed again. Julie resisted the urge to roll her eyes and elbowed him firmly in the ribs instead. "We've been promoted." She gestured at her epaulet. "We're directly under you now, and we've been given six months to train the rest of the department in our methods."

"Wow, really?" Bianca snorted. "Kaplan finally realized that one overworked CO can't be responsible for *everything* in this department?"

"Apparently?" Julie mumbled.

Bianca leaned forward and spoke in a husky purr. "I hope you'll have better luck with them than I did." She rummaged in the piles of files for a few moments before extracting three enormously thick ones and pushing them across to Julie. "Here's all the info you need."

Julie grabbed the files and opened her mouth to ask Bianca how much she wanted to be involved in the training, but the succubus was already turning back to her computer. "Good luck. Bye." She reinserted the lollipop.

Julie stared at her for a few seconds, but Bianca frowned at her screen and began to type furiously.

They left the room, and Taylor let out a breath. "Well, I guess we won't get a lot of help from her."

"Judging by your reaction to her, that's not a bad thing." Julie raised an eyebrow.

Taylor let out a sheepish laugh and rubbed the back of his neck.

"This has been one long-ass day. I can't believe I woke up in Fernwood Deep this morning." Julie glanced at her phone for the time. "I'd better get home to Mom and Lillie. We'll get back to it on Monday?"

"Monday," Taylor agreed. "See you."

Julie let out a long breath of relief as she pulled up Genevieve's parking brake and took the key out of the ignition, hearing the familiar rumble of the garage door closing behind her. *Home, sweet home.* She sighed and grabbed Hat from the passenger seat.

Ah, yes, Hat commented. *So much nicer here than in the gorgeous, luxurious tour bus you had for two nights in the middle of actual Fairyland.*

You know that saying "Fairyland" is politically incorrect, right? Julie slammed Genevieve's door and grabbed her inadequate overnight bag from the trunk. *Besides, I love this place.*

She tossed her bag on the bottom step and plodded to the back door. When she swung it open, the air was filled with the scent of something spicy and homemade and Mexican cooking. Julie's mouth watered.

"Oh, hello, dear." Lillie was on the couch, Pookie on one side and the cat on the other. She muted the TV and gave Julie a wide grin. "I'm so glad you're home."

"Come on in, Julia!" Rosa bustled into the living room, beaming from ear to ear. "I'm making tacos. I hope you're hungry!"

"Starving," Julie admitted, coming inside. She tolerated a huge hug from her mother and rumpled Pookie's ears as the little dog danced around her feet.

Rosa withdrew, studying Julie closely. "You look exhausted, honey. Do you know what you need?"

"No, but I'm sure it's something gross," Julie mumbled.

"Oh, honey, don't be like that." Rosa squeezed her arms. "Green tea will give you a wonderful boost! Sit down with Lillie. I'm almost done making dinner."

Julie shook her hands off gently. "I can help."

"Nonsense. You've had a very long few days, and you look exhausted. Sit!" her mother commanded, then hurried back to the kitchen.

Julie sagged onto the couch beside Lillie. Pookie jumped onto her lap, stretched luxuriously, and curled up. "How are you feeling, Lillie? How's the chest?"

"Fine, dear. Just fine." Lillie patted Julie's knee. "Tell me, how was your 'work trip?'"

Julie narrowed her eyes. "It *was* a work trip."

"Oh, I have no doubt about that, dear." Lillie leered. "But I'm sure you and that very handsome young man had time to fit in some extracurricular activities."

"Lillie!" Julie's blush felt like someone had set her face on fire.

"I'm teasing you, dear." Lillie cackled, squeezing her knee. "Although it was worth it to see the look on your face."

Julie shook her head, groaning.

Lillie smiled. "Teasing aside, tell me about your trip. I hope you were able to have *some* fun, dear."

"Oh, trust me, I did." Julie grinned, wishing she could have taken Lillie to Beltane. The old lady would have loved it. She lowered her voice. "Don't tell Mom, but I sampled a little wine."

"Look at you!" Lillie gave her a playful swat on the back of her head. "Seems like you're finding your inner hellion after all."

"Aren't you going to lecture me about breaking the rules?" Julie raised an eyebrow.

Lillie sat back, her hands resting on her lap. Her lips pursed. "There are some moral rules in life that you should never break, dear. Rules that are irrefutable and cast in stone. Rules like not murdering people."

She smiled. "But other rules are a little fluid, a little bendy. You've gotta take the spirit of them and understand what that means for your conscience and your morality. Then you gotta live your life with the volume turned all the way up, true to what you believe and fearless of what anybody else thinks of you." Lillie's grin widened. "We always did, and what a life it was!"

Her eyes wandered to the picture on the mantelpiece, the one with her late twin, and Julie's heart twisted. *What a life it was!*

I hope I can say that too someday, she murmured.

Hat chuckled. *I think you're on track.*

CHAPTER TEN

Taylor's fist came so fast that Julie almost didn't see it. She ducked under his arm and landed a pair of brisk punches in his ribs, one-two.

"Oof!" Taylor stumbled back, wheezing and clutching his ribs. "I didn't think you'd see that one coming."

Julie laughed breathlessly, bouncing on the balls of her bare feet, hands still held up. "I learned a thing or two."

"Yeah, I see that," Taylor grumbled. He held up his fists again, grinning. "But you're still no Aether prince."

Julie rushed him, her attack quick and high. Taylor fell for it, dodging and aiming his blow for her midriff, but she had slipped aside. Taylor's leg flashed out far too quickly for her to see, and Julie stumbled. He followed it up with his knee to her ribs, sending her rolling over the floor.

Before she could recover her balance, Taylor was behind her. He threw his arms around her neck and put her in a chokehold. Stars swarmed in front of her eyes. Julie grabbed his forearm, fighting to break his grip, but it was like trying to move an iron bar.

Except iron bars didn't have nerve endings. She felt his skin brush her lips and sank her teeth into it.

"*OW!*" Taylor squealed, letting her go and scrambling away from her. "Did you just *bite* me?"

"Not hard." Julie grinned at him. "Just enough for you to feel it."

Taylor rubbed his forearm, glaring even though there were no marks on his skin. "You *bit* me!"

"Hey, you said anything goes when you need to get out of a rear naked choke." Julie held up her hands. "And like you said, I'm no Aether Elf prince."

Taylor scoffed, but before he could come up with a good retort, an elegant figure strode onto their mat. "Getting your ass kicked by an uneducated human, are you, little brother?"

Ilsa's eyes sparkled at Julie as she said the words, and Julie returned her grin. Taylor whipped around, eyes wide. "Where are your guards?"

"All over the gym." Ilsa waved a hand. "Relax, Tay. I have permission from Captain Kaplan to come and spar with you."

Julie spotted several paranormals in blue uniforms lurking in the corners of the gym.

Taylor relaxed. "Okay." He raised an eyebrow. "Tired of your private trainers?"

"Tired of my suite, more like." Ilsa laughed. "Mind if I cut in?" She looked at Julie.

"He's mad at me anyway." Julie sniffed. "I think I hurt his feelings."

Taylor scoffed.

"I'll take a water break." Julie waved a hand. "You two do your thing. I need to watch and learn anyway."

"That's a good idea." Taylor went over to the edge of the mat and retrieved a fistful of training daggers. They were carved wood wrapped in padding but still packed a punch, as the fresh new bruise on the inside of Julie's thigh could attest. "I think Julie could do with a lesson from a master swordswoman."

He tossed one of the daggers at Ilsa, who snatched it out of the air with easy grace and whipped it to and fro, her wrist almost fluid. Taylor threw her another, keeping two for himself.

"Oh, this is gonna be *good*." Julie sat down beside her backpack at the edge of the mat, fishing out her water bottle.

Hat chuckled. "Who are you betting on? The heir?"

Julie watched as Ilsa and Taylor circled one another. Ilsa was low to the ground, her feet catlike in speed across the mat. Taylor held his daggers close to his body, eyes trained on his sister. He had four inches and fifty pounds on her, but Ilsa moved like a shadow.

"Yeah." Julie crinkled her nose. "Sorry, but I think he's about to get his ass handed to him."

Ilsa rushed forward with such speed and silence that Julie almost missed it. The princess' steps were quick, almost skipping, and she slashed at Taylor's chest with one dagger. When he responded with a blow of his own, she spun, blocking both his daggers with one of hers and swiping the tip of the other neatly across his abdomen.

"A bit slow, little brother," Ilsa teased, facing him again.

Taylor's cheeks were flushed, but he grinned. "You barely touched me. I'm still fighting."

Ilsa's grin widened. "We'll see how long that lasts, little—"

Taylor charged. Ilsa slipped aside like water as he struck at her shoulder, but she didn't dodge his second dagger, and it hit her hip.

"That would have hurt if this was an Aether blade." Taylor chuckled.

"Yes, but not enough to stop me." Ilsa charged at Taylor with a series of slashes and thrusts that never seemed to end. Each strike fluidly followed the one before, no energy wasted, no moment unguarded.

Taylor danced back, looking for a gap and finding none. He held his crossed daggers up to protect his face as Ilsa landed blow after blow on his daggers and forearms. She didn't back down, and neither did he, skittering this way and that, looking for an opening.

At last, he spotted one. Ducking to the left, he struck at her legs. Ilsa skipped aside, jumped over his twin daggers, and leaped onto his back. Locking her legs around his hips, she threw an arm around his neck and flung herself backward. With a yelp of shock, Taylor fell. There was a sickening thump when they both hit the mat. Taylor's daggers slid out of his hands. Ilsa had both her wooden blades pressed against his throat.

"Uh, I yield," Taylor squeaked.

Ilsa chuckled and bent forward to give her brother a kiss on the forehead before she released him. "You did well, Tay. I haven't seen you spar this well in a long time."

Taylor got up, rubbing his throat with one hand as Ilsa retrieved his daggers. "I haven't sparred this often in a long time." He glanced at Julie.

"You must be pretty good if you've gotten my brother on his toes." Ilsa flashed her a smile and handed Taylor's daggers back to him. "Another round?"

"Not right now." Julie stood up. "It's ten to nine, Taylor. We'd better get started with those PR and training ideas we want to flesh out today." She met Ilsa's eyes. "Tomorrow?"

Ilsa grinned, nodding. "Tomorrow sounds good. I'll teach you a few tricks with the daggers."

Julie laughed. "I've already learned a few new ones."

Taylor groaned as he stashed the daggers in his duffel bag. "Oh, great. Now I'll get my ass kicked by you, too."

Ilsa stuck out her tongue at him. "See you tonight, Tay?"

"See you," Taylor returned.

Ilsa waved goodbye and headed back to her suite. Two of the

guards slipped out of the door in front of her. The others bunched tightly around her as they left the gym.

"What's happening tonight?" Julie hooked her backpack over her shoulder.

Taylor zipped up his duffel bag. "I'm staying with Ilsa to keep her company. I got the feeling she was really lonely over the weekend, and it's not like there's much waiting for me at home."

"Except for your luxurious royal suite," Julie quipped.

Taylor shook his head.

Julie chewed the end of her pen, studying the scrawled list in front of her. She jotted another line. "So, we'll put ads in the *Avalon Chronicle*. When do you want to do that?"

Taylor glanced up from his computer screen. "How about Wednesday? We wanted to do that presentation tomorrow."

"Okay." Julie scribbled on her notepad. "We can go visit the billboard agency about putting up signage in Avalon then, too."

"Good thinking." Taylor typed on his keyboard for a few seconds. "Next, we need to talk to some of the recruits about making that video."

Julie grinned. "You know who'd be perfect? Those Montana Weres. They'd be adorable on a video."

Taylor laughed. "Are we going for adorable? I think we should just interview Blake. He's got that whole strong-and-silent thing going on."

"Mmm, yeah." Julie sighed. "And he's sexy to boot. That helps."

"You think strong and silent is sexy?" Taylor raised his eyebrows.

Julie shrugged. "Maybe."

Taylor glanced at his reflection in the glass at the front of the painting that hung over their desks, an ugly Renaissance-era representation of a mermaid with strategically arranged curls. "What about Ellie? Didn't you want to talk to her?"

"Oh, yes. I was thinking we could do multiple videos. One from each of the PMA branches. You know, military, agents. Even someone from logistics. I was thinking about how Pereletok said her yetis weren't suited to work in the PMA. We need to showcase our diverse need for all the types of paras."

"Good thinking," Taylor agreed. "Okay, I'll talk to the Weres this afternoon, and you'll talk to Ellie? Maybe over lunch?"

Julie ran a hand over her hair, thinking, *I don't want to miss lunch with you.* That sounded crazy, so she pushed the thought aside. "Perfect."

"Cool." Taylor typed some more. "Hey, do you think we should check in with Bianca?"

Julie snorted. "She didn't seem all that interested. I did send her an email saying we'd be brainstorming this morning. She could have come if she wanted to, but she just sent me a bunch of red rose and kissy lips emojis in response."

Taylor pulled a face. "Okay." He checked the time. "We'd better get down to the conference room for that meeting with the other recruiters." He paused. "Are you sure this is a good idea? I mean, we've barely met any of them. I'm not sure they're going to be happy about our promotion, considering we haven't been here as long as some of them."

Julie pushed back her chair. "If they wanted to be promoted, they should have tried to recruit more paras, hmm?"

Taylor shrugged. "True." He unplugged a flash drive from his computer.

"What's on there?" Julie asked, popping Hat onto her head. She was wearing her uniform, and Hat obligingly turned into a smart peaked cap in matching emerald green.

Taylor tucked the drive into his pocket. "Evidence."

"Be cryptic, then." Julie snorted.

They headed to the ground floor conference room in which

Kaplan had told them about the urgent need for more recruits. Julie fussed around the room, setting out bottled water and straightening the chairs while Taylor plugged his flash drive into an odd machine that whirred like a projector but glowed with yellow runes.

"It's fine, Julie. Don't worry. The place looks great," he told her.

"I've never been the chairperson of a meeting before, okay?" Julie nibbled on her pinky fingernail.

Taylor shrugged. "Neither have I, but I suppose we'll get used to it now that we're officers."

Julie touched the golden epaulet and felt marginally better.

You fought an army of angry yetis with less worry than this, Hat remarked.

Julie ran a hand over his brim. *Yeah, well, that was different. More straightforward.*

The first recruiter to step in was a vaguely familiar orc wearing a bright red curly wig. She nodded at Julie but said nothing as she took her place. Julie was almost surprised when more paranormals flooded into the room. Not everyone she'd emailed came, but most of the one hundred fifty that were supposed to be there had come. She'd half-expected no one would show up.

Taylor closed the doors with a flick of his wrist from where he stood beside Julie. They slammed shut, and the group of paras didn't react. They were whispering among themselves. A few shot glances at Julie, and the orc frowned under her red curls.

"Hey, everyone." Julie stepped forward.

The room fell silent. All eyes were on her, except for a bored male Were leaning back in his chair two seats down from where Julie stood. He was gazing at his phone, probably less surreptitiously than he thought.

Julie cleared her throat sharply. The Were looked up but didn't put his phone away. His eyes had slit pupils like a cat's.

"Thank you all for coming." Julie swallowed. "As you know from the email Captain Kaplan sent last night, we've been asked to provide six months of training for all of you, starting now. Before we—"

"You?" The snort came from a graying dwarf sitting at the top of the table. "Training *us*?" Her eyes narrowed. Julie noticed a few wispy strands of gray beard clinging to the center of her chin.

Taylor raised his chin. "Did you not receive the email, Gruda?"

Gruda blinked. "Of course I did."

"Good. Then you know that this is what Captain Kaplan ordered." Taylor smiled smoothly, but his eyes didn't crinkle the way they usually did.

Gruda shut her mouth.

Julie cleared her throat again. "As I was saying, before we get started with training, I want to hear from the rest of you. I'm sure you all have ideas about how we can boost department productivity, and I'd like to hear them."

There was silence around the table. The Were went back to his phone. Gruda glared moodily at the bottle of water in front of her.

Tough crowd, Hat commented.

Taylor glanced at Julie, who took a deep breath. "How about you?" She pointed at a Woodland Fae near the front of the group, a young male with a smattering of freckles on his nose and enormous dark eyes. Two tiny antlers protruded from his curly blond hair.

"Uh, well, we could, um...we could…" He froze.

Deer in the headlights. Hat snickered.

The Were piped up, eyes still on his phone, "We could just keep doing our own thing the way we have for our entire careers instead of attending a hundred pointless meetings like this one."

There was a mutter of agreement from the rest of the group.

Julie felt a flush creeping up her neck. "Okay, sure. So none of you wants to earn thirty thousand dollars in recruitment bonuses in a single day?" she shot back.

The Were looked up. Gruda's frown disappeared.

"Thirty thousand dollars?" The Woodland Fae gasped. "That's six recruits in one day. It's impossible."

"Oh, it's more than possible. It's probable, using the right strategy." Taylor stepped in and flicked a switch on the projector-thingy. "This is a timeline of our recruitment efforts over the past month."

Julie smothered the self-satisfied smile that threatened to rise to her face as Taylor gestured at a bar graph on the projection. He pointed first at the bar, which was at the number six. "These were werewolves who used to be juvenile delinquents. They were harassing a centaur's horses in Montana," he explained. "We gave them another option. They all joined in a single day."

"This dry spell here occurred when we were helping rescue Malcolm Nox." Julie pointed at an empty spot on the graph. "Those same Weres helped us free him, even though they were only a few days into training."

"This is the recruits we got in the past week." Taylor pointed at the high numbers at the end of the graph.

"Six griffins on Wednesday, and on Thursday, eleven various woodland paras." Julie grinned. "We get a five-thousand-dollar bonus per recruit. You do the math."

The Were put his phone down and leaned forward. "Okay. I think we might be ready to do some listening now."

Julie grinned. "I thought you might."

Obnoxious though Sam, the Were who was addicted to his phone, had been at the beginning of the meeting, he'd had some good ideas. Julie turned them over in her mind as she followed Taylor to the buffet line in the cafeteria. Sushi today, it seemed.

She piled her plate with maki rolls, fashion sandwiches, and salmon, grabbed soy sauce and chopsticks, and was on her way to their usual spot at the end of the middle table in the large room when Taylor touched her arm.

"Okay, see you after lunch." He grinned. "I hear the Weres have arrived."

It was difficult not to hear them. They piled into the room, all six of them in wolf form, yipping and snapping at each other's ears. Only Isaiah was calm, pacing quietly ahead of them.

"See you." Julie watched him go, wondering why it felt weird, and shook herself. She scanned the room for Elspeth Feathertouch, her first recruit, and spotted the elegant dark-haired young para sitting at the back of the room, hunched over a file.

Julie headed over to her. "Hey, Ellie."

Ellie looked up, and her massive amber eyes widened. "Julie! It's nice to see you."

"I see you're busy." Julie nodded at the file. "Is this a bad time?"

"For the girl who changed my life forever?" Ellie grinned. "Never. Have a seat." She closed the file and pushed it aside, but not before Julie noticed the picture clipped to the front page: a handsome Aether Elf who looked like Benedict Woodskin would if he put on fifty pounds.

"How's the agent life treating you?" Julie dipped a maki roll into the soy sauce.

The half-human, half-Woodland Fae beamed. "It's got its dangers, but I love it. I can't believe I thought I wanted to be a *model* a few short months ago." She shook her head.

"I'm glad you've found your niche." Julie gestured with her chopsticks. "And that the paranormal world seems to be treating you well."

"Oh, yes. You know, there was a time, even after I was sure I wasn't fully human, that I wanted nothing more than to be a normal person. I tried to wish away my paranormal side. Ignore it. It was *awful*. I could never fit in. It was like the human world just didn't work for me."

Julie thought about her life before she joined the PMA. Before she even knew paranormals existed. Lonely, unemployed, and looking for love online... Her stomach twisted.

The human world just didn't work for me. Julie swallowed hard.

"Embracing who I really am was life-changing." Ellie hesitated. "You okay? You look a bit pale."

"I'm fine." Julie forced a smile and took a bite of sushi. "So, I have an ulterior motive for lunching with you today."

Ellie raised an eyebrow, and the corner of her mouth quirked up. "I can't blame you. I'd need to have a good reason to skip lunch with Taylor Woodskin, too."

Julie ignored the heat that crept into her cheeks. "I have a favor to ask."

"Sure." Ellie dipped a fashion sandwich in soy sauce. "Anything for you."

Julie laughed. "We want to make recruitment videos. You know, to get people's attention and hopefully get more recruits. I was wondering if you'd be okay with being interviewed for a video. Just to show how lives can change by joining the PMA and finding a purpose."

Ellie was nodding vigorously before Julie finished talking. "Yes. Yes! Absolutely. I would love to."

Julie smiled. "That's great news. I'll send you an email with the details?"

"Sure. I'll clear it with my bosses, but I'm not slated for undercover work, so I'm sure it'll be fine." Ellie smiled.

"If you're not going undercover, what are you working on?" Julie asked.

Ellie waggled her eyebrows. "Oh, it's top secret." Her words were playful, but she put one hand firmly on the closed file, and she didn't show Julie what was inside.

Julie yawned widely, then clicked on the next field in the recruitment report she was busy with.

"I wish we'd filled these out in the minivan on the way home like Hat suggested," Taylor grumbled, typing at his desk across from her.

"I know, right? For once, Hat was right about something." Julie typed in a date.

Hat snorted from his hook by the door. "Wow, a priceless magical artifact thousands of years old had good, wise ideas! Who knew, right?"

Julie snorted and printed her report. She fished it out of the printer and scribbled a signature. "Autograph, please, Prince Taylor?" She waved the paper in his direction.

"Only if I can have yours." Taylor nodded at the printer as it spat out another report.

"Done." Julie signed the report and handed it to him. "Was that the last one?"

"Yeah, I think so." Taylor punched both reports and tucked them into a file. "Finally. What time is it, anyway?"

Julie glanced at her phone. "Shit. Half past five." She groaned. "I promised Qtana I'd visit her in the hospital today, and as it is, I'll only get home around eight in the traffic."

"Not if you leave a little later. You'll miss rush hour." Taylor shut off his computer and got to his feet. "Why don't you come and have dinner with Ilsa and me in the cafeteria? Then we can both visit Qtana. I haven't seen her in a while, and I feel bad about it."

"As you should, you horrible human being." Julie picked up her backpack.

Taylor raised his eyebrows. "I'd take offense if I *was* a human being. Now, are you coming to dinner, or are you going to keep insulting me?"

"I'd love to come. Thanks." Julie grabbed Hat. "Let me call Mom and let her know."

"Good luck." Taylor grimaced.

Julie had told him her mother constantly worried that she was working too hard. "Oh, don't worry. I'll tell her that I'm going to dinner with friends. She's always telling me I need more friends."

Taylor laughed. "Tell her you're going to dinner with *me*. That'll make her happy."

Julie moaned. "Don't remind me."

As predicted, her mother was overjoyed that Julie had friends to go to dinner with. She ended the call and tucked her phone into her pocket as they stepped onto the elevator. She yawned again while it clanked downward.

"Tired?" Taylor's voice was swallowed by a yawn of his own.

"It's late. What a day." Julie rubbed her face. "I think I'm going to need caffeine."

"Coffee at six in the evening?" Taylor raised his eyebrows.

"Don't judge me, dude. I don't have elven superpowers," Julie snorted. *Or do I? How would I know? What am I?*

"Julie?" Taylor prompted.

She realized the doors had opened and shuffled through them.

"Are you okay?" Taylor asked.

She forced her best smile. "Oh, yeah. I'm fine."

CHAPTER ELEVEN

Ilsa watched in fascination as Julie sipped from a huge steaming coffee mug. "Coffee *and* chocolate brownies for dessert? Are you ever going to sleep again, Julie?" The elf princess laughed.

Julie laughed. "At least I'll stay awake on the drive home."

Ilsa took a bite of her brownie. The cafeteria was packed with people at this time of the evening, mostly recruits or soldiers or agents in blue uniforms. Julie noticed Kaplan sitting at the far end of the room, plowing through steak and potatoes, and wondered if he ever went home.

"Where do you live?" Ilsa asked.

Julie sipped again. "Bay Ridge, Brooklyn, in a cool little apartment."

"Brooklyn!" Ilsa frowned. "Is that a rough neighborhood?"

"Some of it, I guess." Julie grinned.

"Sorry." Ilsa shook her head. "I think my royalty is showing. I've seen more of Avalon than Staten Island, and I live here."

Yeah, under lock and key. Julie didn't say it. "I'll have to show you around sometime."

Ilsa's smile crinkled her brown eyes. "I'd like that." She

stretched. "By the way, Tay, my ribs really sting where you got them this morning."

"Sorry, sorry." Taylor laughed. "We won't talk about my lower back. I think you threw it out."

"Don't be a wimp, bro." Ilsa patted his hand. "Hey, Julie, want to spar with me tomorrow morning? I could show you those moves with the daggers."

Julie smiled. "I'd love that."

They finished their dessert, Julie drained the last of her coffee, and Ilsa headed to her suite with her guards. With caffeine crackling through her veins, Julie had just about enough energy to shuffle back to the elevator and hit the button for the medical unit.

Qtana sat up in bed, a laptop propped on her legs. Its screen's blue light reflected in her thick glasses. She looked up as Julie and Taylor came in, and her green-skinned face creased in a smile.

"Visitors!" The troll closed the laptop. "It's nice to see you both. I hear you've been making waves in the recruitment department."

"Making waves or causing shit?" Julie grinned and leaned over the bed to give Qtana a gentle hug. Even though the troll no longer wore bandages around her head, there was still an ugly scar and a purplish bruise across one temple.

Qtana grinned and swept a wing of blonde hair out of her face. "Both, knowing you two."

Taylor chuckled and patted Qtana's shoulder before they took seats. Qtana set her laptop on the table by the bed.

"I hope you're not working." Julie folded her arms as she sat. "You're still on medical leave, aren't you?"

"Oh, yes. And being compensated for all the medical bills, so I don't have to worry about that since it was technically an injury on duty." Qtana spread her arms, indicating the comfortable room.

Taylor snorted. "Technically? It *was* an injury on duty. You were trying to do the right thing when Qbiit attacked you."

"Poor Qbiit." Qtana's face fell. "I know he did bad things, but I'm still sad that it ended with his death at the courthouse."

"'Bad things?'" Julie raised an eyebrow. "He nearly killed you."

"Yes, but he didn't deserve for his head to explode in court from whatever geas was placed on him." Qtana shook her head. "Any news on finding who he was working for?"

Julie sighed. "Nothing yet, but don't worry about that now. Do you still have enough books?"

Qtana smiled at the pile of books on her nightstand, many of them from Julie's ever-growing library at home. "Oh, yes, although I have to be honest. Now that my head is a bit better, I'm fitting in my screen time. Hopefully, I'll be back at it soon. Maybe I can help find whoever was behind all this. The person Qbiit was working for."

Taylor nodded. "Let's hope."

They stayed for a few more minutes, chatting, until Julie spotted the time on the digital clock on Qtana's nightstand and got to her feet. "I'd better get going, or I'll get home really late."

Qtana smiled. "Thank you both for coming. Dr. Olena says I might be out of here soon, and I hope she's right."

"Me too." Julie patted her hand. "Text me sometime."

The troll agreed, and Julie and Taylor left the room and headed down the hall and across the main space of the Para-ER on their way to the parking garage. It was very quiet. Julie could only hear the occasional click of a ventilator or the beep of a monitor.

"I'll walk you to Genevieve," Taylor told her. "I need some fresh air before heading up to Ilsa's suite."

"Uh-huh. Sure you do," Julie sassed.

Taylor scoffed. "Okay, maybe I want to make sure you get there safely. Bite me."

The ER was empty except for the charge nurse at the reception desk, a fae whose rainbow-colored hair shimmered in a ponytail down her back as she scrolled through Facebook on the hospital computer. Dr. Olena was also present. The ethereally pretty Sylthana Elf leaned against the desk, writing on a chart, her lab coat looking rumpled.

Julie glanced longingly at the elevator. She could dart through the doors without saying a word to Dr. Olena, but the elf's shoulders were sagging, and she had dark circles under her eyes. Without wanting to, Julie stopped near her. "Rough day, Doc?"

Dr. Olena's tired eyes brushed over her. "Oh, hey, Julie." She stifled a yawn. "I don't have your results yet."

"That's okay." Julie's toes curled. She could feel the pressure of Taylor's stare in the small of her back. "You look tired."

"I *am* tired. I worked a shift at Avalon General yesterday, and there was another protest. Paras throwing rocks, breaking windows..." She pinched the bridge of her nose. "I put in a lot of stitches. Nothing serious, though. It's just the thought of how much more serious this could become."

Julie cocked her head to one side. "And maybe some of your patients on the Eternity Throne side of things weren't appreciative of being helped by a Sylthana Elf?"

Dr. Olena grimaced. "You could say that."

"I'm sorry." Julie touched her shoulder. "We've still got to get to that lunch date sometime."

Dr. Olena's smile returned. "I'd like that."

When they stepped through the exit, the sky was dark, and the night air was cool.

"It's messed up that people are mistreating Dr. Olena just because she's a Sylthana Elf," Julie grumbled.

"I don't disagree." Taylor hesitated. "Hey, she mentioned results back there, but your medical was ages ago. Are you okay?"

"I'm fine." Julie smiled quickly. "I think we should sit with Dr. Olena every lunchtime if we can. I get the feeling her life has gotten really lonely."

Taylor studied her, and her stomach clenched. She hadn't lied to him. She *was* fine.

She just wasn't human.

He finally looked away, letting it go. "Yeah, good idea."

They walked the rest of the way to the parking area in silence.

It wasn't that the mattress in the small guest room off Ilsa's bedroom was uncomfortable. It was just different. Taylor squirmed, tugging at his sheets. Even though the temperature in the room was perfect, he couldn't decide if he wanted the covers over his feet.

Tomorrow night, I'm sleeping in my own bed, he grumbled, rolling over and stuffing his pillow into the crook between his neck and shoulder. He closed his eyes, feeling his body growing heavier. Slowly, he began to drift away...and Victor Barkhands let out a deafening snore.

Taylor's eyes snapped open. Across the room from him, the burly elf was stretched out on the bed pushed against the opposite wall.

Victor snored again.

"Victor," Taylor hissed.

He snored like a chainsaw cutting a banshee in half. Taylor groaned and pulled his pillow over his head. *Ilsa better appreciate this.* Victor might be one of the most trusted guards among the Aether Elves, but Taylor was beginning to think he'd be better off guarding the gate again, not babysitting Ilsa. He wondered if she'd slept since coming to stay here.

Another snore. Taylor's toes curled. He sat up. "Victor!"

Victor rolled over, muttering in his sleep, and lay on his side. Taylor waited a few seconds. Heavy breathing, but no snoring.

"Success," he muttered, then flopped down and punched his pillow into submission. What time was it? Three in the morning? He groaned, despairing of getting any sleep. And they had so much to do. His heavy eyelids dragged him into a doze.

Another low, rasping sound. Taylor sat upright, furious. *"Victor!"*

The guard snorted and opened his eyes, and his hand went to the twin daggers under his pillow.

"Can you stop snoring, please?" Taylor hissed. "I think you have sleep apnea."

Victor glared at him. "Go to sleep, Your Highness."

"I'm trying, but I can't—" Taylor stopped as Victor held up a hand, eyes wide, and sat up straight.

They were silent for a few tense minutes. Taylor glanced at the door to Ilsa's room; it was still closed. He strained his senses, hoping they would heighten in this quiet room the way they'd done in the peace and openness of Montana, Fernwood Deep, and the yeti lands.

But he didn't need super-senses to hear it. Something low and hissing like furniture scraping on a hardwood floor, and it wasn't Victor who'd made the sound.

Victor was out of bed, gripping both daggers. He gave Taylor a pointed look, then jerked his chin to Ilsa's bedroom door. Taylor nodded. He picked up his own daggers from his nightstand and crossed the floor on silent feet as Victor headed through the other door into the main suite.

Opening the door silently, Taylor let out a soft breath of relief. The room was empty except for Ilsa, lying on her back, head pillowed on one arm as she slept. He picked up her daggers from where they hung on the wall and crouched beside the bed. "Ilsa," he murmured. "Wake up."

Her eyes snapped open. Seeing his face, she sat up immediately and took the daggers from his hands. "What?" she mouthed.

"I don't know. Sounds like someone's in the suite," Taylor muttered. "I think we should—"

The night erupted in light and sound. The bedroom door exploded, bursting into the room in a shower of splinters. Victor's heavy body landed on the floor among the wreckage of the door with a terrible thud. As soon as he'd fallen, the elf was back on his feet, muscles rippling in his bare torso, metal flashing in both hands.

"Wraith!" he thundered.

Ilsa drew her daggers. The wraith soared into the room with a shriek that rattled Taylor's bones. It floated near the ceiling, looking like a humanoid wearing a transparent gray cloak a few inches too long for them, except that when the wraith turned toward Ilsa, there was no face under the hood. Only blackness and a glowing white slash where its mouth should be. The slash opened, and another shriek rushed through the room.

Victor stepped between Ilsa and the wraith. "Protect the crown princess!" he barked.

Taylor rushed forward, daggers held out, as the wraith swooped toward his sister. He slashed at the creature, feeling a faint tug as the tip of one dagger blade found its solid body. Screaming, the wraith twisted to face him, growing less transparent. Already, the slash he'd cut in its side was closing and disappearing.

It screamed and dove toward him. Taylor spun and danced, striking hard with two blades. At the last instant, the wraith almost disappeared, turning so transparent that only its outline remained. Taylor's blades slashed through empty air, and the wraith passed through him. He felt no impact, only an icy chill between his cells.

"Call for reinforcements!" Victor yelled as he threw himself at the wraith with both daggers. The creature slipped through him and charged at Ilsa, growing more solid as it approached. She dodged masterfully, rolling under it and striking upward with both blades and opening two black slashes on its belly. It shrieked and slowed down, writhing in the air, but the slashes were closing. Even Aether steel couldn't really hurt it.

"Taylor, call them!" Ilsa shouted breathlessly. Her knuckles were white as she clutched her daggers.

"Right. *Right.*" Taylor scrambled across the room as Victor faced off with the wraith, slapping the red panic button by the door with the hilt of one of his daggers. He spun back into the fight as the wraith turned solid and flung itself at Victor with supernatural speed. Victor slipped aside and dealt it two brisk stabs with the daggers, opening two holes in its flanks.

Screaming, the wraith rose. Its cuts were closing, but it was slower now. Taylor saw transparency shimmer around its edges and saw his chance. He rushed at it, daggers outstretched, yelling in anger.

The yell was a mistake. The wraith whipped around, that empty face trained on him, and swooped.

Its shoulder slammed into his ribs, flinging him backward and knocking the breath from his lungs. However, he still had his daggers, and he plunged them both into the wraith's back with all his strength. Its cry reached a new pitch that tore at his ears as it reared. Taylor gripped the daggers hard, but his back slammed into something solid—the wall—and darkness clouded his vision. His limbs felt heavy and disconnected, like they belonged to someone else.

Ilsa's shriek cut through his spinning head. *Ilsa!* He scrambled to his feet, shaking away the last of his dizziness. Victor stood in front of his sister, blood streaming from a cut on his face. The shattered remains of the lamp from Ilsa's nightstand lay on the floor around their feet. Ilsa had lost one dagger, and she clutched the other, eyes glittering with rage as she watched the wraith swoop across the room.

It reached a framed painting on the opposite wall. Tendrils rose from its front, and it seized the painting and flung it at Ilsa in a whip-quick movement. She rolled aside, and the frame slammed into one of the bedposts so hard that shattered glass hissed out of it and the shards buried themselves in the wood of the closet door.

Taylor's daggers lay on the floor near where the wraith now hovered, its body fully solid and the color of stone. He rushed toward them, and at the same instant, the wraith dove and grabbed the daggers with its tendrils. It could throw them with deadly speed. Victor stepped in front of Ilsa, shielding her with his body, his eyes ablaze, and Taylor skidded to a halt. Could he wrest them away?

He felt a tickle behind his ear. *Blood? No!* Taylor's heart lifted. He reached behind his ear and pulled out something the size of a toothpick.

"Hey, asshole!" he yelled.

The wraith whipped around to look at him as he raised the toothpick, which instantly transformed into a six-foot staff with a huge blue gem glowing at the tip. Taylor spun it, concentrating his power, and a burst of blue fire leaped from the gem. The wraith shrieked, and the daggers clattered out of its grip as blue flames wrapped around its body. Even as chunks of it broke off and melted, it turned toward Ilsa, its movements sluggish, and lunged for her. The blue flame intensified, and the wraith melted into a heap of ash that drifted to the floor at Ilsa's feet.

Ilsa looked down at the ash, then prodded it with one toe and let out a breath. A grin spread over her features.

"Well, look at you, little bro!" she exclaimed.

Julie's mouth was dry as she threw Genevieve around another

corner. The Mustang's 429 V8 Cobrajet engine roared with fury, tires squealing as they skidded across the asphalt.

Angry honking filled the air. She didn't care. Changing gears, Julie jammed her foot down. Genevieve responded with a rising roar and flew down the street, eating up a block in seconds. The streetlights made faint hissing sounds as they whipped past them.

"Easy. Slow down!" Hat yelped, his brim flexing as he struggled to stay on the passenger seat.

Julie ignored him. The light in front of her turned yellow. She stomped harder and Genevieve surged forward, pinning her back in the leather bucket seat as the car swished across the light.

"I guess the word's gotten out that you have an FBI badge," Hat grumbled. "Not even the cops are going to help me now."

Taylor's text throbbed in Julie's mind. Her phone's buzz had woken her half an hour ago, but she'd missed his call. When she'd picked up her phone, his message had seared itself into her mind.

Wraith attack on Ilsa. It's dead now, but there's trouble.

Julie hadn't bothered to answer. She'd just thrown on jeans and a sweater, grabbed Hat, and scrambled into Genevieve.

The familiar street leading to HQ was in front of them, open and empty. Julie's fingers flexed on the wheel as she sped the last few yards and stomped on the brake. Genevieve screeched to a halt in a cloud of smoke at the gatehouse.

"Let me in, Fred!" Julie yelled, flashing her ID badge.

The listless dwarf at the gate blinked at her once, then hit the button. The gate slid open, and Julie drove up to the front doors. Lights glowed in the third-floor windows, but the rest of the building was dark, except for the brightly lit medical unit.

Medical unit. Julie's stomach twisted.

She retrieved Hat from the seat, threw him onto her head, and left Genevieve at a run. She dashed across the lobby.

"Wait. Wait! Genevieve!" Hat yelled.

Julie snorted. "If she gets stolen, I'll personally have Fred's hide." She reached the elevator and scrambled inside, pressing the button for the third floor as a best guess.

Stepping into the office in the dark was weird. The only light came through Kaplan's office door, standing open on the other side of the floor. Panting, Julie jogged to the doorway and stumbled into the office.

Relief washed through her. Taylor and Ilsa stood side by side in front of Kaplan's desk. Taylor had a reddening bruise over one eye, but his arm was around Ilsa, a muscle standing out in his cheek as he clenched his jaw. Ilsa's arms were folded. Julie noticed two slim daggers sheathed on the belt at her waist.

Kaplan looked up from behind the desk. "What are *you* doing here?"

Taylor turned. The muscle in his jaw unclenched. "Oh, hey, Julie. I texted her."

"Because you thought she'd be useful?" Kaplan snapped. His eyebrows stood out in all directions, and Julie noticed that he was wearing a red PMA t-shirt and boxer shorts.

Taylor held Kaplan's gaze. "Maybe."

The captain sighed, shaking his head.

"Really, Taylor," a well-educated voice snapped. "Why would you send this kind of information via text? You know that's not safe!"

Benedict and Georgina sat in the leather armchairs by Kaplan's desk. Georgina was pale. Benedict's brow was a mass of lines. He didn't look at Julie. Instead, he glared at Taylor, his mouth turned down.

"Father, I—" Taylor began.

"I have no interest in your explanation," Benedict snapped.

Taylor hung his head, nodding silently. He let his arm slip off Ilsa's shoulders and clasped his hands behind his back like a schoolboy being chided.

Julie felt a pang of heat behind her sternum. *Oh, you're gonna be sorry you said that!* she raged, stepping forward.

Whoa. Whoa! Hat cried in her mind. *Now's not the time. He is the King of the Aether Elves, remember? There are other things to attend to right now.*

Julie knew he was right, but she had to flex her fingers a few times before the heat in her chest dissipated. She turned to Taylor. "What happened? Are you guys both okay?"

"We're fine." Ilsa reached out and patted Julie's hand. "Thank you for asking and for coming. You're so kind."

"A wraith snuck into Ilsa's suite," Taylor explained. He nodded at the tall, familiar elf guard standing in the corner of the room. "Victor, Ilsa, and I fought it off."

"You did most of the fighting off." Ilsa grinned widely and gave Taylor a dig in the ribs. "Where did you get that magic staff, anyway?"

"Uh, from the SPTM." Taylor's face grayed.

Kaplan's eyes narrowed. "Didn't you requisition that staff weeks ago for rescuing Malcolm Nox?"

"Yeah," Taylor admitted.

Kaplan sighed, waving a hand. "Well, at least you put it to good use."

Benedict glared daggers at Taylor. Julie glared right back, listening as her orb training told her about wraiths. *Considered by humans to be appearances of the undead, wraiths are spirit creatures capable of phasing in and out of a solid or gaseous state at will. They are known for being naturally aggressive and capable of moving through walls, thus often finding employment as professional killers.*

"Professional killers," Julie echoed. "Wait, so this was a hitman? Hitwraith, anyway?"

"More than likely." Kaplan's voice held the low thunder of a growl. "Wraiths seldom act for their own causes. Someone must have hired this one."

"Where is it now?" Julie asked. "Can we question it?"

"We might have if your friend here hadn't reduced it to a useless pile of ash," Kaplan snapped.

Benedict's glare intensified. Ilsa put a hand on Taylor's arm, frowning. "He had no choice, Captain. He saved us."

"We both know you had it handled, sis." Taylor squirmed out from under Kaplan's glare.

Julie folded her arms. "So, there's no way of finding out who hired it." She half-expected Benedict and Georgina to protest that she was even speaking right now, but Benedict was too busy death-glaring at Taylor. Georgina simply stared at her wordlessly.

"Not right now," Kaplan conceded, "but I'm going to find out. A far more pressing matter is how the wraith got into Ilsa's suite."

Julie hesitated. "I'm guessing the walls of her suite have some kind of magic on them to stop wraiths from going through."

"They do." Kaplan nodded. "The suite is supposed to have some of the strongest warding spells in the universe on it."

"*Supposed to*," Georgina sneered.

Benedict rounded on Kaplan. "Your people are corrupt, Kaplan. You clearly have no control over your own IT department, not after what happened with the troll Qbiit. Your warlocks must be as corrupt as your IT is, and..."

Kaplan leveled a long glare at Benedict, whose voice trailed off.

"Rest assured that a thorough internal affairs investigation was carried out after the Qbiit debacle," Kaplan snarled. "And I'm going to call in IA first thing in the morning."

"Call them now!" Benedict barked.

Kaplan laughed. "Your Majesty, if you think I can summon three Sphynxes to work at four in the morning, you clearly know nothing about cats."

"What about security cameras?" Julie asked. "Don't we have any footage?"

"The IRSA 4000 was in control of the cameras," Taylor told

her. "Since we found out that Qbiit was tinkering with the IRSA to make recruiting more difficult and weaken the PMA, it's been undergoing an overhaul. Obviously, this is going slowly without Qtana."

Julie grimaced. "So, no footage?"

Taylor shook his head. "No footage."

Benedict flew to his feet. "It is abundantly clear that the crown princess is not safe in this building. I demand that she goes home with me right now!"

Kaplan gave him a long unemotional look. "So, you'd rather take her to the Aether Compound, where you don't have any fully warded protective suites, even knowing that wraiths are involved?"

Benedict shut his mouth.

"I didn't think so." Kaplan turned to Julie, Taylor, and Ilsa. "Woodskin, get your ass down to the ER to have that bruise fixed. Princess Ilsanthia, I suggest you return to your suite. I will meet with IA first thing. In the meantime, I've sent extra guards there, and my most trusted warlock is recasting the wards on your walls."

Ilsa glanced at her parents. Benedict let out a breath and got up. "I will permit this. For now." He glared at Kaplan. "But I suggest you improve your agency's performance, Captain." He swept out of the room, Georgina trailing after him.

CHAPTER TWELVE

Julie's eyes felt like they'd been filled with sand. She blinked at the report on her computer screen, the numbers scrambling and dancing in front of her eyes.

Taylor made a soft sound in the back of his throat. When Julie glanced at him, he was also staring at his screen, his fingertips probing the spot on his temple that had been an ugly black bruise just this morning.

"You okay?" Julie asked.

Taylor looked at her. His eyes were red. "Yeah, just sleep-deprived."

"Same." Julie stifled a yawn. "I wondered if your head was okay, though. You're poking it."

"Oh, yeah. It's itchy. Really irritating." Taylor rubbed the spot. "Not sore anymore though, thanks to Dr. Olena."

Julie yawned again.

"Not enough caffeine?" Taylor teased gently.

Julie snorted. "Nope. I'm glad you're all okay, but it bugs me that there are more questions than answers." She frowned. "I wonder if the Sphynxes will talk to you."

"Kaplan sent me an email. They're interviewing me just before lunch." Taylor stifled a yawn.

"Good." Julie frowned. "I need a word with Horusiris."

"You do?" Taylor raised his eyebrows. "Why?"

Julie looked at her screen, stomach clenching. *Curse you, sleep deprivation.* "Just wanted to find out if they've gotten any further in finding who Qbiit was working with."

She could feel Taylor's eyes boring into her, but before he could ask anything more, her phone rang. Mom. For once, Julie was relieved to see her name on her phone. Anything to get out of this conversation. She grabbed her phone and answered. "Hey, Mom." She held the phone a little away from her ear, waiting for her mother's overexcited squealing of her name.

"Julia, can you talk?" Rosa's voice was low and urgent.

Julie's heart flipped, and she sat up straight. "Mom, what's wrong?"

"I'm sorry, honey." Rosa sucked in a shaky breath. "Lillie's back in the hospital."

Julie gripped the phone, and its edges dug into her fingers. "What happened? What's wrong with her?"

"I don't know, baby. I just know that…" her mother's voice cracked, "she fell. I called the ambulance. They're taking her to Maimonides again."

"I'm on my way." Julie jumped to her feet, ended the call, and grabbed her jacket and Hat.

"What's up?" Taylor was already reaching for his bag.

"Lillie's in the hospital. I've got to go." Julie shrugged on her jacket and slammed Hat onto her head.

Taylor grabbed his keys. "I'm coming with you."

"You've got to talk to IA, and Ilsa needs you." Julie took a deep breath. "You need to stay here."

Taylor froze. "But…"

"It's okay, Taylor. I'll be okay." Julie snatched Genevieve's keys. "Just talk to Kaplan for me, please."

"Okay," Taylor mumbled.

Julie didn't have time for the hurt on his face. She shoved the door open and raced for the elevator.

Hat bounced on Julie's head, dreading the prospect of another near-death experience—sorry, drive—to the hospital in Genevieve. He sighed. *I guess I'll have to be an emergency light again.*

Please, Julie pleaded, crashing through the lobby. *I need to get there. Now.*

Hat squeezed his crown more tightly around her head. *I'm right here for you, Julie.*

Thanks.

Hat sensed a buzz in Julie's backpack. Her phone. News about Lillie? Maybe he could tell her. Save her having to pull out her phone and check it in this hurry. He connected to her phone and skimmed her text messages.

The newest one wasn't from Rosa, though. It was from Dr. Olena.

Can we meet urgently? Your blood results are in.

Hat's brim curled as she dashed out of the front doors and headed for the parking garage at a dead run. This would have to wait. Lillie needed Julie's attention now.

Forgive me, Julie, he whispered in the privacy of his mind and deleted the text from her phone.

When Dr. Haynes stepped into the waiting room, there was no sign of his usual dimpled smile. Instead, his mouth was a grim line, and he held his tablet like it contained a ticking time bomb.

Julie's stomach twisted. She scrambled out of the armchair where she'd been sitting, clutching her mother's hand. "Doc," Julie gasped. "Is she okay?"

"Lillie is stable right now." Dr. Haynes took a deep breath and ran a hand over his stubble.

Julie clung to Rosa's hand to stop herself from shaking. "What's wrong with her? Why did she collapse?"

Dr. Haynes gestured at the armchairs with his clipboard. "Let's sit down."

Julie's heart was beating in the wrong places in her body. She sagged into a chair, swallowing hard. Beside her, Rosa did the same. Her face was ashen.

"Lillie's symptoms were caused by an ischemic cerebrovascular attack." Dr. Haynes kept his voice soft and low. "An embolus—a blood clot—in one of the major vessels leading to her brain. The clot blocked blood flow into her brain, causing her to collapse. Since you acted so quickly, Mrs. Hernandez, we were within the window of administering TPA—a clot buster, basically—which broke up the clot and restored blood flow to her brain in time. There wasn't any tissue death."

"She's okay now?" Julie quavered.

Dr. Haynes hesitated. "She feels okay, and she's alert and talking, which are great things. However, the imaging has shown us damage in one of her cranial arteries."

Julie fished for knowledge. She was sure she'd read about this, but her thoughts felt scattered and slow. All she could remember was that a cranial artery was a major blood vessel to the brain. "What does that mean?"

"It means that Lillie has a brain aneurysm." Dr. Haynes spread his hands. "It has a high risk of rupturing and causing a hemorrhagic stroke—internal bleeding into the brain."

"But you can fix it," Mom insisted. "You can do surgery and fix it, can't you?"

Dr. Haynes' mouth turned down at the corners, and Julie's

stomach dropped through the floor. She felt a long way away, the world distant and fractured. Dr. Haynes' voice reached her dimly through the ringing in her ears. She caught only a few words. "Location of the aneurysm." "Advanced age." "Inoperable."

"There's really nothing you can do?" Julie croaked. "Nothing?"

Dr. Haynes shook his head. "I'm truly sorry, Miss Meadows. It's out of our hands."

Rosa's hand trembled in hers, then steadied. Julie stared at the tile floor between the cute brown boots she'd grabbed in her mad hustle to get out of the house this morning. Lillie had complimented her on those boots when she'd brought them home, though she had added that they could have used a few more inches of heel and maybe some spiked studs. Julie had laughed while she fed Pookie. Why hadn't she savored that moment longer? Why hadn't she stayed longer that evening before retreating to her apartment?

Through the haze, she heard her mother ask Dr. Haynes how long Lillie had left.

"It's impossible to tell. Hours, perhaps days." Dr. Haynes' eyes dwelled on Julie for a moment, then returned to Rosa. "We'll keep her comfortable, but when the aneurysm ruptures, there won't be anything we can do. We will make sure she isn't in any pain, but she will die quite quickly once the rupture takes place. I'm so sorry."

"Can I see her?" Julie asked, raising her head.

"Of course." Dr. Haynes got up. "Let me take you to her."

Julie took deep breaths as she and her mother followed the doctor to the same private room Lillie had stayed in when she'd had pneumonia. Somehow, she managed to hold back the tears as the door swung open. Lillie was sitting up in bed, her white hair pulled into a neat bun, sipping tea from a hospital cup.

"There you are, dear." Lillie lowered the mug. "I told them not to keep you waiting for so long."

"Hello, Lillie." Julie had much more to say, but those were the only words that would come out. She sat on the edge of the bed.

Lillie smiled. Her eyes looked far too bright to be hiding an aneurysm. "Come on in. I'm sure you're letting me out soon, Doctor?"

Dr. Haynes hesitated by the door. Julie's heart squeezed. "Lillie, you're..."

"Dying? Yes. I know." Lillie replaced the cup on its saucer and gently set it on her nightstand. "I've been waiting for this for a long time, dear." She patted Julie's hand. "But I'm not dying here in the hospital, thank you. I watched my poor dear twin go through that, the Good Lord rest her sweet soul, and it's not the way I'm going to go. Not with tubes down my throat and heaven only knows what else being done to me. I would like to go home to Pookie and Fluffy and Genevieve and you."

Julie looked at Dr. Haynes, who stepped forward. "I can't keep you here against your will, Lillie. You have the capacity to refuse treatment if you like, but you will need someone to stay with you and take care of you."

Julie straightened. "I will."

Rosa met her eyes. She gave her a gentle smile but said nothing.

"I'll call in sick and stay with you." Julie put a hand on her landlady's knee.

Lillie smiled. "I'd like that very much."

Dr. Haynes nodded. "I'll prescribe medication that will keep you comfortable, Lillie." He hesitated, then retrieved a business card from his pocket and held it out to Julie. "If you need any support, Miss Meadows, call this number right away."

Julie fumbled it into her pocket, thanking him. Dr. Haynes headed off to get Lillie's discharge papers ready. Nurses arrived to take the IV out of her arm and get her ready to go. Julie found herself standing in the hallway with her mother.

Rosa put an arm around her shoulders. "Honey, do you want me to stay with you, or do you want this time for just you and Lillie?" Her eyes were soft, though tears glimmered in them.

Julie tried to breathe. Instead, a sob clutched her throat, and she covered her face with her hands, tears coming thick and fast. Rosa said nothing, just wrapped her arms around Julie and waited as the tears flowed.

When she could speak again, Julie whispered, "I want to be with Lillie, Mom. I just want to be with Lillie."

"Then that's what we'll do, baby." Rosa kissed Julie's forehead like she was a little girl. "You know you can call me any hour of the day or night and I'll be there, okay?"

Julie nodded.

"That's my brave girl." Rosa laid a hand on Julie's cheek, her smile lifting the corners of her eyes. "You know I love you."

"I love you too, Mom," Julie whispered.

Rosa pulled out her phone and walked away. "Hey, Ernesto, honey? Can you pick me up from the hospital?"

Julie sagged into one of the armchairs.

I'm here for you, Hat murmured.

Thanks. Julie sucked in a breath. *Can you tell Kaplan I won't be at work for the rest of the week?*

Already done, Hat assured her.

Julie pressed her hands into her hair. She'd rather fight a thousand yetis than go through this.

Julie tucked her t-shirt into her favorite pair of studded black jeans. The shirt was black and edgy and had the words No Shits Left To Give on the front. She'd bought it on a whim one day, knowing Lillie would get a laugh out of it, but she'd never had the courage to wear it until now.

"Lillie's going to love it," Hat told her from where he hung next to her mirror.

Julie blinked away tears, taking deep breaths. Her eyes were very red. She'd promised herself one night to cry, but that was over. It was time to keep moving. "Thanks, Hat." She hesitated. "I feel bad for leaving you here today."

"Don't." Hat laughed. "I need a break from your craziness."

Julie stuck out her tongue at him. She swiped Genevieve's keys from the kitchen table and headed downstairs. Lillie was already stepping out the back door, and Julie had to laugh when she saw the old lady. There was no sign of her floral housecoat today. Instead, Lillie was wearing a leather jacket covered in spiked studs. Her white hair was loose around her shoulders, and she'd found a pair of leather boots somewhere that went well with her usual black mom jeans.

"Look at you, Lillie!" Julie held down her tears so her grin could escape. "Are you sure you want to take Genevieve instead of a motorcycle?"

Lillie threw back her head and laughed. "Nonsense, dear. I'm not missing out on a drive in my one true love today."

She walked up to Genevieve. While the hospital had sorted out Lillie's discharge yesterday, Julie had taken the car in for a full wash and detail. Genevieve's black-and-pewter body gleamed in the morning sunlight filtering into the garage. Even motionless, the world around the car seemed to blur. Her pointed nose and long slanting lines cried out for speed.

Lillie shuffled up to Genevieve, her gait slow and halting. She rested a gnarled, wrinkled hand on the hood and patted it. "Hello, old girl," she murmured. A smile lifted the deep folds around her mouth and cheeks, and for an instant, Julie wasn't looking at an old lady and a classic car. She was looking at a young girl, all slim curves, bursting with life, touching her brand-new Mustang for the first time. The intervening fifty years melted, and Lillie let out a laugh that bubbled with youth and mischief and potential.

She turned to Julie, her eyes very clear. "Let's drive." Her voice was hoarse and urgent.

Julie's smile came more easily this time. She twirled the keys around her finger and helped Lillie into Genevieve. When they peeled out of the garage, she stomped on the gas a couple of times so Genevieve's engine roared.

Lillie's grin was as wide as the morning sky.

The sunny morning had given way to a stormy midday, but it was as though Genevieve craved the howling wind. She whisked down the freeway, her sonorous engine snarling, the windscreen wipers flapping from side to side as rain splattered against her flanks. A crack of thunder split the sky, and lightning leaped from cloud to cloud.

"Look at that!" Lillie cackled, gazing up at it.

Julie smiled. "Seems like you prefer the storm to sunshine."

"Sunshine's boring, dear." Lillie waved a hand. "This is where you really come alive. At the edge of a storm."

Julie slowed and took a ramp off the freeway. "One last stop before we go home?"

"Sure," Lillie agreed. She patted her stomach, laughing. "As long as it isn't to get more clam chowder. I think I might explode!"

"Not this time." Julie took a breath to suppress the flutter of nervousness in her stomach. She stopped at a red light, then squeezed through several blocks of traffic and turned left. The Manhattan Bridge stretched in front of them, almost seven thousand feet of engineering spanning the East River.

Lillie was very quiet as Julie pulled over and brought Genevieve to a gentle stop. The storm raged, and the river bucked and lashed against the supports of the bridge. There was almost no traffic. Julie kept her hands on the wheel and looked at

Lillie. "I recognized the bridge from your picture of you and your sister."

Lillie's face was frozen. "I haven't been here in years."

Julie's gut twisted. "We can go home if you'd like. I just thought—"

"No." Lillie held out a hand. "No, I'm glad we came. This was our spot." She let out a soft laugh. "It was where we came when the husbands and kids were driving us wild and we needed to take Gennie out for a spin."

Julie waited, giving Lillie space in case she wanted to talk more about her sister. Instead, the old lady sat in silence for a few moments, then unbuckled her seat belt and opened the door.

"Lillie!" Julie gasped. Stopping here was illegal, let alone getting out and waltzing down the road.

Lillie ignored her. She closed the door, strode out into the rain, and walked up to the bridge's rail.

Julie's heart thundered. She scrambled out of Genevieve, slamming the door. "Lillie!" she yelled, buffeted by wind and rain. "Where are you going?"

Lillie had reached the rail. She gazed into the leaping gray of the river, foaming as it battered against the bridge, driven by the wind. Her white hair was whipped and wild. When Julie caught up with her, she was smiling.

"Feel that storm wind, Julie!" Lillie spread her arms, allowing the wind to snap at her leather jacket and press it against her withered frame. "Look at that lightning!"

A thunderclap shook the world. Could you get struck by lightning on a bridge? Julie thought you could. "Lillie, we should go back."

Lillie turned to her, eyes clear, the smile on her face coming straight from the seventies. "Feel the wind!" she shouted again.

Julie obeyed. She turned her face into the wind, enjoying its breathtaking force and the raindrops pelting against her face.

The vehicles that swished past honked, and Genevieve's wipers wip-wopped against the windshield.

Lillie gripped Julie's arm with surprising strength. "You're a storm, Julie."

Julie stared at her. "What?" she yelled over the wind.

"You're a storm, not a ray of sunshine," Lillie shouted back. "You're a woman. You shake the world and water the earth. You hear me? You can destroy things and grow them. Don't turn your thunder down for anyone. No one. Do you understand, dear?" Her eyes searched Julie's, her tone low and urgent.

Julie swallowed, her heart thudding with the wind and the words and the look in Lillie's eyes. "O-okay," she stammered.

Lillie beamed widely. "You're going to do great things, you know. Don't forget that everyone is important. And don't ever stop living your beliefs out loud, no matter what anyone says." Her cackle was caught by the wind. "Always be a hellion."

Lillie let go of Julie and turned back to Genevieve. The storm had darkened the sky, and the city lights glimmered around them. Genevieve's headlights stretched into the rain, droplets shining on her paint as the wind whipped them across her smooth lines.

"I know I was," Lillie whispered. She turned to the rail, reached into the rain, and looked down into the water. "I'll see you soon, sis." She murmured the words almost inaudibly.

Julie put a hand on her arm. They stood in the rain together, listening to the thunder and the crashing water. Then Lillie got back into Genevieve.

Julie was soaked as she scrambled into the driver's seat, but she'd brought beach towels, and they dried themselves a little. Lillie was laughing like a schoolgirl. "We need to do one more thing before we go home."

Julie grinned. "Yeah? What's that?"

Genevieve's engine roared. Despite the gray sky, it seemed like the raindrops parted to let the car through, her aerodynamic shape slicing through the storm.

"Yeaaahh!" Lillie whooped. The window was rolled down, and she had one hand outside it. "Punch it, Julie!"

Julie let out a wild laugh. She wasn't sure she was going to survive this, but she wasn't about to deny Lillie's request. She shifted to top gear and flattened her foot on the gas.

Ahead of them, the near-empty interstate stretched to infinity. Genevieve roared across the miles, swallowing them in seconds, her engine screaming, then whining. Julie watched the needle go to one hundred. One hundred ten. One hundred twenty.

"Go, girl. Go!" Lillie hollered.

Julie's hands were white-knuckled on the wheel. It vibrated in her grip, the little silver horse shape trembling. One hundred thirty. One hundred forty.

One hundred fifty.

The storm raged around them. The car ate up the miles.

Lillie Griswall laughed and laughed.

Julie wasn't sure her heartbeat would ever return to normal. She put Genevieve in park, still trembling, and slowly unstuck each of her fingers from their death grip on the steering wheel.

Lillie grinned and patted her shoulder. "You look shaken up, dear."

"I-I think my life just flashed in front of my eyes," Julie croaked.

Lillie let out a peal of laughter. "That was called living, dear."

Julie snorted. She got out, wobbled on shaky legs to the passenger side, and helped Lillie out. When she opened the back door, Pookie bounded wildly around Lillie's feet, yipping with excitement.

"There's a good puppy," Lillie crooned. "Good little puppy."

They'd brought Indian food for dinner, and they ate it in front of the TV while watching *Judge Judy* reruns.

"What an asshole," Julie grumbled as Judge Judy chewed out some luckless dude who'd tried to steal his girlfriend's car.

Lillie took another bite of naan. "He sure is, dear. Don't you go running around with men like that, okay? Stick with that hottie from work."

"Lillie!" Julie laughed.

The old woman cackled.

The credits rolled, and Lillie turned off the TV. "I think I'm going up to bed."

"Okay." Julie rose. "Do you want a cup of tea to take with you?"

"No, thank you, dear. I'm okay." Lillie paused and turned to Julie. "I wanted to thank you for everything you've done for me, dear."

"Done for you?" Julie had to swallow her tears. "Lillie, you're the one who changed my life. You...you mean so much to me." She blinked rapidly. "You made all my dreams seem within reach."

"Don't be sentimental, dear. It's unattractive." Lillie patted her shoulder. "I just wanted you to know that I lost my inner hellion after my dear sis died. You gave it back." Her eyes grew misty. "Thank you."

Julie couldn't force any words through the giant lump in her throat.

"Don't you worry about a thing, either." Lillie squeezed her shoulder. "You'll be well taken care of when I'm gone."

Julie tried to sniff, but it came out as a sob. Lillie laughed and wrapped her in a soft hug that smelled like lavender and leather. "Cry it out, dear. Then carry on."

It took all her strength not to cry at that moment. She returned Lillie's hug with warmth.

"Goodnight," she croaked as Lillie headed upstairs.

The old lady turned back and waved gently. "Goodnight, dear."

CHAPTER THIRTEEN

Julie slept on the couch.

She couldn't face her apartment, not even with Hat in it. She stopped in long enough to grab a pillow and tell him where she was spending the night. Then she stretched out in front of the TV, cuddled Pookie in her arms, and watched *Judge Judy* until she fell asleep with Fluffy the cat in a purring little curl behind her back.

When she woke up, Pookie had disappeared. She sat up slowly, groggy, her phone's alarm chiming madly on the coffee table, waking her up to go to work. She slid the stop button and sat up, rubbing her hands over her face, which burned with exhaustion.

There was a text from Taylor.

Things okay there? Do you need anything?

He'd sent a funny video of a goat trying to jump into a wheelbarrow and tipping it over.

She ruffled her hair as she gazed at the screen but didn't answer. Leaving the phone on the coffee table, she stumbled into the kitchen and made a pot of tea. Pookie's food bowl was untouched. Julie checked again that both doors were closed. The little dog had to be in the house somewhere.

She added a pinch of chamomile to the tea and plenty of milk and sugar, just like Lillie liked it, and headed upstairs, carrying the saucer in one hand and the cup in the other.

"Lillie?" Julie placed the cup on the saucer and knocked gently on the bedroom door.

There was no response. A bone-deep shudder ran through Julie, and the cup rattled loudly against the saucer. Tears clawed at her throat. She choked them away and knocked again. "Lillie, you awake?"

A soft bark came from inside the room. Lillie must have gotten up in the night to let Pookie in with her. That meant she was okay, right? That had to mean that she was fine. She just needed to be woken up, that was all. Woken up with a nice cup of tea to start the day. One more day.

There was another soft bark. Julie sucked in a breath and pushed the door open.

Lillie lay on her back with her eyes closed. The pretty floral bedspread was tucked over her torso, left arm pillowing her head, right arm above the bedspread on her chest. Pookie was curled in the crook of Lillie's arm, looking up at Julie. Her tail didn't wag. In the soft sunlight filtering through the white curtains, Lillie's face was utterly still, her eyes closed.

Julie took deep breaths as she gently set the cup and saucer on the nightstand. When she stumbled around to the other side of the bed, Pookie let out a soft whimper.

"Lillie," Julie whispered, crouching beside the bed.

She put a hand over Lillie's, and it was cold. Colder than life could ever be.

It was stupid since she already knew, but Julie reached out and pressed her fingertips to the place where the carotid artery in Lillie's neck should have been bounding with life. There was nothing, only cold skin.

"Please," she murmured, her words hitching in her throat. "Oh, Lillie, please! Just one more day. One more drive."

Lillie had taken her last spin in the Mustang she'd loved.

Julie sat on the couch with Pookie in her arms. Someone had brought her something in a hot mug. Tea, coffee; she didn't know. It had long since stopped steaming, full and forgotten on the coffee table.

There were people in the house. Medics and others. They kept leaving the back door and the garage door open, and Pookie might run into the street. Lillie was going to be angry.

Lillie was dead.

Pookie whined, then licked Julie's chin. She reached up, dimly aware of the heat and dampness on her cheeks, and wiped a tear away.

The couch sagged beside her. "You okay, honey? Hungry?"

Julie blinked. It was her mother. She'd been here for a while. "No, thanks," Julie got out.

"Okay." Rosa rested a hand on her knee. "I don't want you to worry about a single thing, baby. I'll sort out all the arrangements, okay?"

"Okay." Julie swallowed hard. "Thanks, Mom."

Her mother put an arm around her shoulders. "She loved you very much, you know. And she knew that you loved her. Even if her family had abandoned her, she was so loved."

Julie broke down and wept.

Everyone else had left. Rosa had bustled around, herding them away. A few of Lillie's friends from bingo, Genevieve's mechanic, Ernesto, and her mother. The family hadn't come.

It had rained in the night, even though the sun shone on the graveyard now, highlighting the damp, wilted flowers on the surrounding graves. Julie's senses were filled with the smell of freshly turned wet earth. She took a deep breath as she crouched in front of the headstone, but her tears seemed to have been cried out in the days before the funeral. Her eyes were clear as she read the inscription on the headstone.

LILLIAN CATHERINE GRISWALL

BELOVED FRIEND

Even though nearly eighty years separated the two dates on the headstone, Julie couldn't shake the feeling that they hadn't been nearly long enough.

"I guess this is goodbye," she whispered.

There was no sound except the background rush of traffic that was never far away in New York City.

Julie swallowed again. "I'll never forget you, especially not when I'm behind the wheel." A smile tugged at her cheeks. "And I won't forget what you said. I'll always be a hellion."

She straightened slowly. She had thought it would be difficult to walk away from Lillie's grave, but it wasn't. The shell that was buried in that grave wasn't Lillie. She had been far more than that, and she wasn't here anymore. She'd gone somewhere else. Julie had been to Avalon. If she could believe that, she could believe there was a place where Lillie lived on.

She wished that place could be here, but it was not. She pushed her hands into the pockets of her blazer and trudged across the wet dirt to the cemetery gate.

Genevieve was parked in the lot, shining in the sunlight.

Taylor was leaning against her, but when he saw Julie come through the gate, he straightened and strode over to meet her. He didn't ask her if she was okay.

"Sushi or shawarma?" he asked instead.

Julie managed a smile. "Sushi."

"No pressure."

She stopped suddenly, a weight crushing her chest, and sucked in a breath, trying not to cry.

Taylor draped an arm around her shoulders and squeezed. His arm was lithe and firm around her, and that fresh earth-after-rain smell filled the air.

"C'mon. Let's go," he murmured and led her away.

Julie looked at the PMA building, staid and blockish in the pale morning light, and took a deep breath.

Sure you're ready for this? Hat asked softly. *Kaplan did say you could have a few more days if you wanted them.*

I'm sure. Julie squared her shoulders. *I need my routine again.*

Even if that routine includes getting your arse kicked by an Aether Elf in whose arms you cried most of yesterday afternoon? Hat enquired.

Julie snorted, striding up to the gym. *Wow, thanks for the reminder! I definitely didn't feel awkward enough.*

Just trying to lighten the mood, Hat chuckled, and his crown squeezed her head gently.

Julie shook her head. Taylor was waiting by their usual mat, sitting cross-legged beside his duffel bag. He scrambled to his feet when he saw her. "Julie, hey! How are...um, how are you?" he stammered.

Julie's toes curled. She set her backpack on the floor and pulled off Hat. "I'm fine, thanks! How are you?"

"I'm okay." Taylor smiled far too widely.

This is going well, Hat commented.

Shut up! Julie hissed. She cleared her throat. "So, more dagger work today?"

"Oh, no. I thought you needed a little pick-me-up, so I grabbed these from the training room." Taylor grinned as he picked up two wooden swords. Each was four feet long and had a wide, sturdy hilt.

"Swordwork?" Julie took one. "More guards today?"

"Not guards." Taylor spun his sword in his hand with lazy ease. "Your first time sparring with longswords."

Julie raised an eyebrow and gripped the hilt in both hands. "This could be interesting."

"I'm hoping so." Taylor stepped back.

What's that supposed to mean? Julie groaned as she raised her sword into plow guard.

Taylor lifted his sword over his shoulder—ox guard—and struck. Julie blocked with her blade, gasping at the force with which he struck, and stumbled back a step. Taylor's sword juddered down the length of hers and slammed into the crossguard, then stuck.

"Sorry." Taylor hurriedly stepped back, lifting his sword away. "I came at you too fast."

"No, no, it's okay. I just…I'm off my game." Julie tried to smile.

Taylor lowered his sword. "That's okay. Do you want to do something else? Just run through the guards again?"

"No, it's fine. Try that again." Julie raised her sword across her body in plow guard.

Taylor nodded but hesitated. "Your feet are wrong."

"Sorry." Julie put her dominant foot in front and turned out her other foot to provide a steady base.

"It's okay. Don't apologize." Taylor took a breath. "I'm going to do the same strike again."

Julie nodded. Moving in slow motion, Taylor raised the sword into ox guard and sent a strike trailing toward her blade. She blocked it and twisted her wrists, trying to turn the blow into a wind, but he didn't have enough momentum. Instead, his sword slithered down the length of hers and knocked painfully into her shin.

"Ow!" Julie jumped back.

"Sorry! Sorry." Taylor held out a hand. "Are you okay?"

"I'm fine," Julie spat. "I'm not a fragile flower, Taylor. Don't treat me like a damsel in distress."

His face fell. "Okay. Sorry."

"I didn't mean..." Julie sighed. "Let's try that again."

"Don't tell me you're teaching this poor girl longswords, Taylor?" Ilsa chuckled behind her. "We both know that you're better off sticking to daggers."

Taylor's face grayed with embarrassment. "Hey, Ilsa."

They turned. The elf princess stepped onto the mat. Her hair was pulled back in a ponytail. Victor and a couple of other guards had spread out around the gym.

"It's good to see you, Julie." Ilsa offered her a gentle hug. "I'm glad you're back."

"Glad to be back." Julie smiled, and it came easily this time. "So, what were you saying about Taylor and longswords?"

Ilsa grinned. "Just that I'm a more suitable candidate to teach you."

"What Ilsa isn't telling you is that I flunked my military training in twelfth grade because I was totally useless at longswords." Taylor laughed. "I have improved since then, you know, Ilsa."

"Yes, but you're still not living it down." Ilsa winked. "Lend me your sword?"

"Sure." Taylor tossed it to Ilsa, who caught it with dangerous ease. She spun to face Julie and struck hard and fast out of ox guard.

With a yelp of surprise, Julie brought up her blade. Wood thundered on wood, and Julie loosened her wrists, allowing the swords to spin in a circle together until Ilsa's pressure on Julie's sword weakened. Then she broke the wind and quickly struck at Ilsa's knees. Ilsa blocked just as quickly, grinning.

"See? You've got this." She stepped back. "Now I'll show you how to block out of a wind like that."

"Get her, Julie!" Taylor cheered.

Julie laughed at him. Ilsa snorted, hands on her hips. "Excuse me, sir. Whose side are you on?"

Taylor cupped a hand by his mouth and spoke in a stage whisper. "I just think Julie needs all the encouragement she can get."

"Hey!" Julie protested, laughing. It felt good to laugh again. She turned to Ilsa. "I really appreciate this, Ilsa, but don't you have more important things to do than train some human?"

Ilsa shrugged. "I've been preparing for the rest all my life. At least, trying to prepare for it."

"Do you have to fight something?" Julie asked.

"I don't know." Ilsa rested the tip of her sword on the ground and leaned on the hilt, the corners of her mouth drooping. "Little is known about the test. We're told that it has a physical component, so I've practiced every martial art I could since I was a kid. Some sports, too."

"I mean, a swordfight does seem more likely than shooting hoops," Julie agreed.

Ilsa shook her head. "It's frustrating, not knowing."

"I'll bet. Why doesn't anyone know?" Julie asked. "Surely it would help people if they could prepare better for the test? The pass rate must be pretty bad."

"Actually, a lot of people have passed it. A lot of royals have to," Ilsa told her, shifting her weight from foot to foot. "Nobody can talk about it, but those who pass are often deeply changed."

Taylor nodded. "In a good way. Every king and queen in the seven royal families has to have passed the test to be eligible for the throne. That's one reason Ilsa has to take it. Otherwise, she won't be able to rule when our parents pass away."

"Oh." Julie blinked. "Then Julius Nox has taken it?"

"Exactly. But like everyone else who's passed the test, he's under a geas. He can't tell you what the test is or how to pass it," Ilsa explained. "It's to prevent cheating."

"Seems harsh." Julie frowned. "Since all you know is that there's a physical component."

Ilsa grimaced. "There's more than that, but not a lot more. You're supposed to be just, wise, and pure of heart."

"Whatever *that* means," Julie shot back.

Ilsa chuckled. "Exactly." She stepped back. "Okay, human, let's spar."

Julie ran a hand through her damp hair, then tossed her backpack over her shoulder. "I didn't see Ilsa in the showers," she told Taylor. "Where are her guards?"

Taylor, also freshly showered, looked up from his phone. He was leaning against the wall, waiting for her. "Ilsa went up to her suite to shower and change."

"Clearly she's too good to shower with the commoners." Julie sniffed. "I'll have to tell her what I think about that."

Taylor laughed. "Yeah, because my sister is *so* arrogant and snobbish."

"Dreadfully so," Julie joked. She fell into step beside him as they left the gym and made for the main building. "No connection with ordinary people. Thinks she's better than others just because she's a noble."

Taylor's grin widened. "Awful."

Julie chuckled at him. "Hey, in seriousness, I know she's going to pass the test."

"I hope so." Taylor's smile faded. "She's the only member of my family who has any time for me. I don't know what I'd do without her."

"She's going to pass," Julie repeated firmly. "Just, wise, and pure of heart? Sounds like Ilsa to me."

A ghost of Taylor's smile returned. "Yeah, you're right."

He pushed the lobby door open, and they strode into the elegant hallway.

Uh, Julie? Hat began.

What's up, Hat? Julie asked.

He took a deep breath. *I didn't want to tell you while Lillie was sick, but there's a message you should know about.*

A message? Julie frowned. *Are you keeping something from me?*

Before Hat could answer, a deafening sound ran through the lobby. Julie ducked instinctively, grabbing Taylor's arm. It was a wailing alarm, and it filled the air with a solid wall of sound. Thundering feet followed.

"What's going on?" Julie yelled.

The cafeteria doors crashed open, and a stream of soldiers and agents in blue and red uniforms poured into the lobby. More slammed in from outside. They skirted the elevator and piled into the stairwell.

"Oh, no," Hat muttered.

"Hat, what is it?" Julie gasped. "What's happening?"

Taylor's eyes were wide. "I've never seen this. A *full* mobilization of the PMA?"

"That's because it only happens when there's a threat to the Eternity Throne," Hat growled.

Six young men in blue uniforms rushed past. It took Julie a few seconds to recognize the Weres jogging in perfect unison with Isaiah at their head.

"Where are they going?" Julie asked.

"To the military wing. There's a portal there to the Eternal Throne for emergency deployment," Hat told her.

Julie raised her eyebrows. "Apparently, there's a lot I don't know about. What are we supposed to do?"

Taylor shrugged. "We're recruitment. We just need to stay out of the way."

"Stay out of the way?" Julie snorted. "We should at least check on Ilsa. I mean—"

Hat gasped. The sound was so loud and sudden that Julie and Taylor jumped. Julie didn't think she'd ever heard Hat gasp before. Ice drenched her veins.

Hat shouted the words. "There's a wraith in the building!"

"A wraith?" The color drained from Taylor's face.

Julie stared at him. "Ilsa!"

"Go. Go!" Hat yelled. "Get to her suite!"

They set off at a dead run, shoving through the crowds of soldiers. Julie bumped against someone with dark hair—Ellie—and mumbled an apology, then shouldered through a crowd of dwarves. Taylor reached the elevator first and slapped the up button. The doors slid open as Julie reached it, and they piled inside. Taylor hit the button for Ilsa's suite. It beeped and turned red.

"What's going on?" Taylor slammed a fist into the button. "Open!"

"We don't have her pass," Julie gasped. "It won't. Should we take the stairs?"

"The stairs won't take us to her suite." Taylor hit the button again. "Come on. Come on!"

"Give me one minute and I'll fix it," Hat growled.

Julie put a hand on Taylor's arm. "Easy, Taylor. She'll be okay." She wished she could inject more conviction into those words. Taylor was trembling under her touch.

"There!" Hat yelled in triumph.

The doors slid open. Taylor lunged out, reaching behind his ear for the staff, which blossomed into its full length as he swung it around in a vicious arc. Julie raised her fists, wishing she'd brought her gun.

The main area of the suite was empty. A book lay splayed

open on the coffee table, an empty mug beside it. Nothing was out of place.

"Ilsa?" Taylor yelled.

"She might be in the shower." Julie stepped forward. "I'll go check."

Her heart thrummed in her ears as she crossed the floor and reached the bedroom, then knocked once. "Ilsa? It's me."

She pushed the door open, and it swung drunkenly on one hinge. Julie's heart froze.

The beautiful canopy bed was torn to pieces. Feathers floated desolately in the air. The canopy hung in sad tatters from its frame. A vicious set of claw marks spanned the wall. The nightstand had been tipped over and a shattered lamp lay beside it.

Julie's gut flipped when she saw a smear of blood on the sumptuous carpet.

"Taylor!" Julie's voice trembled far more than she wanted it to.

Taylor crashed into the room, fire blazing around the gem on the end of his staff. He froze, eyes wide. "No. *No!* Ilsa." The words sounded like they'd been strangled out of him.

"Look at this." Julie stumbled over to the side of the bed and scooped up two small items. "Isn't this Ilsa's elevator pass?"

"That's right." Taylor groaned, shrinking the staff and tossing it behind his ear again, then covering his face with his hands. "She was here. Oh, Julie, she was *here*."

Julie stared at the claw marks in the wall and down at the other item in her hand: a wristwatch. It was heavy and expensive-looking, with a snakeskin band. "This isn't hers, is it?" She held it up.

Taylor glanced at her, shaking his head dumbly.

Julie turned it over in her hands, her breath catching. There was an inscription on the back.

My dear son,
    I wish you all the time in the world.

J. N.

"J. N. *Julius Nox!*" Julie clutched the watch. "Taylor, this is Malcolm's. He was here, too."

"Those must be his claw marks in the wall," Hat reasoned.

Taylor pressed his hands into his hair. "No, no, no, no. They took Ilsa. What are we going to do? What *can* we do?"

"I don't know." Julie sucked in a breath. "We need to call Kaplan. We...we need the whole PMA."

"She's my sister, Julie." Taylor was sobbing. "She's my *sister*."

"There's no time to call Kaplan," Hat snapped. "I don't sense any portal magic here. They must have used the elevator. It's the only portal engine nearby. I can get it to take us to the last place it was opened, but we need to use it before anyone else does."

"How will we get her back? We don't have an army!" Taylor yelled.

"There's no other choice." Hat kept his voice low. "We have to go, Taylor. Now."

Taylor's wild eyes met Julie's. She touched his shoulder briefly. "Come on, Taylor. Let's do this."

The elf took a deep breath, closing his eyes. When he opened them, they narrowed. "*Let's do this.*"

They hurried into the elevator. "Which button do I press?" Julie asked.

"Wait." Hat hummed furiously on her head.

The elevator jolted hard. Julie stumbled and almost fell to her hands and knees. Taylor's shoulder slammed into the wall. The buttons all flashed at once, a chorus of beeping filling the elevator, and the doors slid open.

CHAPTER FOURTEEN

This wasn't the PMA building. They were looking out into a dusky forest without green leaves or towering dryads or soft undergrowth. This forest was a mad tangle of thorns and bushes and gnarled trees, bent as though they had been viciously twisted by uncaring hands. Cobwebs dangled from the trees, stirring softly in the wind that howled mournfully through the forest, making branches clack against each other like bones.

"Look," Taylor whispered, pointing.

Julie dragged her eyes away from the woods and looked beyond them. A hilltop rose from the trees, and a sagging wooden farmhouse stood upon it, sharply silhouetted against the twilit sky. There were no lights in any of its windows, and many of them were missing glass, staring at Julie like dead eyes.

"Well, shit," Julie mumbled. "Ending up in the para version of *Unsolved Mysteries* wasn't in my plans for today."

Taylor let out a breathless laugh. "You did find out that Avalon isn't all sunshine and rainbows at Beltane in Fernwood Deep."

"This is a long way from Fernwood Deep," Julie pointed out. She took a step forward. "I bet she's in the haunted house."

Taylor swallowed.

"Are ghosts real?" Julie asked.

"Depends on your definition of real." Taylor tentatively poked the nearest tree. It didn't do anything. It just sat there being a tree, which was worse.

Julie took a shuffling step forward. "Elaborate?"

Taylor pulled out his magic staff and clutched it, full-sized, in both hands as they stepped into the woods. "Are they the spirits of dead people? Not really. Are they mindless armies of violent terrors unbound to the laws of physics, controlled by a powerful dark magician? A necromancer? Absolutely."

"Great," Julie muttered. "Fantastic. Are these trees going to attack us?"

"They do feel malicious." Taylor kept a wary eye on the largest one nearby as he stepped over a rotting log.

"They're too old and gnarled to do anything except scare you," Hat told them.

Julie scrambled over the same log. "Thanks, Hat. Reassuring."

Taylor swiped at some cobwebs with his staff. A spider the size of his head popped out of the tree in front of them and landed heavily on the ground. Skittering on its eight legs, it whirled to face them, raising two front legs in a defensive posture.

"Ugh!" Taylor raised his staff.

"No!" Julie grabbed it. "Most spider species are harmless."

Taylor stared at her. "*Earth* spider species. And they're not usually the size of a basketball."

The spider saw its chance. It spun and scuttled into the undergrowth.

"If that comes back and kills us, I'm blaming you." Taylor held the cobwebs aside with his staff.

Julie ducked through. "You won't be blaming anyone. You'll be dead."

The word echoed through the woods. *"DEAD, dead, dead, dead."*

"This place is giving me the heebie-jeebies." Julie shoved aside a bunch of thorns, wincing as it tugged at her clothes. "Do you know where we are?"

"Your guess is as good as mine. Avalon is bigger than Earth. I've never seen anywhere like this before." Taylor labored through the thorns, swatting at them with his staff. "I was expecting to find myself in the Sylthana castle, or maybe in some Dark Moon League hideout, but this isn't elf country."

"Me too," Julie admitted. "That doesn't mean they didn't do it."

"Probably not," Taylor agreed. He sighed. "I should have seen this coming."

"How so?" Julie paused at the edge of a murky pond that bubbled like tar and smelled like roadkill. She began to skirt it, pushing aside dry branches.

Taylor grabbed a branch and held it back for her. "I'm not supposed to tell you this, but I'd better fill you in on what's happened in the para world since you took time off."

"Divulging secrets of the throne to a lowly human, are we?" Julie ducked under a branch and jumped over the last scrap of pond to reach the other side.

Taylor chuckled as he scrambled after her. "You're not lowly." He took a deep breath. "I found out the reason for the guards arresting people in Avalon Village, like Iris told us about last week."

"Oh?" Julie paused, glancing back at him. "What was it?"

He passed her and headed up a winding footpath crisscrossed with spiderwebs. "My uncle was kidnapped."

"Your uncle? Taylor, I'm really sorry! Why didn't you say something? I could have helped look for him." Julie jogged to catch up.

Taylor sighed. "The whole PMA's looking for him already. He's the Aether Councilor to the Eternity Throne—the guy Shae works for. He'd been kidnapped when we went to Julius' council; that's why Shae was there. Asshole didn't even tell me."

"Are you close to your uncle?" Julie asked.

"Uncle Arion's cool, but I don't really know him. He pays more attention to the crown princess. Don't think he could pick me out of a lineup." Taylor shrugged. "No one knows why he was taken, but I was scared that Ilsa would be next. Still, I figured she was safe at the PMA. I think that was why Julius insisted she move there. And Uncle Arion wasn't the only one."

Julie paused. "Someone else went missing?"

"Yeah, and it's weird." Taylor frowned. "Someone kidnapped Prince Lotan off the streets of Avalon in broad daylight."

"Lotan? That Sylthana heir?" Julie stared at him. "Why would the Dark Moon League take him?"

"There have been mutterings on social media that Lotan isn't 'strong enough to lead the Sylthana Elves back to their rightful place of supremacy.'" Taylor enclosed the words in air quotes. "It could still be them."

"Weird." Julie snorted.

The path got steeper. Taylor dug his staff into the ground with each stride. "Oh, and someone tried to assassinate Julius Nox when he was being driven home from the opera."

"What? Is he okay?" Julie demanded.

Taylor laughed. "Obviously. He's a badass. They didn't catch the guy, though."

"Or girl." Julie raised her chin.

Taylor spread his hands. "Or girl."

"It sounds pretty hectic." Julie frowned. "Like someone's trying their best to start a war."

"You've got that right." Taylor nodded. "Whoever they are, they're making their move."

After pushing through the last of the forest, Julie stepped onto the foot of the hill. A chill ran through her body.

"Dude, you said they weren't the undead, so why are there gravestones everywhere?" she squeaked.

Taylor stumbled out of the woods beside her, clawing cobwebs off his face. "Ew! Get it off get if off get it off!"

Julie grabbed the spiderwebs and pulled them off. "Little arachnophobic there, are we?"

Taylor dusted the last bits of cobweb off his shirt and straightened, trying to regain some dignity. "Oh, the gravestones? They're traditional."

Julie shivered. The hillside was ringed with them, and they weren't pretty, well-carved gravestones in neat rows with inscriptions. These gravestones jutted out of the hillside like a crackhead's teeth, all at odd angles, none the same. Crypts were dotted among the gravestones, stone-gray in the twilight.

"Creepy as shit," Julie assessed.

"You can say that again." Taylor looked up at the haunted house.

On cue, lightning blazed in the dark sky beyond.

"Great." Julie snorted. "We're doomed."

"Ilsa's doomed if we don't go up there." Taylor clenched his fists and raised his staff, blue fire licking at the gem. "Let's do this."

They stepped forward in unison. Julie kept her fists raised, wishing she'd had time to fetch the magical gun she'd used when they'd rescued Malcolm from the yetis not long ago.

"We really have to stop having to rescue Malcolm," she hissed.

"I'll tell him that—" Taylor stopped short, shivering visibly. Goosebumps appeared on his neck.

Julie felt it too—a dreadful icy chill stabbing at the pit of her stomach. She turned to Taylor. "What was…"

The crypt doors all slammed open at once, the *cracks* echoing through the still air.

"Crap," Julie opined.

A hiss behind her made her whirl. Dirt sprayed out of the

nearest grave, and something gray and horrible crawled out of it, limbs bending at the wrong angles. Hollow white eyes stared at her. It had no nose, but when it opened its mouth, it was filled with a ring of sharp blackened teeth.

"Ghoul!" Taylor yelled, raising the staff. A blue fireball exploded out of it and hit the ghoul in the face. It squealed and fell over backward, then turned into ash.

"Look out!" Julie screamed. "Scary things!"

Creatures poured out of the crypts and circled above them like a flock of bats, flickering from transparent blue to solid gray and back, their eerie screeches echoing through the air.

"Wraiths," Taylor snarled. He raised his staff, and the fire intensified.

More dirt burst out of the surrounding graves. Ghouls crawled toward them, snarling. They looked like Voldemort if Voldemort had been cooked in acid for a week or so. Taylor blasted blue fire into the wraiths and ash rained down on them, but hundreds still swooped through the air.

"A little help, Hat?" Julie yelled, raising her fists.

Hat sighed. "Okay. Reach into me."

"What, like, telepathically?" Julie stepped back and pressed against Taylor as one of the ghouls crawled nearer.

"No, you idiot, with your hand!" Hat yelled.

There wasn't time to argue. Julie pulled him off her head and reached inside. Instead of feeling the crown of the black fedora, her hand slipped in past the elbow and struck something hard and round.

The hilt of a sword.

Julie pulled it out.

"Ooh," Taylor gasped.

"Ooh" was right. The sword was long and straight, and its basket hilt was an intricate network of wrought iron covered in runes. The thin blade was patterned with runes, and it sang in the air as Julie swished it, leaving glowing blue trails.

"It's called the Soul Cleaver. Bit fanciful, but it works," Hat told her. "Oh, and don't tell anyone I can translocate items from the Warehouse."

There was a strangled roar, and the nearest ghoul launched at Julie. She plunged the Soul Cleaver into its chest in an arc of blue. Screeching, the ghoul fell backward and exploded into ash.

Taylor shot another blast of fire, but it fell far short of the rising wraiths, who were flying faster, a tornado of fury above their heads. Julie slashed at another ghoul. "Get them, Taylor!"

"The staff doesn't have enough range for me to pick them off from here!" he gasped. "If they all attack at once—"

"I got you," Hat barked.

Julie held Hat out to Taylor upside down. Tucking the shrunken staff behind his ear, Taylor reached inside and drew out a longbow. Six feet of yew strung with horsehair, patterned with the same runes as the sword. A quiver followed, filled with arrows that glowed blue.

"The quiver never runs out," Hat announced. "You're welcome."

Taylor tested the bowstring with two fingers and grinned, then pulled the strap of the quiver over his head. "*Now* we're talking."

"Let's get these spooky nasties!" Julie cried. She slammed Hat back onto her head and spun to face the nearest ghoul. "Come at me!"

The ghoul lunged at her, and she lunged back, slashing its face. It burst into ash. Two more charged her legs. She stabbed one in the eye and kicked the other in the face. It fell back, yowling, and she slashed its throat. Ash piled up around her as the ghouls kept coming.

"Make for the house!" Taylor shouted, drawing the bow. It creaked for a second before he let the arrow fly. It sailed through the air, leaving a blue arc, and slapped into one of the wraiths at the top of the flock. It plummeted, its shriek fading as it scattered into ash.

Julie punched a ghoul in the jaw and raked the sword across its chest, then turned toward the house. A wall of ghouls blocked her path, all snarling mouths and empty eyes.

She let out a scream and rushed them, swinging her sword. The ghouls charged forward. Julie slashed the blade across three of their throats as they plunged at her, but the fourth came out of nowhere and threw its arms around her chest, exposed muscle twitching in its face as its teeth snapped at her throat. She yelled and flailed, but it was too close for her to get it with the sword. A second leaped for her face. She plunged the sword into its guts, and ash showered her. She grabbed at the face of the ghoul on her chest and shoved her fingers into its eyes. It threw back its head, screeching, but its grip around her chest was like iron, and she couldn't breathe. Teeth slashed fire across her forearm. She screamed, yanked her hand back, and stumbled backward as she fought to keep her feet. The other ghouls were closing in.

A blue arrow lanced through the sky, piercing the ghoul between the eyes. It gave a last shriek and exploded.

"Thank you!" Julie yelled. Blood ran hot down her arm as she slashed the charging ghouls, trampling the ashes to make headway.

"No problem," Taylor panted. He loosed an arrow into the circling wraiths, then spun, plucked an arrow from his quiver, and plunged it into the back of a ghoul as it lunged at him.

Hacking and slashing as hard and fast as she could, Julie fought back the tide of ghouls. Sweat and blood trickled down her skin, but they just kept coming, throwing themselves at her as their brethren fell to ashes under their feet. Claws and teeth snapped at her as she chopped off limbs.

Stomping on one ghoul's face and pinning it under her foot, Julie plunged her blade into the chest of another. Shaking ashes out of her eyes, she looked up. "We're almost there!"

The haunted house was a few yards away. Taylor glanced at it and lowered his bow. "I think we can—"

The wraiths' shrieking intensified, shaking the very air. Julie gasped and raised her free hand to her ear. Taylor gritted his teeth. They both looked up. The ten wraiths that were left were forming a vortex.

"They're going to swoop at us!" Taylor yelled.

"RUN!" Julie screamed.

Slashing the ghouls with sword and arrows, they bolted for the house and reached it in a matter of moments. Diving under the porch, Julie spun as the wraith vortex plunged toward them.

"Here!" Taylor yelled. "Blast them with this!" He tossed the staff to her. It grew to its full length in mid-air, and Julie caught it one-handed, then held up both sword and staff, shrieking in defiance.

The wraiths were solid gray and moving at a speed that would plunge them *through* this house to their deaths. Julie held up the staff. Even though she could only use its pre-charged fire-blasting spell, it was better than nothing. She brandished it at the wraiths, and a tongue of blue flame burst from the gem and slammed into one of the wraiths. It exploded into ashes, but there were more coming.

Taylor drew five arrows from his quiver. He nocked them all on the string, some of them quivering as he held them in place with magic, and Julie heard him mutter, "Here goes nothing."

The bowstring twanged, and five arrows arced toward the plummeting wraiths. Taylor held out a hand, teeth gritted, sweating. In mid-air, the arrows veered off, each sailing into a different wraith. Ashes filled the air and swirled around the four remaining wraiths. Julie screamed and blasted fire at one, then slashed another in the face with her sword. Ashes surrounded her, filling her eyes and covering her face.

Gross, gross, gross! Julie spat out ashes.

A shriek split the air. Julie wiped ashes from her eyes with the back of her sword hand. The last wraith had stopped short and was hovering above the ground, its empty face turned toward Taylor. He whipped an arrow from his quiver and threw it. The wraith dodged too late, and it exploded into ashes.

"Crap," Julie commented. "That was intense."

Taylor shook ashes out of his hair. "Let's not do that again, ever. Okay?"

"Deal." Julie tossed his staff back to him. "Thanks. That was pretty cool."

Taylor tucked it behind his ear and faced the closed door. "Ready to see what's inside?"

"Sunshine and unicorns?" Julie guessed.

Taylor snorted. "We can always hope, although maybe not unicorns. I'd rather face an army of ghouls and wraiths than *those*." He stepped forward, raising a boot to kick the door down.

The door slowly swung open with a long, drawn-out moan of rusted hinges.

Goosebumps rose on Julie's arms. "Yeah, okay. Because what this situation really needed was the creepy factor cranking up another level."

They stepped over the threshold into an entrance hall that was far bigger than anything that would have fit into the ramshackle farmhouse. Even in the semi-darkness within, Julie could see that the dusty floor was marble. Dim, twisted shapes surrounded them. Statues? They weren't moving, and cobwebs draped them all. They heard skittering near the ceiling. Julie held up the glowing Soul Cleaver and spotted a nest of bats above them, all leathery wings and little scratching claws.

"What's next, zombies?" she muttered.

A wail rose from the darkness and echoed around the entrance hall.

Taylor stopped and nocked an arrow. "Worse."

"What's worse than something that wants to eat your brain?" Julie snorted.

The woman came out of nowhere, and she was levitating. She appeared above the marble floor, her face ghostly pale among the cloud of black hair that floated around it. Tearstains streaked her ashen cheeks, running from red-rimmed eyes, and the bare feet that dangled three feet off the floor were covered with grave dirt. Her ragged black dress hung from a bony frame, tattered and stained.

Taylor drew his bow. "Something that wants to eat your soul."

Banshee, Julie's orb training explained helpfully. *Known as harbingers of death, these are deeply emotional creatures drawn to comfort the dying. Neutral throughout history, banshees exist in a state of compassion and sorrow.*

The banshee threw back her head and screamed. The sound rattled Julie's bones, making something primal and cold twist within her.

Yep, sounds real compassionate. Julie took a step back, lowering her sword hand to her hip in plow guard.

"There!" Taylor yelled, pointing.

Julie glimpsed a gaunt male figure at the top of the stairs, then a deep rumble shook the hall. The banshee screamed again, holding up her twisted clawlike hands. The hall trembled again, and the statues lining both sides began to move. They were jerky and stiff at first, then gained speed. Dust and cobwebs trickled from their bodies as they stretched their stout limbs.

"Golems!" Hat screamed.

The gaunt man at the top of the stairs shouted something Julie didn't understand and the statues froze, their blockish heads turning toward Julie and Taylor. In unison, their eyes opened, glowing with an unearthly neon-green light.

Hat hummed on Julie's head.

"You'd better be sending an SOS to the PMA right about now!" Julie gasped.

The golems stepped off their pedestals and charged. Julie tried to count them as they rushed forward, but there were too many.

Julie slashed at the nearest one, expecting it to explode into ash like the ghouls had. Her sword bounced off its stone belly and came back toward her with a force that made pain lance through her arm. She stumbled back, gasping. The golem drew back a fist the size of a cantaloupe and launched a long, sweeping blow. Julie ducked, then rolled out of the way of a giant foot that came stomping toward her. She felt Hat growing on her head, enclosing her ears. A nose guard grew down the bridge of her nose, and metal clanged when she rolled over.

Strike for the chinks! Hat shouted in her mind.

She shook her head as she rolled to her feet. Four golems surrounded her, and she couldn't see Taylor. *What chinks?*

The first golem, which had a strange floral design on its forehead, took a lurching step forward and swung a haymaker in her direction. As Julie dodged, she spotted it: a glowing line of green light where its shoulder met its torso. Striking hard and fast from plow guard, she drove the tip of her sword into the chink. The golem's arm crumbled and turned to gravel. It stumbled back with a roar of pain.

Oh, those *chinks.* Julie whirled to face the next one, spotted the line of light where its neck and torso joined, and struck. Her sword slashed into the spot, and the golem's head crumbled. It collapsed to its knees, headless and lifeless. Julie heard the scrape of stone on marble behind her, whirled, raised her blade—

The golem's fist landed in her solar plexus. Julie's feet left the ground and her breath exited her lungs in a hard *whump*. Her limbs flailed at nothing, fingers twitching on the hilt of her sword as gravity sucked her back to the floor.

She landed on her lower back with a bone-rattling crash and skidded across the dusty floor. Stars popped in front of her eyes and the ceiling spun above her, filled with panicked bats swooping among the rafters. Sword. Where was her sword? She felt the hilt. Still in her hand. *Okay.* Okay, but she needed air. Her ribs twitched, but no air would come.

Golems loomed in her vision. She bent her knees, dragged her feet closer, and rolled onto one elbow, but her chest was on fire, and her breath wouldn't come. There were three of them, one with a missing arm, closing in around her, their eyes glowing and their feet thumping on the marble.

Get up! Hat shrieked. *Get up!*

She tried to roll onto her knees, struggling for a sip of air, but the floor tilted, and she fell back on one elbow.

"Julie!"

An arrow slashed through the chink in the neck of the nearest golem. It slapped a giant hand to its throat, eyes widening as its head turned to ash.

Taylor burst between the other two, grabbed Julie's arm, and hauled her to her feet. The movement forced her nerves back to life. Air rushed into her lungs, and her head cleared as she raised her sword. They had their backs to the staircase at the end of the room, and the golems advanced. Many remained, and the banshee hovered behind them with her tortured eyes fixed on Julie and Taylor.

"Are you okay?" Taylor yelled, nocking another arrow.

"Just winded," Julie croaked. She raised her sword. "Let's kick some golem ass."

Taylor let the arrow fly. It hissed, straight and true, toward the nearest golem's neck. The stone creature moved with unthinkable speed. It plucked the arrow out of the air and crushed it in a giant fist.

"Shit," Taylor spat. He shoved the bow into his quiver and grabbed his staff instead. Sending a plume of blue fire spitting into the golems, Taylor swiped the staff right and left, surrounding them with an arc of flame.

The golems trampled through the fire, their hands balled into fists.

Julie glanced behind her. The gaunt man was still up there.

Necromancer, Hat hissed. *The most evil kind of wizard there is.*

"Taylor, behind us," Julie croaked, eyeing the nearest golem. "Shoot him. I'll cover you."

Taylor glanced at her, then nodded. He switched his staff for his bow again, nocking an arrow. Julie struck at the nearest golem, slashing her blade into the chink behind its knee; it fell to its knees, foot crumbling, and the golem behind it tripped hard and fell close enough that she could stab it in the shoulder.

Taylor screamed.

Julie whipped around. Taylor's bow and arrow clattered to the ground. His feet kicked at thin air, eyes wide, his throat wrapped in the long white fingers of the banshee.

"Taylor!" Julie screamed.

The necromancer's cackle echoed through the hall as the banshee rose, Taylor borne helplessly upward. His face turned scarlet as he clawed at the hands locked around his throat.

Do something! Julie shrieked at Hat.

On your left! Hat yelled.

Julie dodged as the golem struck at her. Its fist missed her face, but the golem behind it didn't miss. Its blow hammered into her back, sending her flying forward. She landed heavily on her hands and knees, and pain jolted through her limbs. Her sword skidded out of her hands.

She rolled onto her back. The golems kept advancing, and Taylor was twenty feet off the ground near the ceiling of the hall, his struggles growing weaker, his face going from red to blue—

Glass shattered, and light poured into the hall. The golems froze, looking up, and the air filled with roaring and feathers.

Six griffins swooped into the hall, each wearing a collar with a glowing golden pendant that filled the hall with warm light. Their amber eyes were afire, their claws outstretched and fangs flashing as they roared their battle cries.

NO! Hat screamed.

Julie looked up. The banshee had let go of Taylor. He fell, limp and lifeless, hair whipping around his face.

CHAPTER FIFTEEN

"*Taylor!*" Julie shrieked.

A griffin swooped under Taylor's falling form. Julie saw a flash of feathery wings and got a glimpse of armor, then thin arms plucked Taylor out of mid-air and pulled him to safety over the griffin's shoulders.

"Gotcha!" Bianca yelled from the griffin's back.

Four griffins landed soundlessly and charged at the golems, their claws slashing at the chinks in the golems' limbs. Ash filled the air. Above them, a griffin seized the banshee in its claws and they tumbled over and over in the air, scratching and screaming like fighting cats. Julie let out a roar of fury and beheaded the golem in front of her, then kicked aside its falling body as she ran across the hall to where Bianca and her griffin had landed.

"Taylor!" Julie exclaimed.

"He's okay. He's okay," Bianca soothed.

Taylor slithered down from the griffin's back, face ashen. He had red lines on his neck where the banshee had clutched him.

"Are you okay?" Julie grabbed him by the front of his shirt.

"I'm fine," Taylor croaked. "Where's my bow? I didn't shoot him."

"Who?" Bianca demanded.

Julie pointed. The necromancer was still at the top of the stairs, skinny hands clenched into fists as he watched the griffins tearing his golems apart. Green light oozed from his hands and curled around his fingers.

"My bow," Taylor wheezed. He took a step forward, and both knees buckled.

Julie threw an arm around his chest, barely catching him. "Taylor?"

"Dizzy." Taylor grunted and sagged to the floor.

"Stay with him," Bianca ordered. She threw a leg over her griffin's shoulders and slid to the floor, and her leathery wings unfurled. "I've got that bitch."

Julie stood over Taylor, sword in hand. The griffin leaped into the sky to assist his companion, who was still locked in battle with the banshee. Griffins and golems filled the hall's floor, fighting hard, and fur and ash flew. Bianca strode toward the middle of the fight. Red light oozed from her wings and horns and fingers.

The necromancer strode down the staircase, his green light intensifying.

The fight parted before Bianca like the Red Sea. She kept walking, her leather boots clopping loudly on the floor, her wings spreading wider and red light balling and crackling between them.

"She's not armed," Julie hissed, putting a hand on Taylor's shoulder. "Should I throw her my sword?"

Taylor managed a strangled chuckle. "I don't think she needs it."

There was a feline shriek. One of the golems had seized a griffin by its wings and lifted her into the air above its head, then flung her toward Bianca. The griffin flew through the air, helpless, wings and tail lashing uselessly. Bianca held out a hand, and the griffin was surrounded by tendrils of red light that carried her gently over the succubus' head and lowered her to the ground. Bianca's eyes were still fixed on the necromancer. She mounted the staircase in sure strides.

The necromancer let out a yell. Raising his fists, he thrust them toward Bianca, and green light exploded out of them and hurtled toward the succubus. She stepped aside, and the light arced past her and slammed into two of the golems, exploding them.

Before the necromancer could ready another blast, Bianca ran up the stairs. She jumped, planted the soles of her boots against the railing, and shot a blast of red light at him from the side. The necromancer barely dodged as Bianca somersaulted onto her feet again and raised both hands.

Red light formed two long whips, the tendrils dancing above her head. The necromancer flung an arc of green light into her stomach. The whips disappeared and Bianca was thrown back, boots skidding on the floor, hands scrabbling for purchase, wings flailing. She thumped to a halt against the rail of the staircase and fell on her face, then her beating wings dragged her back to her feet.

She flipped her blonde curls out of her face and spat a mouthful of blood on the floor. Her blue eyes locked onto the necromancer, and she grinned.

He let out a yell and punched his fists toward her. When the green light shot toward Bianca, she responded with a red blast of her own. The two blasts met halfway between them and erupted into a crackling ball of power, yellow arcs of electricity spurting from it. The ball grew and filled the hall with dancing light. Bianca's grin widened. She took a step toward the necromancer and the ball edged closer to him, red creeping through the yellow and the green light growing dimmer.

The necromancer gave a defiant shriek and stepped forward,

and a fresh pulse of green light traveled into the ball. It glowed yellow for an instant. Then Bianca roared, tossing her horns and curls, and a burst of red light crackled from her. It surged through the ball of light and struck the necromancer with a blinding flash.

There was a deafening crack. The necromancer was thrown back and he slammed into the floor on his back, flailing as he skidded.

"Look!" Taylor coughed. "The golems!"

The golems' movements turned jerky and slowed. The nearest one was throwing a punch at a griffin's face. Its fist slowed, and the light in its eyes dimmed. The golem became a statue once more. The light winked out, and it stood motionless, as did every other golem in the room.

From above them came a terrible wail. Julie looked up. The banshee, one arm clutched in a griffin's claws, tore free. She looked around the hall wildly and vanished into thin air.

"It's over, necromancer." Bianca's voice echoed from the top of the staircase. She strode toward the necromancer, who was struggling to his feet.

"My powers," the necromancer gasped, shaking his hands. "My *powers*!"

"They're gone." Bianca grabbed a pair of handcuffs—magic-nulling restraints, Julie remembered—from her belt and slapped them on him. When she hauled him to his feet, he looked far less like the scary wizard he'd been a few minutes ago. He drooped in his dark robes, a stooped and balding figure with a paunch.

"Get back to the portal and take him to the PMA," Bianca commanded. "And you two. Get yourselves to Dr. Olena."

One of the griffins came up and snarled at the necromancer. He trembled as the griffin seized his arm in her mouth and dragged him out of the farmhouse. Two griffins followed, one with a drooping wing, one limping on a front paw.

Bianca strode up to Julie and Taylor, slapping her hands clean. "Kaplan was right. You two *are* trouble."

Taylor struggled to his feet, coughing. "My sister is in here somewhere."

Bianca's eyes met his, and she nodded. "Let's find her."

"Are you okay to walk?" Julie asked.

Taylor nodded. "Feeling better," he rasped.

"Amazing how being able to breathe does that to you," Hat commented.

Bianca led the way across the hall, and they mounted the staircase. The griffins' collars made the hall look old and abandoned instead of haunted, although the frozen golems all over the floor were still creepy.

"How did you *do* that?" Julie asked. "Take away his powers?"

Bianca laughed over her shoulder. "A necromancer's powers are rooted in evil and death." She held out a hand, palm up, fingers wiggling, and a ball of red light formed over her palm. "Succubi are creatures of love. Neither death nor evil stands a chance against that."

Two halls split off from the top of the stairs. Bianca closed her hand, and the red light disappeared. "I'll take the left, and you take the right. We shouldn't be attacked by any more nasties now that the necromancer is gone."

Julie nodded.

Shouldn't, Hat grumbled.

"Let's have some light in any case." Taylor pulled out his staff, and the gem's blue glow illuminated a long hallway carpeted with a geometric pattern.

"Why is *The Shining*'s carpet in here?" Julie demanded.

Taylor shrugged. "Where do you think they got the idea?"

"Whatever, man." Julie gripped her sword. "I'm just saying, if I see twin girls, I'm killing them with fire."

"Not a fan of scary movies?" Taylor guessed as they slunk down the passage, their feet almost soundless on the carpet.

Julie snorted. "My life is scary enough, thanks."

Taylor chuckled.

The first door led to a room containing hundreds of porcelain dolls with dead glass eyes.

"Nope." Julie slammed the door. "Nopity-nope-nope. No way and no how. It's not happening. I'm not going in there."

"Let's try this one." Taylor pushed another one open.

The door swung inward with a long creak, and they were in a huge old ballroom, all black drapes and candlesticks and cobwebs. Two humanoid paras huddled in the center of the room, staring at the three inert golems that surrounded them.

"Malcolm!" Julie yelled.

The vampire jumped to his feet. "I told you they'd come!" he declared triumphantly.

A tall figure rose beside him, tossing a silver braid over his shoulder. Lotan. "Who are you?" He sniffed, staring at Julie.

"Your rescuer." She beamed at him. "You're welcome."

"How did you find us?" Malcolm asked.

"Magic." Julie wiggled her fingers. "Where's Ilsa?"

"I don't know." Malcolm's face fell. "They separated us. The necromancer said something about a family reunion."

Taylor's eyes widened. "Uncle Arion." He swallowed. "Come on. We've got to find her."

With Malcolm and Lotan hot on their heels, they hurried from room to room. Many were empty, although one was full of clown suits, which gave Malcolm the heebie-jeebies.

"I'm just saying." The vampire shuddered. "Something's just not right about clowns."

Taylor's face was pale. "Where *is* she?"

The blue glow of his staff illuminated a low door at the end of the hallway, all wood and wrought iron. It had a massive keyhole, but when Taylor pushed it, it swung open. The smell of mold and wet rock filled the air.

"Let me go first." Julie brandished the Soul Cleaver and

ducked through the door, holding up the sword. Blue light filled the small stone cell. Chains shone on the walls, and there was trash heaped in the corners. On the far side of the room was Ilsa, hands chained above her head.

"Ilsa!" Taylor gasped and pushed past Julie.

"Hey, little bro," the elf princess croaked. A weak smile flitted across her face.

Beside her, a burly male elf was chained just as she was. His face was gaunt and pale, and his wrists had been rubbed red by the shackles. "Taylor?" he gasped.

"It's okay, Uncle. We're getting you out of here." Taylor ran up to Ilsa and grabbed at the shackles.

"Free him first." Ilsa nodded at Arion. "He's been here for a long time."

"Let me help." Malcolm hurried up to Taylor. "I can pick those locks with my claws."

"How come you know how to pick a lock?" Ilsa teased.

Malcolm raised an eyebrow. "Are you complaining?"

"Maybe there are keys in these trash heaps." Julie held up the Soul Cleaver and used its light to pick through the nearest pile. There were a lot of bones and rags, the corpses of a few rats, and something else—an egg-shaped object the size of a watermelon in purest black. Obsidian, Julie realized. She hesitantly reached out and brushed the cold black surface. It was hard and smooth.

"What is this?" she murmured, putting down her sword. Gripping it with both hands, she lifted it out of the trash.

"Oh." Hat sighed. "Oh, that's not good."

Julie looked down at the obsidian object. She could barely see her reflection in its surface.

"It's a dragon egg," Hat murmured.

"Whoa." Julie held it tightly and stared into it. She remembered the first time she'd seen a dragon on her first trip to Avalon, a huge beast with glittering scales and broad wings. She could still see that giant eye looking into hers and smell the smoke it huffed into her face as it swooped over her. It had been the most beautiful thing she'd ever seen, and the memory made her heart pound. "So, the necromancer took it from its parents."

"Yes," Hat sighed.

"Poor thing." Julie smoothed a hand over the surface, wondering if she'd been taken from her real parents, too. She pushed the thought aside. *Mom and Dad* are *my real parents*. "We will take it back." She pictured the tiny dragon within, curled up snugly, tail wrapped around it, tiny wings furled against its back.

"I'm sorry, Julie. That's not going to happen." Hat paused. "The dragon inside is dead. The necromancer must have killed it."

Julie's world jolted and she sagged to her knees, the egg in her lap. "Why?" she gasped. "Why would anyone do that?"

Ilsa came closer and rested a hand on Julie's shoulder. "I don't understand it either."

"It was helpless," Julie cried. "It never did anything wrong, and it could have had a wonderful life." *A life like Lillie's.* Tears choked her throat as memories crashed over her head like a tidal wave. *Oh, Lillie.* Today had been the first day she had almost been able to forget about going home to an empty house tonight.

She swallowed hard, conscious of everyone looking at her, but one tear escaped. It slid down her cheek and landed softly on the surface of the egg. She reached over to wipe it away, but the tear sank in, absorbed into the egg.

"I'm so sorry," she whispered, "I didn't..." She paused. Had she seen a glimmer of color on the egg's surface? Silver?

"Look!" Taylor gasped.

The egg's surface rippled. It felt the same in her arms, but something briefly danced within, silver and black like moonlight on water.

Silence fell in the cell.

Hat cleared his non-existent throat. "My bad. Looks like it just needed some love."

The Para-ER was the fullest Julie had ever seen it, not least because two of Dr. Olena's patients were griffins. They sat on comfortable beds on the floor, their wings and paws being bandaged.

Taylor flinched when Dr. Olena touched the black bruises forming on his throat.

"Sorry." The elf winced with him. "These are nasty." She checked the pulse oximeter on his finger. "I can't believe you weren't killed."

"It was a close thing." Julie shifted her weight. She was sitting on the hospital bed next to Taylor.

"Isn't that heavy?" Dr. Olena asked. "You can put it down, you know. It's not a chicken egg. It doesn't need to be kept warm."

Julie's arms tightened around the egg. They ached with its weight. "No, it's okay. I think I'll hold onto it."

Dr. Olena shrugged. "Suit yourself." She wiggled her fingers, and blue light gathered between them and threaded onto Taylor's bruises. They rapidly faded.

"How's Ilsa?" Taylor croaked.

"Shhh. I'm busy," Dr. Olena grumbled. "But she's fine. Got a broken ankle in the fight, but it's fixed, and I sent her to a private room to rest for the night. It will take Arion a few days to recover, but he's basically fit."

"And Kellian?" Julie asked. "She looked rough when Bianca found her in that house while we were rescuing Ilsa and Arion."

"I think it was mostly phone withdrawal symptoms." Dr. Olena shrugged. "Once she had her phone back, she perked up remarkably."

"I can't believe that that necromancer kidnapped so many of the heirs." Julie shook her head.

Dr. Olena nodded. "Saving them might stave off the war a little longer. A good day's work for you two."

The bruises on Taylor's throat had vanished. He cleared it, then rubbed a hand over the skin. "Thanks, Doctor. That was uncomfortable."

Dr. Olena turned to Julie. "How do those stitches feel?"

Julie flexed her forearm. "They pull a little, but they're okay."

"Good. I'll prescribe Tylenol for a few days." Dr. Olena paused, glancing at Taylor. "Do you have a minute to go over your results, seeing that I can't seem to get you to come down here?"

"They're back?" Julie frowned.

Hat coughed. "Oh, yes. I didn't tell you about the text message."

"Text message?" Julie pulled him off and glared at him. "Have you been tampering with my phone?"

Hat, now a black fedora, squirmed in her hands. "I wouldn't call it *tampering*. You had other things to attend to."

Julie sighed. "Sure, Doc. We can talk about them if you want. In the lab, maybe?" She glanced at Taylor, who frowned.

Before Dr. Olena could respond, Taylor's phone buzzed. He pulled it out. "Oh, great. It's Kaplan, and he wants to see us right now. Like, *right* now. You, Bianca, and me."

"Clearly, they dealt with the emergency at the Eternal Palace, whatever it was," Julie grumbled.

"I have no idea about that." Dr. Olena shrugged. "It's okay. We'll talk later."

Julie clutched the egg firmly in her arms as she and Taylor headed for the elevator. The elf looked at her, raising an eyebrow. "Hey, is everything okay with your blood results? Seems like Dr. Olena's run a lot of tests."

"Oh, yes. Everything's fine," Julie mumbled. Now wasn't the time to tell him that she wasn't human.

Not because Taylor wouldn't understand but because she didn't.

Kaplan glared over the desk, his amber eyes drilling into the egg in Julie's arms. "Is anyone going to tell me what you're doing with *that*?"

Julie sank into one of the armchairs, her legs exhausted. "It's a dragon egg."

"I can see that it's a dragon egg," Kaplan barked. "What are *you* doing with it?"

Taylor gestured at the other empty chair, allowing Bianca to take it. She cocked an eyebrow at him, smirked, and sashayed into it, leaving the elf to stand.

"We found it in the haunted house," Julie told Kaplan. "It's still alive, and it needs to go back to its parents."

"Amazingly, Meadows, I was able to draw that conclusion by myself," Kaplan growled. "Nox!"

Malcolm popped his head around the door. Apparently, being kidnapped didn't mean he could have a day off work. "Yes, Uncle Jack?"

"Take that thing to the Warehouse for storage until it can be returned to the Lords of the Deep." Kaplan pointed at the egg with a pen.

"What? No!" Julie clung to it. "You can't put it in *storage*. It's alive. It needs to be nurtured."

Kaplan huffed. "Do I have to keep reminding you that we are shorthanded as a military agency, Meadows? We're a little short on dragon nursemaids."

"I'll take care of it." Julie tipped up her chin.

Kaplan held her gaze for a few moments, then sighed, shaking his head. "Fine. If you're that overprotective, you'll have to take it back to the Lords of the Deep, too."

"I will." Julie looked at the egg. "I won't let anything happen to it." She stroked it with a thumb. "But first, I want to see the necromancer's interrogation."

Kaplan's eyes narrowed. "Need I remind you, Meadows, that you're in no position to make demands after you and Woodskin made an unauthorized excursion into a highly dangerous situation, placing yourselves, the heirs of multiple thrones, and the agency as a whole at risk?"

"Sir." Bianca folded her arms. "Woodskin and Meadows were acting on my orders."

Kaplan glared at her. "*Your* orders?"

"Yes. I am their commanding officer, am I not?" Bianca raised an eyebrow.

She is cool after all, Julie thought.

Hat snickered. *I'd argue that she's more* hot *than cool.*

Julie rolled her eyes.

Kaplan spread his hands. "Very well." He hesitated, gazing at Julie. "I will be interrogating the necromancer with Hartshorn's assistance. You two may watch."

"Thank you, sir," Taylor gushed.

Julie held the egg tighter.

Kaplan got to his feet and huffed. "Yes, Meadows, you can bring the egg."

He swept out of the office with Bianca right behind him. Julie followed on tired limbs.

"Can I carry it for you?" Taylor held out his arms.

"No." Julie hugged it, lowering her voice. "It was cool of Bianca to cover for us."

"She's better than I gave her credit for." Taylor smiled.

"I don't think Kaplan would have punished us." Julie patted the egg. "Considering how many lives we saved."

Taylor laughed. "I'm not sure he sees it that way."

"Hurry up, you two," the captain barked from the elevator. "I'm ready to hang the Dark Moon League up by their ankles."

Julie hurried into the elevator. "Do you think they're behind this, sir?"

"Them, or some other connection to the Sylthana Elves." Kaplan hit the button.

"Lotan was kidnapped, too," Julie pointed out.

"Kidnapped and unharmed. The perfect cover." The weretiger folded his enormous arms. "Either way, we'll soon find out. We finally have someone we can get solid intel out of."

CHAPTER SIXTEEN

Horusiris sat on the table in the small room next to Julie, looking through the one-way mirror into the interrogation room. The Sphynx purred, and his hairless front paws kneaded the table in front of him. He didn't blink his pale eyes as he stared into the room.

Julie ached to ask him what species she was. She had a feeling Horusiris knew and had known for a long time. However, Taylor sat next to her in one of the uncomfortable plastic chairs the room was furnished with, so she stayed quiet, holding the egg steady in her lap.

Kaplan paced in front of the window, hands behind his back, holding a file in one of them.

Under the brutal fluorescent lighting and wearing an orange jumpsuit, the necromancer had lost his intimidating edge. Now, with the remains of his quiff straggling over his balding head and his dark eyes darting around the room, he looked about as scary as someone's emo teenager who'd never grown up.

"You will regret treating the Great Ouroboros this way!" he hissed, but as he spoke, his eyes darted to the corner of the room, where Bianca lounged against the wall, arms folded.

Kaplan whirled and slammed the file on the steel table in front of the necromancer, and his words came out in a tiger's snarl. "Save the theatrics." He leaned forward, his nose inches from the necromancer's face. "Your name is Kevin Greenlaw, and you have a rap sheet of petty crimes as long as my arm." He opened the file and flipped through it. "Starting with disfiguring enchantments of a fellow student at the first warlock school you ever attended. It gets worse from there."

Kevin leaned back in his chair, eyes wide. The farther he leaned back, the more Kaplan leaned forward.

"Regardless of what you do, you're headed for the Locker," Kaplan growled. "The only thing you have the power to affect is how long you spend there." He flopped back into the chair opposite Kevin, folding his arms. "Now sing, little birdie."

"Okay, okay!" Kevin tried to hold up his hands but flinched when the handcuffs yanked at his wrists. "I'll tell you everything, but I don't know much. I swear it."

"Don't know much, do you?" Kaplan snapped. *"Don't know much?* How can you kidnap five of the heirs to the seven royal families without 'knowing much?'"

"It wasn't my idea, okay?" Kevin spluttered. "I was just doing what I was told."

"What was that?" Kaplan demanded.

Kevin took a deep breath. "Someone offered me the opportunity of a lifetime. I'd only been doing petty necromancy like you said. A ghoul here, a wraith there. Mostly scaring people. Bachelor parties, that sort of thing. It's not easy to find work as a warlock when there's so much stigma against necromancy."

"Stigma against necromancy?" Taylor raised an eyebrow. "That's like saying there's a stigma against murder or grand theft auto."

Julie snorted.

"But my boss saw my talent. They knew I could do bigger

things." Kevin's eyes gleamed. "They gave me the resources I needed to really shine."

"Someone paid you to do this?" Kaplan snarled.

Kevin nodded. "Oh, yes. Handsomely, too—life-changing money. I had everything I needed at my disposal. All I had to do was hire some mercenaries to kidnap those heirs and steal that dragon egg, then keep them hidden in the house."

Julie gently stroked the egg's surface. "It's okay," she whispered. "You're okay. No one's ever going to hurt you again."

Kaplan leaned forward. "Who hired you?"

Kevin raised his chin. "I won't tell. They'll break me out. They'll get me out of this. They'll—"

Kaplan lunged to his feet and slammed his hands on the table on either side of Kevin's. His roar ripped through the interrogation room and made everyone jump, even Bianca.

"Who hired you?" the weretiger thundered. Red and black fur sprouted on the backs of his hands.

"I don't know! I don't know!" Kevin held up his hands, whimpering the words. "I don't know, okay? I never met them. They never told me. I don't know who it was!"

Julie snorted. "A likely story." She touched the stitches on her forearm with her fingertips.

"He's telling the truth, I'm afraid." Horusiris got up and stretched, his tail curling over his back.

"Then how did your employer contact you?" Kaplan growled, the fur on his hands receding.

Kevin trembled, swallowing hard. "I...don't know." He frowned.

"Don't play games with me, necromancer," Kaplan rumbled.

"He's not playing games," Horusiris murmured.

"Another geas?" Julie asked, shoulders slumping.

The Sphynx stretched his hind legs this time and yawned massively, showing off white teeth. "Oh, not this time. This feels like a mind-wipe."

"So, that's it." Taylor folded his arms. "We're not going to get any information out of the guy who kidnapped my *sister?*"

Julie put a hand on his arm. He was trembling with rage.

"Not necessarily." Horusiris chuckled. "We have...ways of clarifying memories." He began to lick his paws.

"Remind me not to get on your catty side," Julie muttered.

Very droll, Hat grumbled.

Kaplan slammed out of the interview room, leaving Kevin to stare at Bianca. She gave him a little wave that made him jump in his chair. The door to the observation room crashed open, and Kaplan stormed in.

"Tell me that that necromancer hasn't been mind-wiped, Sphynx," he barked.

The Sphynx purred. "You want me to lie to you?"

"I thought so." Kaplan pinched the bridge of his nose with two enormous fingers. "We'll have to work on his memories. It's going to be a long process." He huffed and pressed the button for the intercom to the interview room. "Take him back to holding, Bianca. We're going to take a different approach."

He shot Julie a glare. "Meadows, Woodskin, get some rest. You've caused enough trouble for one day."

Horusiris and Kaplan left, talking in low voices. Bianca hustled Kevin off to Holding. Taylor held the door for Julie as they left the room and headed down the hall to the elevator.

"Want a ride home?" Julie asked.

The elf shook his head. "It's okay. I'll have dinner with Ilsa in her hospital room first. Check that she's okay."

You should go with him, Hat murmured. *Dr. Olena was desperate to talk to you.*

Julie's stomach knotted at the thought.

I know it's frightening, but don't you want to know for sure what species you are? Hat asked.

"Uh, Julie?" Taylor waved a hand in front of her face. "You okay?"

Before Julie could answer, her phone rang, chiming loudly in the elevator's enclosed space. She plucked it out of her pocket, hugging the dragon egg with one arm. The sight of her mom's name on the screen teased a breath out of her tense chest, and a smile tugged at her lips as she raised the phone to her ear. "Hey, Mom!"

"Hello, my sweetest baby. How's your day been?" Rosa asked.

Julie smiled. *Well, I fought an army of ghouls and wraiths and golems, and there was also a necromancer and banshee involved. Taylor almost got killed, but our succubus boss came to our rescue just in time, so we* did *retrieve some of the most important people in the world.* "It's been fine. Good, actually."

"That's good news, honey. I'm glad you went to work today. It was the right choice," her mother told her. "Are you on your way home?"

"What time is it?" Julie asked.

"Just after five, honey, but don't worry if you're still at work. I just didn't want to bother you while you're busy."

"No, that's okay. I was just leaving."

"Okay, good. I wanted to run something past you, but feel free to say no if you like."

I could get used to Mom being this nice. Julie chuckled inwardly. "What's up, Mom?"

"Ernesto misses me, baby. Do you think it would be okay if he came to pick me up tomorrow morning?"

Julie blew out a slow breath, thinking about that empty house.

Hey, you won't be alone, Hat reminded her.

"Yeah, sure, Mom. That's fine." Julie shifted her grip on the egg. "I'll be home soon. I can help you pack if you want."

"That would be amazing, sweetie. I'll order pizza," her mother offered.

Julie smiled. "That sounds great. See you later, Mom."

"Bye, honey."

Julie hung up, tucked the phone back into her pocket, and

glanced at Taylor. "I'd have loved to come with you to see Ilsa, but I need to get home and help Mom pack."

"Of course. No worries." Taylor smiled.

The elevator trundled up to the lobby. Julie passed the egg to her other arm. When the doors slid open, she stepped out. "Bye, Taylor."

"See you tomorrow to take that egg back to its people." Taylor hesitated. "Hey, Julie?"

"Yeah?" Julie turned back.

Taylor shifted his weight from foot to foot. "You know you can call me anytime, right? If the house starts to feel empty, or anything." He cleared his throat.

Julie nodded. "I know. Thanks."

Taylor's cheeks grayed. He nodded and hit the button, and the elevator doors slid shut.

Cardboard boxes were all over the spare room in Lillie's house. Even though Julie knew that all of her mother's stuff had made it here in those boxes, the thought of packing everything into them again seemed impossible. She tried to squash a gigantic floral bedspread into one of the boxes, but it kept unfolding and sprawling out on the floor.

"Are you *sure* this is the right box for this, Mom?" Julie grunted, wrestling it down again.

Rosa was bubble-wrapping a bedside lamp. "Of course, honey. It arrived in that box, didn't it?"

"I don't know. Did it?" Julie grabbed the packing tape off the bed.

Rosa held up the bubble-wrapped lamp. "Do you think it's okay like this, or should I add another layer?"

"It won't fit into the box if you do that." Julie pummeled the bedspread into submission and squashed the top of the box down over it. "What did you need your bedside lamp for, anyway? Lillie has hundreds."

"I do like my creature comforts, honey." Rosa tucked the lamp into a box. "Need a hand there?"

Julie was trying to tear a strip of packing tape off the roll with her teeth. "Mmmhmm."

Rosa came over and squashed down the box's lid while Julie taped it securely. It bulged dangerously on the sides, and Julie had visions of her mother's bedding floating all over the U-Haul truck that would pick up her stuff.

"There!" Rosa stepped back, hands on her hips. "Fits perfectly."

"If you say so." Julie straightened and stretched her back. She glanced around the room, which had full cardboard boxes everywhere. Soon it would be quiet and empty and dusty again, the way this guest room had always been.

The only difference was that the living room would be the same, and the kitchen and Lillie's bedroom. The house seemed so quiet without *Judge Judy* in the background.

There was a soft chirp, and Fluffy walked into the bedroom. He arched his back against Julie's knees but didn't purr.

"Hey, buddy." Julie scooped him into her arms and buried her face in his thick white fur. "I miss her too." She blinked furiously against the tears that burned her eyes. "I-I guess I'll have to pack up all of Lillie's things soon."

Rosa put a hand on her arm. "It all depends on the estate, honey. Are you sure you don't want me to stay until that is settled?"

Julie raised her face out of the cat's fur, cuddling him in her arms. She shook her head, swallowing tears. "It's okay, Mom. You've got your life to get back to, but thank you so much." She swallowed again. "I don't know what I would have done without you."

"Aw, honey, what else are mommas for?" Rosa hugged her and the cat. "You sure you'll be okay?"

"I'll be fine." Julie nodded. "I'll call you if I'm not."

"That's my baby girl." Rosa beamed. "Want to take a break for some tea?"

Julie shook her head and lowered Fluffy onto the bed. "It's okay. I'd rather keep going if it's all the same to you. I've got a long day at work tomorrow."

"Seems like they're *all* long days," Rosa grumbled. She opened the closet door and took out a few dresses on hangers, including a little black number Julie didn't want to imagine on her mother's body.

Julie tugged her mother's suitcase out from under the bed and opened it. "What's that supposed to mean?"

"Just that you've been burying yourself in work since Lillie got sick, honey." Rosa gave her a pointed look as she folded one of the dresses. "I hope you're not off on another trip."

Julie cleared her throat. "It's just a day trip."

"Honey!" Rosa shook her head. "You have *got* to give yourself some time."

Fluffy got into the suitcase and sat there with his tail curled around his paws. Julie scooped him out of it and flicked away some of his long white hairs. "It's easier to focus on work than home right now," she admitted.

"That may be true, baby, but you need to be careful with your health. Burning yourself out won't help anyone," her mother pointed out.

"I know." Julie shrugged. "I just have a lot to do, that's all." *Like taking a dragon's egg home to its parents.* The egg was currently wrapped in blankets in Julie's bed, much to Hat's amusement.

"Work isn't everything, baby. Just take care of yourself, okay?" Rosa reached over and squeezed Julie's hand. "And allow yourself to be sad sometimes. It's okay."

Julie nodded, and the lump grew in her throat again. She stroked Fluffy's back, wondering what would happen to him and Pookie now that Lillie was gone. So far, she hadn't heard from Lillie's family.

"And if you have to cut loose sometimes and treat yourself, you do that," her mother added. "Especially when it comes to Tyler."

"Do you mean Taylor?" Julie raised her eyebrows.

Rosa raised a brow. "Don't think I didn't see you sobbing in his arms, baby. Take advantage of that. There's nothing a man likes more than a damsel in distress."

Julie felt her cheeks burning. "Mom! Seriously? I am *not* a damsel in distress!"

"He doesn't need to know that, does he?" Rosa smirked.

Julie groaned. "Mom!"

Rosa chuckled and tickled the cat under the chin. "I'm just saying, honey. Everyone deserves to find true love." Her eyes grew misty. "I've been lucky twice."

Julie smiled. "You know I love you, right, Mom?"

"You bet I do." Her mother returned the smile. "Hey, do you know what would help keep you from burning out?"

"What?" Julie looked at her.

Rosa beamed. "Aloe vera juice!"

Julie burst out laughing, wrapped her arms around her mother, and held her tight.

Julie pulled a handful of sugar cubes out of her pocket. "Hey, Sleipnir. I remembered your sugar this time."

The eight-legged horse nickered in recognition and lipped them out of her hand. His stall in the PMA's parking garage was right next to Genevieve's parking bay. Julie dusted the sugar off her hands, then opened Genevieve's passenger door. The egg was wrapped in a blanket on the seat and secured by the seatbelt.

"Heavy egg." Julie grunted after unclipping the seatbelt, having had to grab the egg to keep it from rolling on the floor.

Hat chuckled. "Need some help with your little one?" He hopped off the dash. *Poof!* The purple beret was replaced by a blue baby carrier.

Julie rolled her eyes and scooped the egg into her arms. "Helpful."

"You don't like the color?" The baby carrier turned pastel pink, adorned with unicorns and flowers.

"Adorable." Julie snorted, feeling a weight she didn't know she was carrying lift from her shoulders. Not the egg, though. That was a weight her aching shoulders were very aware of.

Hat turned back into a beret, and Julie flipped him onto her head before quickly returning both hands to the egg. She shut Genevieve's door with one hip and plodded out of the garage, hugging the egg close.

Automatically, Julie's feet turned toward the gym. She shook her head and turned toward the main building instead. "Nearly forgot we don't have training today, even though I got an extra hour's sleep."

Hat snorted. "In my day, young knights trained with broken limbs, never mind a few little stitches."

"Uphill in the snow, both ways?" Julie quipped.

"Hilarious." Hat scoffed.

"Okay, boomer," Julie teased.

"Hey, who are you calling a boomer?" Taylor stepped out of the cafeteria, holding out a chocolate muffin. "Can I carry the egg for you?"

"No thanks, but hang onto the muffin." Julie grinned. "I'll want that in a minute."

"Deal." Taylor fell into step beside her, heading for the elevator. "Do you know if our paperwork is ready for the trip to the Deep yet?"

"Kaplan said to come and see him first thing. I think he pulled some strings to make it happen quickly." Julie waited, cradling the egg, as Taylor hit the button.

They stepped into the elevator. "I'm willing to bet he's ready to have his best recruiter back with both hands unoccupied." Taylor grinned.

Julie held it closer to her chest.

"Did it sleep in your bed?" Taylor joked.

Julie's cheeks burned.

"Wait, you didn't *really* sleep with a dragon egg in your bed?" Taylor's eyebrows shot up.

"Where else was it supposed to sleep?" Julie demanded. "On the floor?"

Taylor shook his head. "You do know there's a dragon in there, right? A powerful, magical, and practically immortal being?"

"So?" Julie hugged the egg. "It felt safer there."

"Oh, so you have dragon egg telepathy," Taylor commented. "Amazing."

Julie elbowed him in the ribs. He clutched them, laughing. "Ow!"

The elevator came to a halt, and they crossed the floor to Kaplan's office. The weretiger glared at them over his computer screen when they came in. "Here to do your little personal errand on company time, Meadows?"

Julie raised an eyebrow. "I'll be sure to tell the Lords of the Deep that returning their heir to its rightful home is considered a recruiter's personal errand, sir."

Kaplan snorted. "It's far too early in the morning for you to be this sassy, Meadows. Just take the egg back safely and get your ass into your office for once, got it?" He held out a sheaf of paperwork. "The portal to the Deep is in the military wing. You'll need to show this to the guards for them to let you through."

Taylor took the paperwork.

Julie met Kaplan's eyes. "Thank you, sir."

He held her gaze for a moment, nodding. "Dragon escorts will be waiting for you on the other side of the portal. Get your sorry asses down there."

CHAPTER SEVENTEEN

If Julie was expecting a medieval armory rattling with knights, she was disappointed by the military wing.

The elevator had moved nauseatingly sideways to take them there, and when they stepped out into the reception area, Julie blinked at a huge, bustling room with gray carpet and rows of desks. Phones rang everywhere, and paranormals in blue and brown uniforms hustled in all directions.

There were a few curious stares in the direction of the dragon egg before a familiar werewolf pushed through the crowd and strode toward them. "Hi, Julie! Hey, Taylor!"

"Hello, Teddy." Julie grinned at the short, stocky Were. "Are you our guide today?"

"Only to the portal. The dragons will take you from there." Teddy sighed. "I'm so jealous. Isaiah and Chester got to go to the Ice Palace, and you two are going into the Deep. All I get to do is take you down a hall."

They fell into step behind the Were, who led them across the reception area.

"You *did* get to fight an army of yetis when you'd only been in training for a matter of days," Julie pointed out.

Teddy shrugged. "I guess I can't have all the luck." He started down a corridor that ended in a metal gate. "Got your paperwork?"

Taylor held it out. The somber gargoyle manning the gate glared at the papers, then slowly pulled the gate open to allow them through.

"How are the others?" Taylor asked.

"We're all great." Teddy grinned. "Living the soldier life. We're looking forward to doing that recruitment video you told us about."

"Later this week," Taylor promised.

They reached a sturdy barred door guarded by two orcs with rifles slung over their backs and halberds in their hands.

"'Sup, fellas," Teddy chirped.

The orcs didn't return his cheery greeting. They read every page of the paperwork slowly and with laborious attention. Julie's arms were stinging with the weight of the egg when they finally unbarred the door.

Should have gone with the baby carrier, Hat commented.

Julie scoffed, then gasped in awe as the door swung open.

The vast cavern beyond was lit by an eerie blue glow from high above. Green moss dripped from every surface and thickly carpeted its floor. Purple and gray lichen grew like trees from cracks in the stone wall near the portal, and the sound of babbling water filled the air as a perfectly clear stream rushed past the portal. At the far end, Julie could make out a white thread of waterfall as another stream came into the cavern, its distant roar barely audible.

"Whoa," Julie murmured.

Taylor was wide-eyed before the two dragons uncurled from where they lay in front of the portal. Their scales were patterned with the same greens and browns as the cavern floor, so Julie didn't see them until they rose to their feet.

These were smaller than the one she'd seen in Avalon, but

each towered over her head, and their sinuous bodies were easily the length of Genevieve. Neither had wings, but their backs were studded with long yellow spikes. Their six sturdy legs ended in talons that dug into the moss as they turned to face her with a soft rustle as their long tails dragged across the rock.

The nearest one lowered his head, which was almost the size of Julie's body, and gazed at her and the egg. She looked into his enormous eyes. They were blue enough to make the sky look pale and shoddy by comparison, and they made her heart thunder in her chest.

The dragon's voice rumbled in her mind. *Greetings, Julie of the Meadows.*

Julie took a deep breath for what felt like the first time in ages. "Hello," she murmured.

Speak telepathically, Hat murmured. *I'm translating.*

Okay. Julie cleared her throat and tried again. *Hello, Sir Dragon.*

The dragon's long lips twitched, and his fangs flashed in what might have been a smile. *I am your escort to the Augur.* He nodded to Taylor. *Welcome too, honor guard of Julie of the Meadows.*

Taylor shot her a glance, and she did her best to smother her grin. Demoted from Aether prince to a human's honor guard. She wasn't going to let him live this down.

The other dragon raised her head and studied them with eyes as green as her companion's were blue. *Enter.*

Julie stepped forward. Her dress boots thudded on the moss, and she felt a moment's vertigo as the portal gripped her. After her head cleared and she took a long breath, her eyes popped open. She'd been expecting the smell of dirt and stale air in this cave. Instead, the scent that filled her senses was exotic and wild. It was like sage and smoke mixed together.

Now that she was inside the cavern, chill air kissed Julie's skin. She scanned the space and gasped at the sheer size of it. She'd only glimpsed half of it through the portal, looking toward the waterfall. Now, looking downstream, Julie watched the water wind through a vast stretch of landscape filled with moss and lichen.

Heavy, hairy animals grazed in a herd a quarter-mile away. They looked like cows, but when one of them raised its head, chewing the moss, Julie saw that it had no eyes. Instead, long golden whiskers trailed from its snout, stirring gently as they touched the environment. The cow-thing chewed the moss for a few moments before lowering its head and going back to grazing.

The scene was draped in a bluish twilight. When she looked up, Julie expected to see a crack in the cavern's ceiling, letting in the sun. Instead, she saw a rocky roof covered with stalactites. Blue crystals traced through the rock, emitting the blue glow that illuminated the scene.

"Whoa," Julie murmured again.

Are we done staring? Hat grumbled. *Can we maybe pay attention to the* dragons *in front of us now?*

Julie started and turned her eyes back to the two dragons, but she noticed that Taylor was gawping as much as she was. She bowed to one of them, hugging the egg. *I'm here to bring this egg back to its parents.*

The blue-eyed dragon dipped his head. *You are very welcome, Julie of the Meadows. I am Aladabil. This is Minatarva.* He nodded to his companion. *We will guide you to the Augur.*

Minatarva bowed her head in greeting, and the yellow spikes rose on her back. *Nothing shall stand in the way of returning that which was stolen from us.*

Thank you. Julie hugged the egg closer. Maybe it was her imagination, but she thought she could sense a thrill running through it. Did it know it was home? She stroked its surface, and Minatarva and Aladabil watched every movement she made.

This way, if you please. Aladabil gestured with a claw.

A footpath—or cow-thing path—wound through the moss. She stepped forward, and Aladabil paced beside her, with

Minatarva and Taylor bringing up the rear. The terrain climbed steadily toward the cliff with the waterfall, and as they drew nearer, its sound grew louder in Julie's ears.

How big is this place? Julie wondered, noticing for the first time the tunnel mouths set into the walls at intervals. This cavern was big enough to swallow several city blocks.

Think big, Hat told her. *No, bigger.*

At the foot of the waterfall, a limpid pool churned with water so clear that Julie could see the many-colored pebbles at the bottom, even in the dim light from the blue crystals. Small, white fish flashed to and fro in the water, glowing with bioluminescence or magic.

This way, Aladabil rumbled.

The dragon turned his head, indicating a rope bridge just downstream of the pool. Julie kept a firm grip on the egg with one arm as they crossed it since it swayed under their feet. The ropes were woven from strands of dark purple moss, and the wood under her feet was strangely springy.

It's from those tree-like lichens, Hat told her.

You've been here before? Julie looked up at the waterfall, barely feeling the coldness of its spray on her face.

Hat snickered. *There aren't a lot of places I haven't been.*

After they crossed the stream, Aladabil turned to the left and led them toward a tunnel beyond a mossy field full of the blind bewhiskered cows. The tunnel was enormous as well, tall enough for Lillie's house to fit inside, and its walls were streaked with the glowing crystals. When Julie glanced at Taylor, he was grinning, his eyes reflecting the blue light.

"Nice to be on an adventure where nothing is trying to kill us, isn't it?" Julie quipped.

Taylor snorted. "Something like that."

Deep red light glowed at the end of the tunnel, and as they stepped into another cavern, a blast of hot air rushed through Julie's hair. She gasped. This cavern was smaller than the first. Its roof was lower, and the red glow came from a river of lava that poured through a massive crack in the center of the rocky floor. Stone outcroppings sprouted from both sides of the lava river, littered with loose boulders.

Careful. Minatarva ran a claw through the lava, and droplets of the red ooze trickled from her claw. *It's not safe for fleshlings like you.*

Julie swallowed and hugged the egg. *Yeah, I got that.*

Taylor shot her a glare, but Aladabil chuckled.

They followed a rocky path along the lava river in single file. Aladabil's tail swished from side to side as he took smooth, reptilian strides. Julie expected to find nothing alive in this cavern apart from her group, but when they were halfway across the cavern, a skittering sound echoed through the empty space. She jumped, clutching the egg.

Something white and furry skipped across one of the rocky outcrops, hooves resounding on the hard surface.

"Look!" Taylor squealed in excitement, grabbing Julie's arm. "A *goat!*"

The creature had cloven hooves, curving horns, and a beard like a mountain goat's, but Julie spotted long, trembling whiskers sprouting from all four of its legs, feeling their way across the rock. When the mountain goat reached the top of the outcrop, it turned its head. She expected it to have no eyes like the cow-things, but it had two huge, dark eyes that were all pupil like a bush baby's.

A chill ran down her spine. *I thought the Deep was the dragons' fortress.*

Oh, it's much more than that, Hat told her. *The Deep is a subterranean world beneath Avalon.*

Wow. Julie blinked. *So, we've got a long walk ahead of us?*

Should have brought hiking boots, Hat quipped.

Scales rustled on scales to Julie's left, and a black dragon uncurled from the top of one of the outcrops. This one had six legs with webbed claws and a spiked fin running down his back, and when he opened his eyes, they glowed red. Red light shimmered between his scales as though it was emitted by his soul. He slipped off the outcrop and slid into the lava, only his eyes and fin showing, and swam beside them like a crocodile.

Is he friendly? Taylor hesitated.

Minatarva smiled. *He honors the carrier of the egg. None of you will be harmed here.*

The lava dragon raised his head from the fiery river and let out plumes of smoke through both nostrils. He clawed his way onto a rock in the middle of the river, red eyes never leaving the egg. A strange sound filled the cavern, long and slow and deep yet haunting. It was so low that Julie felt it in her bones rather than heard it in her ears. It was only when the lava dragon's chest glowed a brighter red that she realized the sound was coming from him.

Dragon song, Hat whispered.

The sound followed them out of the cavern, down a winding tunnel, and into the next open space. Here, towering mountains rose on either side of them, and the path cut through a valley covered with tall gold fungi that stirred like grass in wind, except there was no wind. The long hyphae moved of their own accord, brushing softly against Julie's thighs as she walked. They emitted a warm glow that filled the cavern with golden light. When Julie looked up, the dark ceiling was so far away that she could barely see it. A flock of bats soared through the air, their clicks and murmurs resounding off the slopes and their furry brown bellies flashing in the gold light.

A new note joined the song of the lava dragon. A winged silver dragon emerged from the mouth of a cave in a nearby mountainside, a song rising from her chest, which began to glow silver. She had sweeping horns that curved up and back like an antelope's.

More of the horned silver dragons emerged from the mountainside as they walked and joined in the singing. Julie heard a melody in the song instead of a tuneless roar. Each time she thought she caught the tune, it changed. It ebbed and flowed, sometimes almost inaudible, sometimes filling her mind with sound.

The path began to climb one of the mountains. Sweat trickled down Julie's face, and her arms shook with the weight of the egg, but neither Aladabil nor Minatarva offered to carry it. She wouldn't have given it to them if they had.

Are we going to see their king or queen? Julie whispered.

Dragons don't have hierarchies the way that other species do, Hat told her. *You're going to see the Augur. He's responsible for the egg.*

Is he its dad or something? Julie asked.

Something like that. Hat chuckled.

A silver dragon stood on the path as they neared the mountain's summit. It was colder here, and Julie shivered as her eyes met those of the dragon. Their gazes locked for a few moments, then the dragon dipped her nose, lips twitching in a smile as she raised her head and joined the song with a pure, high note that rang through Julie's head for a moment before softening to a whisper. The dragon raced out of the path, threw open her wings, and took off over the golden valley.

They had left the glowing fungus behind some time ago, and it was dark as they reached the top of the mountain. Julie panted, sweat prickling her back and palms. The egg weighed three tons or so.

That pink baby carrier would have been very fetching on you, Hat grumbled.

Julie scoffed. *Make yourself useful and tell me why the dragons are singing.*

Aladabil stopped at the top of the mountain. It was not so much a peak as a rim like that of a volcano, Julie realized. She could make out the blue glow of the dragon's eyes. *They are cele-*

brating the return of the egg, he murmured. *We seldom reproduce. Each is a rare treasure.*

Julie cradled the egg. *All life is.*

Aladabil rumbled his agreement, then led them over the rim.

The mountain was hollow.

Beneath Julie's feet, the ground sloped sharply toward a bowl at the bottom, the surface uneven and unforgiving. Claws digging into the slope, hundreds of dragons filled the bowl, singing, their glowing chests illuminating the space in a multitude of colors from deepest red to pure white. Some were smaller, like Aladabil and Minatarva. Others were vast, stretched out along the rim of the bowl, their massive bodies as long as streets.

Julie spotted a familiar pattern of blue, purple, and gold scales. They belonged to a dragon the size of a small house, all sinuous curves, his broad wings folded by his sides. She could feel his amber eyes upon her even from this distance.

Come, Aladabil purred. *The Augur waits.*

He set off down the hill, and Julie followed, slipping and scrambling but keeping both hands firmly on the egg. Near the bottom, her feet almost skidded out from under her. She caught herself on one elbow with a grunt, hugging the egg, and Aladabil grabbed the back of her shirt with one claw and boosted her to her feet.

Beside her, Taylor came to an ungainly halt on his hands and knees. He scrambled to his feet, gray with embarrassment, and swiped his hands clean on his pants.

The many-colored dragon raised his head. The others fell silent, but their glow filled the bowl. He strode forward, smoke curling from his nostrils, his movements smooth and slinking. As he neared Julie, he changed. His wings flattened, sinking into his scales, and his tail shortened, then vanished. He shrank, then rose onto his hind legs. His snout shortened, and sheaves of shining fabric fell around his body. By the time he reached her, he looked nearly human: a seven-foot-tall man with huge amber eyes wearing silken robes in blue, gold, and purple, skin patterned with all three colors faintly glowing on his bald skull.

Taylor's elbow thudded into her ribs. She jumped, realized he was bowing, and did the same. When they straightened, the dragon-guy was still looking at them, a faint smile tugging at his lips.

He seemed to be waiting for her to say something. She stepped forward, holding out the egg with shaking arms.

"I have come to return this egg to your people," she announced.

Her voice rang around the bowl. It was met with a rumble of song, low and deep, that gave her goosebumps.

The Augur held up his arms, robes falling back to reveal more patterns on his skin. "That which was taken from us has been returned!" he thundered. "That which was dead is alive again. Love has conquered death, and this treasure has been restored to us."

There was another burst of song, then a swell of color from the dragons' chests blazed a purple afterglow across Julie's eyes.

"We all felt the egg die," the Augur went on. "Now we feel its presence among us once more."

He lightly touched the surface of the egg, and it rippled silver. Julie waited for him to take it, but the Augur just met her eyes, his smile deepening.

"You have done well, young one," he rumbled. "But we cannot accept the egg."

Julie gasped with the shock of pain that ran through her chest. "But...but it's alive. You just saw that it was alive. It needs to be with its people!" Her eyes stung with tears.

Minatarva gasped.

Julie, your manners! Hat hissed. Taylor was gaping at her.

"I-I'm sorry," Julie croaked. "I didn't mean to offend."

The Augur laughed softly, an animal rumble deep in his chest. "You are forgiven since you are very young." He lowered his hand to his side again. "This egg does not belong to a mother and father the way you do. It belongs to the one with whom it bonds."

Julie's breath caught in her throat, her protest dying on her lips. *Surely not. It can't be!*

The Augur's eyes stayed on hers. "Your love brought this egg back to life. It has bonded to you. It is yours."

Julie sucked in a breath. Looking down at the egg, she felt a wild jolt of excitement that set her heart to thumping in her throat. Panic replaced that almost immediately.

"I...I'm honored," she squeaked. "I really am, but like you said, I'm young. I'm *way* too young to be a mom!" She shook her head. "I don't know the first thing about taking care of babies, let alone a baby dragon. I could be a cool aunt, but I'd mess it up. I'd feed it the wrong foods. I'd set myself on fire, burping it!"

Hat shickered.

"Augur, sir." Taylor stepped forward. "Forgive my intrusion."

"You have a question." The Augur turned his attention to the elf. "Ask it."

"How is this possible?" Taylor glanced at Julie. "I've never heard of a dragon bonding with a human before."

The Augur's smile flickered. "That is because dragons do not bond with humans."

Julie's stomach twisted.

"But once in a while," he went on, "we have bonded with Lunar Fae."

CHAPTER EIGHTEEN

Taylor's jaw dropped. Julie cringed, waiting for him to say something. He just shut his mouth slowly and stared at her.

Lunar Fae. Lunar Fae. Lunar Fae. The words beat through her mind in a wild tattoo. She thought about Penelope, the judge at Qbiit's trial. The fae had been capable of commanding an entire courthouse with a single glance. That wasn't her. Julie didn't have that power.

The unborn dragon in her arms believed she did.

The Augur turned his eyes back to her, his smile steady. "You are afraid, young one, but you will not abandon your charge." It was a statement, not a question.

Julie looked at the egg. "No," she muttered. "I won't. I just want what's best for it." She swallowed. "I want it to grow up with its own people." *The way I should have grown up,* she thought, and instantly felt as though she'd betrayed her mom and dad.

"You are correct in that the egg needs dragon care," the Augur told her. "Even more so when it hatches and becomes a dragonling. Yet at the same time, it needs you, the one to whom it bonded."

Julie blinked back her tears. "So, we negotiate shared custody or something?"

For a panicked moment, she thought the Augur was going to tell her to stay in the Deep forever. Instead, he produced a real smile that displayed his sharp white teeth. "Something like that, young one. You do not know how to care for a dragon yet, but you can learn. At the same time, the egg needs Avalon moonlight to develop, as well as dragon song."

"Then the egg must stay here." Julie forced herself to loosen her grip on it. "And I'll come to see it." She cleared her throat, reminding herself that she was in an assembly of dragons. "If that's okay."

The Augur glanced at the watching dragons. "Very well," he rumbled. "The egg will remain here, and we shall care for it as it develops. The young one will visit every waxing moon and renew her bond with the egg, at the same time receiving guidance on caring for it." He dipped his head. "I am the Augur, and I vow to care for this egg and train this young fae personally."

A rumble of assent rose from the dragons, their chests blazing.

"It is agreed." The Augur turned to Julie. "I will keep the egg safe."

He held out his arms, and although Julie ached with fatigue, she clutched the egg more tightly to her chest. The Augur waited. Slowly, Julie forced herself to extend her arms and gently rolled the egg into his grasp.

It rippled again, black and silver. When her tired arms fell back to her sides, they felt empty.

The Augur dipped his head. "You have our respect and thanks, young one."

Our respect and thanks. All the dragons' voices chorused in Julie's head.

Aladabil rose from where he had been sitting beside Julie.

Come. I will show you the Maw of the Deep, the entrance through which you will come on your monthly visit to the egg.

Dazed, Julie shuffled after Aladabil, who made his way to the rim of the bowl with sure steps, his claws digging into the loose shale. Pebbles shifted under her feet, and she slipped and threw out her hands to catch herself. Taylor seized her arm.

"You okay?" he whispered.

Julie looked into his tender eyes and almost cried. Instead, she nodded.

Hold onto my tail, Aladabil told her.

She hesitated, then gripped one of the big yellow spikes near the end of his tail. It was smooth and hard like a horn and warmer than she'd expected. Taylor did the same with Minatarva, and they were towed up to the rim.

When they reached the top of the bowl, sound swelled to meet them from below: a crescendo of dragon song. The bowl glowed with multicolored light. The Augur had transformed back into a dragon, and he cradled the egg in his front claws as he threw open his wings and leaped into the air. The wind from his wings buffeted Julie as she stood at the top of the rim. He sailed over their heads, swooped into the valley, and was gone.

The Maw of the Deep was a huge round stone set in the side of the cavern. It met the rim of the bowl about ten minutes' walk around the edge. It was covered with runes and inscriptions, and when Aladabil pressed his snout against a runed rock beside it, the stone rolled back.

"Open sesame," Julie quipped.

Taylor scoffed.

As beautiful as the Deep was, Julie took a deep breath of pure, fresh air as she stepped through the round doorway, felt a breeze on her face, and reached out into sunlight.

Goodbye, Julie of the Meadows. Aladabil stuck his head out of the hole and smiled. *May moonlight bless your path.*

Before Julie could say anything, the dragon withdrew, and the stone rolled over the entrance again. Two dragon statues guarded the stone. They towered on either side of Julie, silent and impassive. She rolled her shoulders, rubbed her sore arms, and gazed down the mountainside. Green grass spilled down the slopes on either side of them, and sheep with normal sheep eyes, even if they had gold fleece, grazed just below. An asphalt road wound around the mountain. It looked like the country just outside Avalon Village.

"Okay, now what?" Julie turned to Taylor. "I really hope we're not walking all the way back to the village and HQ."

"Never mind walking!" Taylor burst out. He grabbed her shoulders, eyes sparkling. "Julie, you're a Lunar Fae! How cool is that?"

Julie twisted free of his grasp. "Ow! That hurts. That egg was heavy, dude."

"Sorry." Taylor laughed and let his hands fall to his sides. "Lunar Fae! How come none of us knew?" He frowned. "Is your mom a Lunar Fae too?"

"I doubt it." Julie turned. "I'm starving."

"We can get something in the village." Taylor nodded at a bus shelter next to the road at the base of the mountain. "We'll take a bus back if there are any, or I'll call Kaplan to rescue us."

"Yeah, let's not do that." Julie snorted.

"There's a bus every hour," Hat told them. "The next one's due in twenty minutes. We should make it if you two get walking right now."

Julie wrapped her arms around her torso and started down the mountain, following a worn track that wound down it in a series of switchbacks. Taylor jogged alongside her, words bubbling out of him. "A *Lunar Fae*! Julie, that's amazing. You have the most incredible magic powers, do you know that? Not to mention the ability to bond with dragons!"

Lunar Fae had *not* been at the top of Julie's possible species list. If she was honest, she hadn't made a list, but if she had, Lunar Fae wouldn't have been on it.

"I mean, your magic is clearly dormant, but there's got to be a way we can reawaken it," Taylor babbled. "Dormant magic is a common problem. I was a late bloomer, believe it or not."

"Oh, I believe it," Hat snarked.

"You'll love your powers, Julie. I can't wait to see Shae's face when he finds out." Taylor chuckled. "He's going to grovel and scrape, that speciesist asshole. He'll regret mistreating you."

The corner of Julie's mouth quirked. "That'll be satisfying to watch."

Taylor hesitated, brow furrowing. "Are you okay? You seem...quiet."

Julie shrugged. "I miss the egg." It was true, but not the whole truth.

Taylor stared at her. "You're not as surprised as I thought you would be."

"I didn't know I was a Lunar Fae." Julie chose her words carefully. They were scrambling down a series of steps of different sizes cut into the earth of the mountainside.

Taylor stopped dead at the top of the steps. "But you *did* know you're not human."

Julie turned to him. "Come on, Taylor. We'll miss the bus."

"You found out that you were a different species." Taylor spoke slowly, his face crumpling. "And you didn't say anything?"

Julie looked away.

"That's why Dr. Olena has been bugging you to come see her. That's what the blood tests were all about." Taylor shook his head. "You've known for weeks, and you didn't say a word."

"I wasn't ready to say anything." Julie grimaced. "Now, let's get to that bus."

She marched across the grass with a crushing weight in her chest. Taylor jogged after her. "I can't believe you didn't say anything."

"Why, Taylor?" Julie shot back. "I wasn't ready to share, and I didn't. I wasn't ready to deal with it, and I'm still not. I had a lot going on, in case you hadn't noticed."

Taylor's lips drooped. "I'm your friend, Julie. You could have told *me*. I could have helped you."

"How?" Julie countered. "By making me human again? By explaining how this happened and whether my mom and dad are even my real parents?" She folded her arms and kept walking.

Taylor huffed. "I could just have been there for you, that's all. I just want to help and support you as your partner and friend. You could have told me."

"So, now I owe you because you're being nice to me?" Julie spat.

Taylor stopped, the color draining from his face. "You know I didn't mean it like that."

Julie faced him, trying to undo the knots in her shoulders. "I'm sorry, Taylor. I know you didn't. I shouldn't have said that." She sucked in a breath. "To be honest, I've been avoiding the whole thing, okay? I don't know how to deal with it." She looked down at her hands and realized they were shaking. "Now that I know I'm a Lunar Fae, I still don't know."

Taylor folded his arms. The distant rumble of a bus floated through the still countryside. "I can understand that." He sucked in a breath. "We'd better catch the bus."

"Yeah, we'd better," Julie mumbled.

They walked down the rest of the mountain side by side and in silence.

Julie couldn't believe it was still daylight when the taxi pulled up in front of PMA HQ. She tipped the driver handsomely for his trip from the Central Park portal to Avalon, not that he knew what 110th Street Bridge really was, down to Staten Island. She stretched her shoulders as she got out, working on the stiffness in her arms and back.

"Sore?" Taylor asked, raising an eyebrow as they walked up to the gate.

"You would be too if you'd toted a dragon egg through the entire Deep," Julie shot back. It came out more harshly than she'd meant it to.

Taylor held up both hands. "Okay, okay."

The silence hung between them as they crossed the grounds. Julie checked her phone for the time. How was it only one in the afternoon? It felt like they'd walked through the Deep for hours.

Avalon time runs differently, remember? Hat pointed out.

Fantastic. So my workday will be twice as long, Julie grumbled.

That's not a bad thing. We need to get back to work on those training materials for the recruiters.

When she stepped through the doors into the entrance hall, Julie spotted Captain Kaplan. He stood in front of the cafeteria, arms folded and eyes burning as they followed Julie's steps across the room.

Dr. Olena stood beside him.

"Uh-oh," Taylor mumbled.

"You can say that again," Julie whispered back.

"Is this about, you know, your species?" Taylor asked as they headed for Kaplan instead of the elevator.

Julie snorted. "I'm willing to bet it is."

Taylor said nothing.

Julie pasted on a cheerful smile as she reached Kaplan. "Hey, Cap! How's it hanging?"

"Don't start with me, Meadows," Kaplan snarled. "The paranormal world is teetering on the brink of crisis, the PMA is short-staffed, and the media is bordering on hysterical. Do you know what I *really* don't need to waste my time on right now?"

"Ping-pong?" Julie guessed. "Dodgeball?"

Kaplan jabbed an enormous finger at her. *"You."*

"Ah." Julie noticed that Kaplan's face had new strained lines around his eyes and on his forehead.

"Imagine my joy, Meadows, when Dr. Olena came to my office to inform me that one of my best recruiters has been ignoring her urgent requests to visit the medical unit," Kaplan growled.

Julie took a breath. "I'm sorry, Captain. I had a lot going on."

"Well, now you have this going on, so you're going to deal with it." Kaplan extended an arm to the door, raising a huge bushy eyebrow. "Shall we?"

Julie's heart sank, but she nodded and shuffled to the door. *Great. The last thing I need is Captain Kaplan to be present while Dr. Olena tells me I'm a Lunar Fae.*

He's going to find out one way or another, Hat told her. *Would you rather he found out now or had to tell him later?*

Good point, Julie conceded.

Taylor kept his mouth firmly shut as he trailed after them into the sunshine and across the manicured lawns of the PMA campus to the medical unit.

"I understand your personal life has been in upheaval lately, Meadows, but that's no excuse to ignore Dr. Olena." Kaplan was taking huge prowling strides.

"I know." Julie winced. "I'm sorry this had to take up your time, Captain."

"Is that contrition I hear?" Kaplan barked. "She really is sick, Doctor."

"She's not sick," Dr. Olena soothed. She met Julie's eyes. "I'm sorry for going over your head, but Commander Hartshorn just laughed when I approached her, and—"

"It's okay, Doc. It's not your fault." Julie sighed.

"I could have you suspended," Kaplan growled. "Technically, you still haven't passed your mandatory physical."

Julie stared at him.

"I won't. We need recruits, and I'm no fool. But I *could*," Kaplan added, "and maybe I should have."

Taylor spoke up as they stepped into the unit. "I'm going to see Ilsa."

No one responded. Julie felt a flush creep up her cheeks. The elf shrugged and hurried off.

Ouch, Hat commented.

Not now, Hat.

Dr. Olena showed her to one of the beds in the ER and drew the curtains around it. "Captain, respectfully, you don't have to be here."

"It's okay." Julie took a long breath. "He should know."

"Know?" For an instant, Kaplan's frown faded, replaced by narrowed eyes. "Know *what*?"

Dr. Olena glanced at Julie, who nodded. The Sylthana Elf turned to Kaplan. "Julie's routine bloodwork showed some discrepancies I couldn't explain. I conducted further tests myself, sending some of them to bigger labs in Avalon, and the results just came in. That's why I urgently wanted to speak to Julie. I wanted to let her know what we found."

"I'm sorry for ghosting you, Doc." Julie bit her lip. "It wasn't personal. I just...I had too much going on recently to deal with the news that I'm a fae."

The words slipped out before she could stop them, and Kaplan's bushy eyebrows leaped so high that they threatened to merge with his hairline. Dr. Olena's jaw dropped, too.

"A fae?" Dr. Olena gasped.

"But she's *human*!" Kaplan spluttered, pointing at Julie like she hadn't believed the same thing. "That's her whole thing." He gestured at her with both hands.

Exactly, Julie thought. *I'm the human who became the PMA's best recruiter. That is my whole thing, only now it isn't.*

Maybe your identity doesn't have to be about your species, Hat murmured.

"We all thought so until I saw the bloodwork," Dr. Olena told him. "She *was* raised human."

"My parents are human." Julie folded her arms.

"Are you sure?" Dr. Olena asked.

Julie chuckled. "Trust me. Mom is a lot of things, but a fae isn't one of them. And Dad…" She hesitated. She'd only been thirteen when he died. "I think so," she managed.

Kaplan passed a hand over his face. "Do you know what type of fae she is, Olena?"

Julie kept quiet. *That* nugget she wasn't ready to share.

"I don't. My tests couldn't even tell me she's a fae," Dr. Olena replied. She turned to Julie. "I don't know how you found out, but I'm glad you did. All I could tell was that you have a very powerful glamour on you—a concealment spell." Dr. Olena touched Julie's arm. "I've never seen magic like it, but it explains why you look human to us, to yourself, and to other humans. This is more than the Veil that protects all paranormals from human eyes. This hides your true appearance from *all* eyes, even your own."

Kaplan frowned. "I've never heard of a glamour like this."

"Me neither. We'll need to do more research to determine how to break it." Dr. Olena eyed Julie as though the clue was written on her clothes or something.

Julie stared at her reflection on the smooth metal surface of the table by the hospital bed. Her pixie-cut hair, the features her mother had always called "foxy," and her bright eyes. Were they fake? What did she look like as a Lunar Fae?

"How *did* you find out you're a fae, Meadows?" Kaplan barked. "And, more importantly, did you give that egg back to the dragons?"

"Yes, I did." Julie hesitated. "Well, I mostly did."

Kaplan's eyes narrowed. "What do you mean, 'mostly?' If you dropped it down there and it broke, Meadows, I swear—"

"I don't think dropping it would break *that* shell, captain," Julie interrupted. She paused. "I gave it back to the Augur, but he said...well, he said it had bonded with me."

"A dragon." Kaplan stared at her. *"Bonded* to you."

Clearly, he didn't know that was a Lunar Fae thing. Judging by her expression, neither did Dr. Olena.

It's not common knowledge, Hat told her.

Julie scoffed. *You didn't seem surprised.*

Hat sniffed. *I'm not common.*

"Yes. I have to go back once a month on the waxing moon to interact with it and learn how to care for it." Julie sat on the edge of the hospital bed. "I hope that's okay."

Kaplan threw up his hands. "Sure. Fine. My top recruiter has turned out to be a different species and needs a monthly day off from work to babysit a dragon egg. What's not fine about that?"

Something stirred in the corner of Julie's vision. She jumped up and looked around to see a hairless feline tail swish into nothingness.

"Was that one of the Sphynxes?" Julie spluttered. "Has he been listening this whole time?"

"Eavesdropping menaces," Kaplan grumbled. He pinched the bridge of his nose. "Olena!"

"Sir?" Dr. Olena all but saluted.

"Clear this *fae* for duty." Kaplan waved a hand at Julie. "And send her back to her office to get on training those recruiters."

"Yes, sir." Dr. Olena shrugged. "She is clear for duty in any case. She's perfectly healthy."

"Good. Get to work, Meadows," Kaplan ordered.

Julie nodded. "Yes, sir."

She was ducking through the curtain when Kaplan's voice sliced through the air at her. "And Meadows?"

Julie hesitated. "Yes, sir?"

Kaplan folded his massive arms again, eyebrows drawn low. "This is *not* the end of this discussion."

CHAPTER NINETEEN

"I'm here to offer you a high-paying job with excellent benefits!" Julie told the plushie.

The plushie stood on the middle of a table in one of the conference rooms, which felt eerily empty with only a handful of people in it. Qtana, crouching behind a video camera powered by runes that glowed blue around the lens, gave Julie a big grin and a thumbs-up. Beside her, Taylor snuck a glance at the lines he'd written on his wrist.

The plushie took a few waddling steps across the table. It was a gray creature with four huge flippers and a long neck ending in a vaguely equine head. Hat's voice emanated from its immobile mouth, picked out on the face with bits of thread. "Money?" the kelpie-shaped plushie demanded. "What kind of an idea is that, idiot? Do you really think *money* would motivate a free creature of the ocean? I hunt for my food. I sleep where I like!"

"Too harsh." Qtana straightened up. "You're going to discourage them if you put that into your video."

"That's not even what the kelpie said, Hat," Julie protested.

"Yes, it is," Hat argued.

"Actually, it's not," Taylor told him. "It rolled over and asked Julie where it would keep its money."

Hat sniggered and wriggled his stuffed flippers. "Really? I remember your first attempt at recruiting to be *much* more embarrassing than that."

Julie scoffed. "I've done enough cringing reliving this, let alone re-enacting it, okay? Stick to your lines."

"Fine," Hat grumbled. He rolled over laboriously, his flippers thudding on the wood. "Where am I—" *thud* "supposed to keep—" *thud* "my money?" *thud* "In my pockets?"

"Better. I can edit that in." Qtana smiled.

Julie looked into the camera, ignoring the weird feeling it gave her. "This is why research on your chosen subject is one of the most important things you can do in recruitment. Every paranormal group is different, and more than that, every individual is different."

"Offering species-appropriate incentives can go a long way toward recruiting the rarer paranormals." Taylor stepped up beside her and flashed the camera a Prince Charming smile. "For example, in recruiting the kelpie, Julie would have done better if she had argued that joining the PMA would help protect the freedom of its species. What's more, she could have focused on incentives that were more meaningful to this individual, such as being relocated to an Avalonian sea rather than having to live in a dirty New York harbor."

Julie gritted her teeth but kept her smile in place. "It's also important to work together. Since recruiters work in pairs, the more experienced member of your team should be ready to help, yet also to accommodate the less experienced member's ideas."

"Perfect!" Qtana straightened. "I think I have what I need."

"Great." Julie took a step away from Taylor, not missing the glare he gave her. She picked up Hat and cuddled him.

"Hey!" Hat protested. "I'm an ancient magical artifact! Could you please not?"

"But you're so cute." Julie squished him.

"As if the humiliation of being a stuffed toy isn't enough," Hat grumbled, wriggling determinedly.

Qtana rummaged in her bag. "This has been a fun way to get back to work. Thanks for asking me to help with your recruitment videos while I'm still on light duty. I've really enjoyed doing this for the past week."

"Yeah, so did we." Julie grinned, relieved that Qtana had agreed. That way, she didn't have to spend much time alone with Taylor.

Qtana pulled out something that might have been a DVD, except for the blue runes around its edge. "I edited the footage from the Weres' interviews. Did you want to see?"

"Yes, please!" Julie grinned. "They were amazing."

"Amazing?" Taylor sat on the edge of the table. "I think 'chaotic' is the word you were looking for."

"Don't worry. I sorted out the chaos." Qtana slid the DVD into the projector-like device. "See what you think."

Julie cuddled Hat as the footage played on the big screen at the back of the room. The first clip showed Isaiah looking seriously into the camera, his soft blue eyes intent. "It was a meaningless existence. Nothing we did mattered."

The next clip featured Chester leaning back in his chair and giving a stilted chuckle, arms folded. "All we ever did was cause trouble. I mean, it was stupid, but we'd go into town and turn over trash cans just to annoy people. We'd chase this centaur's horses for kicks." He rubbed a spot on his shoulder. "Real ones, sometimes."

Blake hunched forward in the chair, elbows on his knees, hands interlaced between them. He stared at them, then at the camera. "I missed having a family." He took a deep breath. "I missed having a home."

Soft piano music began to play over the interviews. The next shot was a close-up of Noah, his big green eyes blinking rapidly as he spoke and his voice ringing over the music. "We all felt like there was so *much* of us. So much life. So much strength. But it had nowhere to go. We didn't know what to do with ourselves."

"No matter how much we indulged ourselves, we never felt content," Austin told the camera with serious brown eyes. "Never."

Teddy sat in the chair with one foot hooked over his knee, both hands clasping his shin. He laughed, not looking at the camera. "It was...*boring*."

Abruptly, the music stopped. Isaiah smiled into the camera, his attractive features looking radiant with the angle and lighting. "Then we joined the PMA, and everything changed."

The music returned in a crescendo of instruments and deep voices vocalizing in harmony. A montage of shots played on the screen: the six Weres sparring together, Isaiah swinging a sword in brisk circles so the blade became a flashing blur of steel, Noah working on a computer whose blue light reflected in his bright green eyes, Austin, Teddy, and Blake climbing a wall side by side, and Chester pummeling a punching bag.

"We'd always been friends," Isaiah stated over the montage. "But then we became a team. We became a unit."

"I feel like I'm doing something with my life now," Noah added over a shot of him firing an arrow at a target.

A slow-mo shot showed Blake firing two handguns at a human silhouette and bullet holes appearing in the paper. "I've got a reason to get up in the mornings, you know?" He chuckled, and the shot returned to him sitting in the chair. "I've got a purpose."

"*Nothing* is boring anymore," Teddy added over a shot of him tackling an orc off his feet, throwing him onto a gym mat, and restraining him with his arm twisted behind his back even though the orc was twice Teddy's size.

The second-to-last shot was particularly good, Julie thought with appreciation. A shirtless Chester pounded his fists into a punching bag, his massive muscles rippling under his pale skin. "I found out what my real strengths are." The shot returned to his interview, the strong Were smiling into the camera from inches away. "And so can you."

The music ended, and the screen faded to black with white letters across it.

Join the Official Para-Military Agency.
Make a difference.

"Whoa." Julie turned to Qtana. "That was *incredible*!"

"You're the one who came up with the idea." The troll laughed, and a faint pinkness crept into her cheeks. "And conducted the interview. The Weres really opened up to you."

"We have something of a bond." Taylor grinned. "Fighting a yeti army together will do that to you."

Julie glanced at him. *Or not.* "Your editing really made it sing," she told Qtana out loud. "I love it."

"You made good music choices too, Julie," Taylor pointed out.

If he was trying to suck up to her, it wasn't going to work. Julie gave him a brief smile. "Thanks."

The door swung open, and Ellie poked her head in. "Hey! I'm here for my interview?"

"Of course. Thanks for coming." Julie got up and gestured to the chair in the corner of the room where she'd set up black drapes as a backdrop.

"It's my pleasure." Ellie grinned. "I love this idea." She touched her chin. "Do I look okay? The last time I was in front of a camera was with the modeling agency, and let's just say my look has changed a lot since then."

"You look stunning." Taylor beamed at her.

Julie's stomach twisted for some reason. "Do you want some water or something before we get started?" she asked Ellie.

The newly minted agent shook her head, and her black hair

rippled over her shoulders. It was strange to know that Ellie, who was half-Woodland Fae and half-human, had more *Homo sapiens* blood than Julie did. "I'd better get back to work, so let's get started."

She took her seat, and Qtana brought the camera over on its tripod. Hat turned back into a purple beret. Julie donned him and pulled up a chair next to the camera. She looked at the list of questions she'd jotted on her notepad last week after getting back from the Deep.

"Okay, Ellie, let's get started." She smiled. "Can you describe your life before you were recruited?"

Qtana folded her tripod and tucked it into her bag. "That was amazing," she told Ellie. "I can't wait to edit your footage."

Ellie laughed. "Glad to hear I've still got it," she joked.

"Trust me. You could have been a brilliant model." Taylor grinned at her.

Julie was nauseated. "Thanks again for coming, Ellie. I'm sure we'll get lots of new recruits when we put this video on screens around Avalon Village and on the paranormal internet."

Ellie hooked her bag over her shoulder. "No problem. It's going to be weird seeing my face everywhere, but I'm sure I can live it down." She laughed. "Hey, Qtana, can I help you carry some of that stuff?"

Ugh, no, Julie muttered. *Don't leave me alone and force me to have this conversation with Taylor.*

It's got to happen sometime, Hat pointed out.

"That'd be great. Thank you." Qtana handed Ellie her camera bag. "I'll send you a sneak peek of the footage tonight, okay, Julie?"

"A copy for me, too, please," Taylor added.

"Sure." Qtana nodded. "See you."

"Thanks," Julie called after her.

Then she and Ellie were gone, shutting the door behind them, and it was just Julie, Taylor, and Hat.

Help me out here, Julie moaned.

Oh, no. There is no way on this Earth that I'm getting involved. Hat scoffed. *In fact, I'm going into sleep mode now. Goodbye.*

Hat! Julie wailed, but he had gone still on her head.

Taylor gave her a tight-lipped smile. "I guess we'd better pack this stuff since we're done filming."

"Yeah, okay." Julie picked up the chair and moved it off the backdrop.

"Actually, could you bring that back? I need to stand on it to unpin the backdrop," Taylor pointed out.

"Oh, yeah. Sorry." Julie handed it back.

"It's okay." Taylor took it.

She stood awkwardly to one side while Taylor climbed onto the chair and pulled out the tacks that secured the backdrop to the wall. The silence hung over her like smog.

When he got down from the chair, Julie cleared her throat. "I, uh, I thought I'd go and see Ilsa after we're done packing this stuff up."

Taylor looked up. "That'd be great. She's been lonely since she was taken back to her suite."

"Cool." Julie nodded. "Glad that's okay with you."

"Of course it's okay with me, Julie." Taylor lowered the backdrop to the floor and turned to face her. "Hey, listen. I was out of line. I owe you an apology for how I acted the other day when we left the Deep."

Julie hung her head, staring at her boots.

"A bunch of other days as well lately, come to think of it." Taylor cleared his throat. "I don't know what's gotten into me. I've never been friends with anyone before the way I am with you." He frowned. "I never meant to hurt you. I'm just trying to figure out what real friendship is supposed to look like, and I'm not very good at it."

Julie looked at him, feeling a smile tug at her cheeks. "I was a bit harsh, too," she admitted. "In hindsight, it *would* have been easier for me to deal with if I'd told you about the not-being-human thing from the beginning."

Taylor held up both hands. "You didn't have to. You were correct; it's your right to keep things private if you want to."

"It is, but that doesn't mean it was the right thing." Julie smiled. "You've been there for me through thick and thin since we met. As persistent as an annoying mosquito that won't quit buzzing around your head for the *entire night*."

"And here I thought you were about to be nice!" Taylor clapped a hand over his heart, but he was grinning.

She punched him in the arm. "A mosquito I could learn to lean on a little more in tough times. Better?"

"Barely." He snorted.

She scoffed as she scooped up some of the backdrop. "Stop being difficult and help me to fold this up, Your Highness."

"Whatever, huma…I mean, fae." Taylor turned gray.

Julie snorted. "Let's not even go there, okay? I'm not ready."

"Deal." Taylor picked up the other end of the backdrop. "Hey, you mind if I come along to visit Ilsa? Or do you girls want to complain about me in peace?"

Julie snorted. "I've got a better idea. How about we grab dinner after work? I'm not in the mood for the empty house tonight."

Empty? Rude! Hat gasped.

I thought you were in sleep mode, Julie chided.

Taylor grinned, then smothered it. "Sure. That'd be great. We could go in the BMW."

"Oh, no. Uh-uh. We're taking Genevieve." Julie smiled over the pang that shot through her chest. "I have no idea how much longer I get to drive her, considering she'll probably go to Lillie's kids."

"That doesn't seem fair." Taylor frowned. "Those kids didn't even come to her funeral, and you love Genevieve."

Julie shrugged. "Life's not fair." She thought about what Lillie had said about Julie being taken care of when she was gone and allowed herself to hold onto a vestige of hope. "So, where are we going for dinner?"

"How about that snazzy rooftop bar? The one where we got attacked by a yeti in the parking lot afterwards?" Taylor suggested.

Julie laughed. "How about somewhere we don't need a trust fund to afford? A mid-range steakhouse will be fine."

"Deal." When Taylor smiled, the corners of his chocolate-brown eyes crinkled in that way that Julie could never look away from.

CHAPTER TWENTY

Taylor's cheeks bulged. "I'm gonna need more of these fries."

Julie snorted into her soda. "Dude, if your mom knew you were talking with your mouth full, she would have kittens."

Taylor washed down the enormous mouthful with a generous swig of iced tea. "If my mom knew I was out to dinner with a secret fae at a common human steakhouse, she would shit herself."

"Georgina Woodskin, shitting herself?" Julie raised an eyebrow. "Not ladylike. Maybe explode into the stratosphere."

"Something like that." Taylor chuckled. He raised his hand to the waiter and ordered a second plate of fries with a wide smile before turning his attention back to his rump steak and onion rings.

Julie stabbed a crumbed calamari ring with her fork. "A secret fae," she mused. "It doesn't seem real."

"Not to mention being a secret *Lunar* Fae." Taylor stared at her, then cleared his throat and dropped his eyes to his plate. "We don't have to talk about that, though. I respect your privacy."

Julie snorted. "I thought we'd figured that out. I wasn't entirely in the right, either." She bit her lip. "Honestly, I should have trusted you with the truth a long time ago. It feels good to talk about it."

"I don't get it," Taylor blurted. "Whatever this spell on you is, it's got to be powerful. I never suspected for a moment that you were anything but human, and you know Lunar Fae aren't easy to mistake for something else."

"I've only met Judge Penelope, but she made an impression," Julie agreed. "Maybe I'm not very good at being a Lunar Fae. Maybe that's why I got..." She stopped. What? Abandoned? Given away?

"I'm sure that's not true." Taylor met her eyes. "Maybe your parents are Lunar Fae and under a concealment spell themselves. Maybe you've been Lunar Fae for generations."

The thought lightened the weight on her chest. "Maybe." She smiled. "You know, I could kinda believe that Dad was a Lunar Fae."

"How so?" Taylor stuffed a forkful of steak into his mouth.

"Dad was just one of the coolest people I've ever known. He was a trauma doc, and the one time I got to watch him work, he was in total command of the ER without having to raise his voice. Some of the other doctors threw their weight around and yelled, but people *wanted* to follow Dad's leadership." Julie stared into her calamari. "He was great. I miss him so much."

"How old were you when he passed?" Taylor asked softly.

"Thirteen." Julie raised her eyes, managing a smile. "Feels like yesterday sometimes." She croaked a laugh. "I hope Lillie's teaching him to let his hair down in the afterlife."

"I think Lillie is raising a total ruckus up there." Taylor chuckled. "Giving angels gray hairs and hijacking fiery chariots for joyrides."

Her tears spilled over, but Julie laughed as she wiped them away. "That sounds about right." She swallowed. "Hey, thank you. I haven't talked about Dad in a long time. Maybe not since he died." She took a shaky breath. "It feels good. And talking about Lillie with you? It makes the grief a little lighter."

"That's all I wanted when I argued with you earlier." Taylor's dark eyes held hers, and the corners of his lips twitched up. "I just wanted to make whatever you were carrying lighter."

It was difficult not to stare when his eyes crinkled. Around them, the chatter of voices, the clatter of cutlery, and the soft country music that played through the corny Western-themed steakhouse melted. Even the kitschy cowskin booth they were sitting in disappeared. Julie might as well have been in Fernwood Deep with the wild breeze of a faerie wood blowing through her hair and the music of Bacchus in her ears.

He still smelled like the earth after rain. The thought wandered vaguely through Julie's mind. There was a word for it. Petrichor. Was it cologne, or just the way you smelled when you were a prince of the Elves of the Mystical Dusk?

"Your fries, sir."

They both jumped. Julie giggled and buried her burning face in her soda as Taylor smiled at the waiter who slid the second plate of fries onto the table. Taylor's cheeks were faintly gray. He grabbed some fries and stuffed them into his mouth in an ungentlemanly fashion.

Julie was glad she'd decided to leave Hat in Genevieve. It was hard enough to contain the thoughts that galloped through her mind as madly as the Beltane dance without him snarking in her head.

She stole one of Taylor's fries without thinking about it and shoved it into her mouth. The steakhouse was abruptly back. Someone laughed boozily, and two kids argued at top volume over the toys that came with their meals.

What now? Do I make a stupid joke and we talk about work for the rest of the night? Julie stared at her napkin, smoothing it on the table, then scrunching it.

Then she was back in Lillie's house on the sofa with Pookie

and Fluffy and *Judge Judy* in the background, looking into the old lady's pure blue eyes and hearing her words. *You gotta live your life with the volume turned all the way up.*

Julie looked up at Taylor. At the way the light fell on the soft curve of his hair where it lay in a glossy wing over his forehead. At the elf prince who'd treated her as his equal from the first day, and the words just came out of her. "What are we doing, Taylor?"

Taylor glanced at her. "Um, eating fries?"

"No, I don't mean that." Julie looked away. "You remember what happened in the haunted house with the banshee?"

"You mean the part where I got choked out like twenty feet in the air and almost plummeted to my death before being rescued by a succubus riding a griffin? Yeah, I don't think I'll forget that anytime soon." He chuckled.

Julie bit her lip. "I don't know what I would have done if…if Bianca hadn't been there."

Taylor's eyes held hers.

"I don't know what I would do without you," Julie murmured. "I think that's why we've been fighting lately."

A gray flush crept across Taylor's cheeks, but he didn't look away. "Maybe it's not just because I don't know how to be friends like this," he admitted. "Maybe it's because I don't know how to be…" He hesitated, then blurted the words in a rush. "More than friends."

She couldn't help smiling at him, and he returned it. Something warm and golden filled Julie's chest with rising bubbles, like a cross between melted honey and champagne.

"So, what do we do about it?" she asked.

Taylor spread his hands. "I vote we don't jump into anything since we'd have to report to HR." He grimaced. "And they're gorgons."

"Wait, *actual* gorgons?" Julie raised her eyebrows. "Medusa-style?"

"Something like that." Taylor grinned.

"Okay, that's a very good reason not to rush into anything." Julie laughed. "But I agree with you in any case. I don't want to ruin this."

Taylor nodded seriously. "So, what do we do?"

"I don't know. What do people do?" Julie shrugged. "Go on a date?"

"So, this isn't a date?" Taylor raised an eyebrow.

Julie grinned and grabbed a handful of his fries. "No, this is two paras eating fries."

"Two paras, huh?" Taylor's smile widened.

Julie nodded. When he said it that way, it sounded like something she could get used to.

Sam, the werecat recruiter, strode up boldly to the hologram. It hovered over a circle of runes on the floor of the conference room in the shape of a huge black hound with glowing red eyes. Its edges were grainy, like an old video game.

Julie checked her clipboard. "What's his hologram set to, Hound of the Baskervilles?"

Taylor snorted beside her. "Please. Everyone knows the Hound of the Baskervilles wasn't real. He was a trick by Jack Stapleton."

"Just like everyone knows succubi are evil, seductive spirits?" Julie hissed, raising her eyebrows.

Taylor chuckled. "Touché. No, that's a hellhound."

Julie grinned. "Let's see how Mr. Confident handles it."

Sam had swaggered up to the hound, his green slit-pupiled eyes creasing in a smile. "Good morning, sir." He held out a hand, then let it fall back to his side. "I'm a recruiter from the Para-Military Agency. Have you ever wanted the opportunity to rise to a position of authority? To be able to have other paras do your bidding?"

The hellhound hologram bared its teeth. "I live to serve," it snarled.

"Okay, time out!" Julie walked across the floor, shaking her head. "Sam, did you do *any* research on your subject?"

Sam huffed, dejected, as the hologram froze. "I thought you'd give us simulations closer to our species."

"That's the whole point." Julie stuck her polite smile in place. "You're supposed to learn how to handle species different from yours."

Sam folded his arms. "It makes more sense for each recruiter to work with their own species."

"Does it?" Julie raised her eyebrows. "Is that how a human and an elf recruited a record number and diversity of paranormals in the past couple of months?"

Sam turned away, sighing. "Okay, point taken."

"Go do more research and try again." Julie shook her head.

The werecat stalked away, and Julie looked around the conference room. They'd used screens to convert it into thirty cubicles, each equipped with a hologram and a sweating recruiter trying to convince it to sign on as a PMA recruit. So far, everyone looked nervous, but Gruda had signed an orc by encouraging him to indulge his creative side.

Julie headed to the other side of the room, where she and Taylor had set up a table on a dais so that they could look into the cubicles. Taylor chewed on his pen as he glared into a cubicle where a fumbling vampire stuttered through his pitch. His brown eyes were intense as he watched.

Gross, Hat grumbled.

Hey, you're the one who's listening in on my thoughts. Like them or leave them, Julie told him.

Touchy, touchy, Hat tutted.

"This was a great idea, Julie." Ilsa, still looking pale, sat on a chair behind Taylor's. "It's inspiring to see what you guys are achieving with this department."

"Kaplan will probably be appeased if not impressed," Malcolm quipped beside her.

Julie shook her head. "You can tell your boss I'm not happy that he sent his little office spy to watch my training exercises."

"'Little office spy!'" Malcolm clapped a hand to his chest in mock hurt. "I prefer to think of myself as your personal damsel in distress."

Julie laughed and punched him in the arm, then pulled up her chair and turned her attention to the stammering vampire.

The vampire wiped a bead of sweat from his forehead. "The PMA offers excellent opportunities to develop your powers and use them for the greater good."

The vampire's hologram was in the shape of a unicorn, a massive creature the size of a thoroughbred racehorse with a tumbling mane that fell to her knees. She tossed her horn and turned to the vampire. "Why should I bind myself to another and bend my will to theirs to accomplish that?" She snorted.

The vampire trembled. "There are excellent and comfortable accommodations at our training facilities. Warm stables—"

"Stables!" The unicorn reared. "You would confine me, vampire?" She plunged toward him. The vampire threw up his arms and screamed as the hologram charged at him, then scattered into pixels.

Julie face-palmed. "Does he know it's a hologram?"

"Not all vamps are as brave as I am," Malcolm shot back.

"I'd better go talk to him." Julie pushed back her chair and got up at the same moment Taylor did, and they collided. She thumped into his chest, and he grabbed her arms to steady her. Her heart gave an unwelcome double thud as their eyes met.

"Sorry." She cleared her throat and shuffled away.

"It was my bad. Sorry." Taylor was ash-gray as he pulled away from her.

"Really, you two." Ilsa's laughter bubbled beneath her words. "Get a room."

To Julie's intense relief, her phone chose that moment to ring. She fumbled it out and answered as Taylor hurried off to give the vampire a bolstering speech. "H-hello?" she squeaked.

"Meadows? I want to speak to you and Woodskin five minutes ago!" Kaplan barked and disconnected.

Julie grimaced at her phone. *Shit-shit-shittity-shit.*

Someone's in trouble, Hat sang unhelpfully.

"Let me guess." Malcolm raised an eyebrow. "Kaplan wants to see you in his office?"

"Uh, yeah. How could you tell?" Julie asked.

"There's a certain shell-shocked look paras get when he does that." Malcolm laughed. "You go. Ilsa and I will keep an eye on this lot."

"Thanks, man. I appreciate it." Julie gave him a fist-bump and headed across the floor.

Taylor was in the vampire's cubicle. "You can't show a unicorn your fear. They'll either consider you to be beneath their notice, or they'll think you're a threat. You've got to—"

Julie popped her head inside. "Kaplan wants us in his office."

Taylor groaned.

"Don't show him your fear, either," he told the vampire. "I'll be back."

"Ilsa and Malcolm are covering for us." Julie led him out of the conference room.

"Nice of them." Taylor rubbed his chin as they hustled down the hall. "Julie, do you think he's busting us for, uh, fraternization?" His cheeks went gray again.

Julie swallowed. "How could he? I mean, we only talked about it last night."

"I don't know. Crap. Maybe we're being obvious," Taylor fretted.

Gorgons, Julie thought. *Real gorgons.* Her stomach wobbled. "Do they really have snakes for hair?" she hissed.

The elevator doors slid open, and Julie took an involuntary

step back. Kaplan stood in the doors, and his huge furry eyebrows were wrapped around one another in the middle of his forehead amid a mass of angry wrinkles.

"Get in!" he barked.

Julie would rather have drunk a whole case of aloe vera juice than step into an enclosed space with a furious weretiger, but she shuffled forward. Taylor squeezed into one corner of the elevator and she hugged the other as Kaplan smacked a button and the elevator jolted into motion.

"Before you say anything, Captain," Taylor began, "I just wanted to—"

"I will say what I please when I please," Kaplan snapped.

Julie met Taylor's eyes, and they exchanged grimaces.

Kaplan glared from Julie to Taylor and back. "I gave you two a responsibility if you recall. Your promotion had *strict* requirements, and these included training my recruiters, did they not?"

"Yes, sir," Taylor mumbled, staring at his feet.

Julie swallowed. "Sir, we will in no way allow this to affect—"

"Did your new responsibilities include recruiting more paras?" Kaplan snapped.

Julie stared at him. "Sir?"

"I asked you a simple question, Meadows," Kaplan growled. "You were supposed to be training recruiters. You were assigned other tasks, not recruitment."

Julie stared at him. "But sir, we haven't —"

The elevator doors slid open, and a blast of breathtakingly cold air swirled into it. Julie staggered back with a yelp, and not just because of the cold. She looked out, not onto a featureless mountainside, but onto a mass of yetis, their fur stirring in the cold wind and their eyes resolute above their jutting tusks. Randkluft waved at Julie from the front of the crowd, his face creasing into a wide smile.

"What is happening?" Taylor squeaked.

Kaplan let out a rumble that might have been a genuine laugh.

Julie stared at him. He was...*smiling?* And not in that scary, I'll-enjoy-ripping-your-throat-out way. This smile looked almost happy.

"Like I said, you were supposed to be training my recruiters." Kaplan's grin widened. "Not recruiting yetis en masse." He gestured. "They're all joining the PMA."

Randkluft punched the air. "PMA!" he thundered, his gargling voice forming the syllables with difficulty.

"PMA!" the rest of the yetis echoed.

Julie burst out laughing and caught Taylor's eye. "What can I say? We've got a knack for making people feel welcome."

CHAPTER TWENTY-ONE

Julie pulled another hanger out of her closet and glanced at the cheerful blue-and-yellow sundress. "No," she grumbled, throwing it on the floor. The next hanger held a dressy navy business suit. "Nope." It joined the dress on the floor.

"Someone's going to have to pick that up, you know," Hat pointed out from his spot on her bed.

"What? Who would have known?" Julie shot back. She sighed. "I have *no* idea what to wear."

"It's your first date with him. Let your hair down," Hat suggested. "Wear that little black number you wore for your date with what's-his-face."

"Ew, no." Julie shuddered. "I'm not bringing that bad juju on my first date with Taylor." The words clanged in Julie's head. "Shit, Hat, am I making a terrible mistake?" She ran her fingers through her wet hair.

Hat laughed. "There's only one way to find out, Julie. You have to go for it and see what happens."

"I guess." Julie bit her lip and stood back. "Okay, but seriously, what am I going to wear? We're going to that underage nightclub in Staten Island he suggested." She swallowed. "I've never been to one. I don't even know what it's like."

Hat's brim curled in a shrug. "How about the wool skirt? It's very elegant."

Julie pulled it out and held it against her. She'd bought it for job interviews in the pre-PMA days, and it went from her midriff to her ankles in a single sheet of gray wool. "Yeah, I could see myself going out in this if I was a thousand years old."

"I'm *far* more than a thousand years old." Hat scoffed. "Okay, what about your ballgown? The one you wore to Malcolm's handfasting?"

"Are you nuts? I'm not going to wear a magic blue ballgown to a club." Julie shook her head.

Hat hopped off the bed and waddled over the floor to her closet. Stumbling over a pile of shoes, he used his brim to rifle through her clothes.

"Dude, what are you doing?" Julie spluttered.

"I'm choosing an outfit. I have excellent fashion sense, I'll have you know. I'm the most iconic part of your look." Hat's voice was muffled under her clothes.

"If you say so." Julie leaned against the closet door, arms folded in her fluffy bathrobe and unicorn slippers. "Just stay out of my underwear drawer, okay?"

Hat crawled up to the top of the hangers. Julie didn't allow herself to wonder how. He *was* magical. Unhooking one of the hangers with his brim, he tossed something onto the floor. "There! Perfect," he announced triumphantly.

Julie scooped it up and held it against her body. "I'm not so sure."

"Try it on. It's perfect," Hat gushed.

Carried away by his enthusiasm, Julie darted into the bathroom to do so, then shuffled in front of her closet mirror again. She wasn't sure what she had been thinking when she'd bought this blood-red mini dress a few weeks ago, but it only barely covered her ass. She tugged at the daring neckline.

"Absolutely smoking," Hat cooed.

"That is gross." Julie twirled. "It *is* pretty sexy."

"Taylor's eyes will pop out," Hat told her.

The thought of Taylor knowing she owned a dress like this set Julie's face on fire. "Nope nope nope nope." She rushed to the bathroom to pull it off.

Returning to her bedroom safely bundled in her bathrobe, Julie replaced the dress on its hanger. "You're hopeless," she told Hat.

"Fine." Offended, Hat strutted back to the bed and jumped onto it. "Don't listen to my advice. See if I care."

Julie rolled her eyes. In despair, she pulled out her phone and stared at her mother's name on her contact list for a few minutes.

"Are you sure you want to do that?" Hat asked. "She's going to gloat."

"Yeah, but desperate times call for desperate measures." Sighing, Julie tapped her mom's name and raised the phone to her ear.

"*Juliaaaaaaaaaaa!*" Rosa shrieked. "Hello, baby! Don't you have better things to do on a Thursday night than call your momma?"

"I kind of do, actually." Julie sat down on her bed, hugging herself. "Mom, I need your help."

"What is it, honey? What can I do? Are you okay? Did something happen? Do you need more aloe vera juice?" she shrieked.

Julie's mouth quirked up. "This problem is even bigger than aloe vera juice. I'm..." She took a deep breath. "I'm going on my first date with Taylor."

There was a long silence. Julie thought she heard muted spluttering from the other end of the line. She cringed, bracing herself for the comments, but when Rosa spoke, her voice strained with the effort of trying to sound normal. "Oh, honey, that's lovely. How can I help you?"

Julie felt the knot in her stomach relax. *Mom is always there when it counts, even if she's not my real mom.* She pushed the thought aside. Her mother was as real as mothers got, even if she was a different species than Julie. No amount of DNA could change that.

"I don't know what to wear," she blurted, going back to her closet and tugging on her clothes. "I don't want to be too sexy because this is our first date, and I don't want things to get weird, you know? I also don't want him to think I'm a total goody-two-shoes and button up to my chin. But, like, he does know me since we've worked together for months. Yet, I think there's a side of me he hasn't seen, and—"

"Say no more, honey." Rosa chuckled. "You've come to the right place for support. Let me tell you, dating as a fifty-something widow in New York City is not for the faint of heart. I've got you."

Julie smiled. "I know you do."

"Now, do you still have that blue blouse you liked so much in high school?" Rosa asked.

Julie sighed. "Yeah, but—"

"Hear me out. Remember you showed me that black skirt you bought a few weeks ago while I was staying there? You were very excited about it."

Julie's jaw dropped. "That could work."

Rosa laughed. "Don't sound so surprised, honey. Go ahead. Try it on. I'll wait."

Julie put her mother on hold and scrambled into the blouse and skirt. When she looked into the mirror, she couldn't help grinning. She put the phone on loudspeaker and balanced it on a bedpost. "Mom, it's perfect!"

It *was* perfect, though Julie would never have thought of the combination. The blue blouse was cute and girly, snug in all the right places and floaty in others, with loose, flowy sleeves. It contrasted with the tight midi skirt that clung boldly to her hips, then flared outward, making her legs look even longer.

The look was perfect.

"I told you so, honey." Rosa permitted herself a little smugness.

Julie grinned, twirling. "It's pretty, but it's also fierce."

"Just like you, baby."

"Aw, thanks, Mom." Julie laughed and picked up the phone again. "I'd better go."

"Wear that necklace with the topaz pendant. It'll go well with the blouse," her mother advised. "And be safe, baby, okay?"

"I will. Love you, Mom."

"Love you, honey. Oh, and tell my future son-in-law I said hi."

"Mom!" Julie groaned.

Rosa laughed and hung up.

Julie blow-dried her hair, added the necklace her mother had suggested, and gave herself a last look in the mirror. "I have no idea what I'm doing," she whispered.

"Living your life," Hat told her. "Lillie would be proud."

The thought of Lillie made her eyes sting. She took a deep breath and dabbed them to avoid ruining her light makeup, then her phone binged.

It was Taylor. Six goat emojis in a row.

"What—" Julie began, and her doorbell rang. She hadn't gotten around to getting anything fancier than a bell on a string inside her door, and its jangle made her jump. Swallowing a giggle, she trotted over to the door and pushed it open.

She had been terrified that Taylor would turn up in the midnight-blue suit he'd worn to Malcolm's handfasting. Instead, he leaned against the wall, comfortable in a black button-up shirt and cream-colored chinos.

"Hey." He grinned.

Julie swallowed. "Hey."

They stared at one another.

"Just *go*, lovebirds." Hat groaned. "I'm all too happy to be staying here."

Julie laughed. "See you, Hat." She automatically reached for Genevieve's keys, then paused. "I guess your driver and Rolls are here?"

"No way." Taylor's eyes creased when he grinned. "I wouldn't dream of parting a woman from her Mustang."

If only she was my *Mustang*. Julie pushed the thought away and grabbed the keys. "Okay, Mr. Woodskin. Let's hit it."

They piled into Genevieve and backed out of the garage, then cruised to the end of the street. When Julie turned right, the road past the bodega was open and empty. A green light beckoned at the end, and the black stretch of asphalt called her name.

She flashed a grin at Taylor and stomped on the gas. Genevieve's tires screamed and she sliced through the wind, eating up the asphalt. Her screeching engine was not quite loud enough to drown out their wild laughter.

Even before Genevieve purred to a halt, Julie could hear the thump of music pouring from the nightclub. It looked nothing like she had expected and nothing like the dark, creepy one that regularly attracted police sirens at three in the morning, two blocks from Julie's apartment.

The huge building's neon sign flashed over the door. Through the front windows, Julie looked into a well-lit interior, and the shiny polished concrete dance floor looked like no one had puked on it in the last twenty-four hours.

"You guys do it differently in Tottenville, huh?" she quipped, squeezing Genevieve into the only available parking space halfway down the block between a classic Chevy and a gleaming new Gelande Wagen.

"You're going to like this place," Taylor told her. "The bouncers are pretty strict, so we're unlikely to be vomited on by drunks. And the music is great." He smiled. "That's what we came for, after all. The dancing."

"Yeah, well, I don't think cocktails or shots will hold up when one's first real drink was magic mead from a spring in the Fernwood." Julie laughed.

"True." Taylor got out. "Come on!"

She followed him outside—closing and locking her own door, thank you very much—and they headed down the sidewalk. Julie toyed with the idea of taking Taylor's hand, but he shoved both of them into his pockets, so she folded her arms and walked beside him. Ahead, the music changed. It was upbeat, instrumental, and more complex than the standard thunk-thunk that came from the club in Brooklyn.

"However, they do great mocktails here," Taylor was saying. "We'll down piña coladas all night without the headache tomorrow."

Julie glanced at him. "Sounds pretty good." Was there something chocolatey in his cologne tonight?

The nightclub doors were wide open, and Julie and Taylor were still several yards away when a Starlight Fae strode out of the club. Her silvery-white skin was luminous under the streetlights. She wore her hair in a fancy updo, and a nose ring gleamed in her septum. Her glittering black dress was daringly short.

"Paras come here?" Julie whispered.

"*We're* paras," Taylor pointed out.

She snorted. "You know what I mean."

Taylor laughed. "Yeah, it's pretty popular with paras, especially fae. The music appeals to their taste."

The Starlight Fae hesitated outside the doors and looked around, her blue eyes wide. Her shoulders relaxed and she hurried to the curb, raising her hand for a taxi.

Half a second later, a burly young man stumbled out of the club, followed by two clones. They all wore sagging jeans, gold chains, and band t-shirts. A fug of stale alcohol hung in the air around them.

"Where are you goin' in such a hurry, sexy?" the ringleader yelled after the Starlight Fae.

She tensed. Her soft, transparent wings unfolded from her shoulders, quivering. "I'm going home. Please leave me alone."

"Don't be in such a hurry." The ringleader's red hair shone in the streetlight, as artificial as his smile. "We were just getting started."

The fae's eyes darted left and right as the redhead's cronies flanked him, effectively pinning her against the curb.

"Nothing was getting started." The fae's voice shook. "Just leave me alone."

The redhead stepped forward, only a few feet separating his sweaty bulk from the fae's slender body. "Oh, trust me," he hissed. "Something great was getting started."

"Hey!" Julie yelled, quickening her step. "She told you to leave her alone. Did you hear her, or do I need to open your ears for you?"

Taylor was right behind her as she strode up to the three stooges. They turned, and the redhead's face crumpled into an ugly glare.

"Keep walking, chick," he barked. "This is none of your business."

The fae shot Julie a desperate look.

"She said she wants to go home," Taylor growled. "She's not interested."

"You just keep walking, pretty boy." The redhead sneered as he slapped a chunky fist into his other palm. "You don't want to get involved."

The clones laughed.

"Oh, he doesn't need to get involved." Julie strode up to the redhead and stepped into his space. "I can handle you on my own."

Taylor folded his arms and leaned against a streetlight. "Get 'em, Julie," he drawled.

The redhead laughed and shook his head, about to turn away. "Piss off."

Julie slammed both hands into his chest, shoving him back a step. "No, *you* piss off and leave the girl alone."

The redhead's eyes darkened. "You don't want to do this, bitch."

Julie had taken on elven princesses and multiple werewolves, and that was only in training. She could handle three drunken idiots. "I really do." She poked him in the chest. "Question is, are you up for it?"

The redhead snarled and swung a drunken, loopy fist in her direction. Julie stepped aside and grabbed his arm, helping his momentum along. He stumbled forward and landed heavily on his hands and knees with a roar of pain and indignation.

"Woot woot, Julie!" Taylor cheered.

"Get her!" The redhead struggled to his feet, swayed, and fell back to one knee. "*Get the bitch!*"

Julie beckoned to the remaining two thugs. "Come on, then."

They charged simultaneously. Julie sidestepped one while planting an elbow in his ribs that sent him reeling into Taylor. The elf grabbed his arm and neatly pinned him against the club's wall. The other grabbed for Julie's throat with both hands. She gripped one wrist, spun him, and twisted his arm up behind his back.

"Ow, ow, ow, ow!" the big man bawled.

The redhead had finally found his feet and shot Julie a fearful look. "Let's go, boys!" he gasped, bolting.

Julie let go of her opponent, if you could call him that, and Taylor shoved the third man in the direction of the fleeing redhead. They reeled off, belching and squealing.

"They were gross," Julie commented. She turned to the fae. "Are you okay?"

The fae's wings sagged with relief. "I'm fine, thanks to you." She smiled. "And you, Prince Taylor." She curtsied.

Taylor turned gray. Julie fought to hold in her laughter when a taxi finally appeared, and the fae gave them a last wave before she slipped into the backseat. Turning to Taylor, Julie grinned. "Am I going to have to get used to you being recognized in public?"

"She must be a royalty nut to know who I am." Taylor's cheeks grayed more. "Nice moves, by the way. Who taught you how to fight? He's a good teacher."

"Eh, he's okay." Julie prodded him in the ribs.

Taylor raised an eyebrow. "Wow, thanks." He laughed. "Those three didn't know what hit them."

"All in a day's work." Julie smirked.

Taylor held out a hand. "The day's work is done. Are you ready for an evening's play?"

Julie looked into his chocolate eyes, drawing the scent of fresh rain into her nostrils. "Absolutely," she murmured and took his hand.

As they stepped into the nightclub, the soft instrumental pop playing through the speakers switched to something more familiar. The playful tones of Ed Sheeran's *Shape of You* coursed through the club. This early in the evening, the floor was mostly empty, and neon lights in the ceiling flashed tantalizing blues and purples on the polished surface.

"I love this song," Julie gushed.

Taylor's eyes found hers. "Well, I hope you know how to dance to it."

"I know how to try." Julie laughed.

Taylor grinned. "That sounds perfect."

He took her hand and led her onto the dance floor. It wasn't like dancing at Beltane, but with the elf's dark eyes on hers and his hand on her waist, it was close.

Somehow it was sunrise.

Julie and Taylor leaned on Genevieve's hood, the pewter Mustang shining in the soft gray light as dawn broke over the bay. At this hour, the beach was deserted, a silent sweep of gleaming silver sand.

"I've never danced the night away before," Julie murmured. Exhaustion tugged at her, but her body was filled with electricity.

Taylor grinned at her. "Neither have I."

"Yeah, but you have no life," Julie pointed out.

Taylor chuckled, his eyes not leaving her. "That's changed since you came into it."

The breeze blowing off the water was chilly, or maybe there was another reason Julie scooted closer to him. She tucked herself under his arm, and she had to tip her head back to look him in the eye. "Just a little, huh?"

He dipped his head, and she didn't pull away.

"Yeah, just a little," he whispered, his breath against her lips.

Her heart galloped. Her fingers found his shirt and tugged him closer, and their lips met slowly and gently but with a gathering certainty. He tasted faintly of apples. Not the sour green ones. The thought trickled through Julie's brain, a delicious rush crawling up her spine as she pulled him closer. He tasted like ripe red ones, sweet and rich and fresh.

She pulled back, and his eyes shone when they met hers. The early sunlight played on her cheek, warm and pure. Their hands tangled and fit perfectly.

A breathy laugh escaped her. "I guess we're going to have to face the gorgons."

AUTHOR NOTES RENÉE JAGGÉR

FEBRUARY 1, 2023

Thank you for reading through to the back of book four!

It's cold. There is still snow on the mountains. A friend and I took a drive on old Route 66 through Valentine to Seligman (which was part of the scenery that shaped the *Cars* movie, in case you didn't know), and there was snow on the ground at the end. It was a gorgeous day, though. And did you know that there are still Burma Shave signs in the world? I had heard about but never seen them, but they have several series on that stretch of road. https://www.legendsofamerica.com/66-burmashave/

C. O. L. D.

Thank you, polar vortex! Mostly, I have been huddled on the couch, writing, with alpaca socks on and a heating pad behind me and a blanket on my lap. Not doing much that involves not being near a heat source. Did I mention that it was cold? Went out to lunch yesterday wearing leggings and a fake fur coat just because it came to my knees, unlike any of my jackets. Also Ugg boots. I am bringing back the eighties single-handedly. I could really get into leg warmers.

Jo thinks me huddling on the couch is swell, by the way. She settles into her spot and starts snoring within five minutes. Sometimes, for some inexplicable reason, she decides she MUST be petted RIGHT NOW and climbs onto my laptop. Thank goodness for the editors! She's caused some doozies.

Update on the mead project: let's just say it needs to age more. Haven't made the cyser (apple mead) yet. Bottles and other arcane implements are all sitting in the (cold) dining room, waiting for me to want to go into the (cold) kitchen, where the apple juice is on the (cold) windowsill.

My friends in the UK say that with the temps we're having, they would be at the beach in shorts. I suppose Alaskans would be too. I should ask Craig Martelle about that. Forty-five to fifty degrees is not beach weather to me, but they say it's all about the sun. I will say that on any given sunny day in the UK, regardless of temperature, you see more pale, pasty flesh than at a computer hackers' convention. The Brits are insane!

I wish I had something more interesting to report, but that's my world right now. It's been a quiet month.

The next book is in editing as we speak. And bless my proofreaders! They take care of the Jo-bloopers I miss. I hope you enjoyed the continuation of Julie's journey! Her world will keep changing, as will she.

Until we speak again, I hope your skies are sunny and your days are filled with happiness and good books!

Renée

BOOKS FROM RENÉE

Para-Military Recruiter
(with Michael Anderle)
Drafted (Book 1)
Recruiter (Book 2)
Accepted (Book 3)
Lead (Book 4)
Recruited (Book 5)

Reincarnation of the Morrigan
Birth of a Goddess (Book One)
The Way of Wisdom (Book Two)
Angelic Death (Book Three)
A Cold War (Book 4)
A Battle Tune (Book 5)
Broken Ice (Book 6)
A Torn Veil (Book 7)
Sins of the Past (Book 8)
The Wild Hunt Comes (*coming soon*)

The WereWitch Series

Bad Attitude (Book One)
A Bit Aggressive (Book Two)
Too Much Magic (Book Three)
Were War (Book Four)
Were Rages (Book Five)
God Ender (Book Six)
God Trials (Book Seven)
The Troll Solution (Book Eight)
Winner Takes All (Book Nine)

Callie Hart Series
Thin Ice (Book One)
Cold Blood (Book Two)
Feelings Run Deep (Book Three)

BOOKS BY MICHAEL ANDERLE

Sign up for the LMBPN email list to be notified of new releases and special deals!

https://lmbpn.com/email/

For a complete list of books by Michael Anderle, please visit:

www.lmbpn.com/ma-books/

CONNECT WITH THE AUTHORS

Connect with Renée

Facebook: https://www.facebook.com/reneejaggerauthor

Website: https://reneejagger.com/

Connect with Michael Anderle

Website: http://lmbpn.com

Email List: https://michael.beehiiv.com/

https://www.facebook.com/LMBPNPublishing

https://twitter.com/MichaelAnderle

https://www.instagram.com/lmbpn_publishing/

https://www.bookbub.com/authors/michael-anderle

www.ingramcontent.com/pod-product-compliance
Lightning Source LLC
LaVergne TN
LVHW091720070526
838199LV00050B/2479